THE IRON MAIDEN

Published by Mundania Press
Also by Resa Nelson

The Dragonslayer's Sword
The Stone of Darkness*

Our Lady of the Absolute

(*Forthcoming)

THE IRON MAIDEN

RESA NELSON

Y
Nelson

A Mundania Press Production
Mundania Press LLC
6457 Glenway Avenue, #109
Cincinnati, Ohio 45211-5222

To order additional copies of this book, contact:
books@mundania.com
www.mundania.com

Cover Art © 2011 by Ana Winson
Edited by Erena Kelley

Trade Paperback ISBN: 978-1-60659-282-3
eBook ISBN: 978-1-60659-281-6

First Edition • December 2011

Production by Mundania Press LLC
Printed in the United States of America

10 9 8 7 6 5 4 3 2 1

ACKNOWLEDGEMENTS

As always, thanks to all the great folks at Mundania Press for all their help.

Also, as always, many thanks to fellow writers Tom Sweeney and Carla Johnson for their spot-on insight, advice, and brilliance.

A few years ago, my friend Andy Volpe said, "Hey, you should call your next book The Iron Maiden." I loved the title but had no idea what it meant with regard to my characters and the story I wanted to tell. Part of the great fun in writing this novel was discovering who the Iron Maiden is and what the name means. Thanks to Andy for giving me a great title.

When I attended the 29th annual Medieval and Renaissance Forum at Plymouth State University in Plymouth, New Hampshire, two presentations really struck a chord with me. Dr. Roberta Milliken of Shawnee State University presented a paper called "Women's Glory, Women's Wickedness: Hair as Symbol in the Writings of the Church Fathers," and Dr. Raymond Eichmann of the University of Arkansas presented a paper entitled "The 'Priestess' in the French Fabliaux." Each presentation sent my head spinning. Even though these academic topics had no direct connection with the type of fantasy I write, I immediately began connecting the dots between the historical research being presented and Book 2 in my Dragonslayer series. A very special thanks to Dr. Milliken and Dr. Eichmann for giving me permission to take inspiration from their presentations and create something of my own. For the record, I don't write historical fiction, and I take a lot of liberties as a fantasy writer, so I don't claim to use their research findings—I'm simply inspired by them to think in a new and different way. If you ever have a chance to hear Dr. Milliken and Dr. Eichmann speak, don't miss this great opportunity. Their research findings are fascinating. I also recommend Dr. Eichmann's books: *Cuckolds, clerics, & countrymen: medieval French fabliaux* and *The French fabliau*, both of which I found through my local library's interlibrary loan system. Dr. Milliken has written a new book called *Ambiguous Locks: An Iconology of Hair in Medieval Art and Literature*, which should be published by the time you have this novel in your hands.

CHAPTER ONE

Don't move, Astrid told herself. The crumbling foliage danced in circles around her. Underneath the familiar scent of the forest—the tangy pine, the rotting and new wood, the rich earth—was the distinctive briny smell of lizard. One step on a crackling leaf would give away her position. If the lizard lay in wait nearby, it would be at her throat before she knew it.

Alone in the woods, no help would come to Astrid. She turned her head slightly into the oncoming breeze, cold and sharp. Brown and brittle leaves with curled edges drifted loose from their branches and swirled around Astrid like strange, dark snow in the cold breeze.

Lizards were huge and crafty things, and anyone other than a dragonslayer called them "dragons," not "lizards." Their hunting strategy consisted of digging a trench by the side of a path, lying low and hidden inside that trench, and then springing out if anything juicy passed by. Despite their size, lizards were quick and agile, often catching those who assumed otherwise off guard.

This time of year, they migrated from Astrid's home in the Northlands to the southern regions. Although she'd been a dragonslayer for only a few months, Astrid knew what to do because of DiStephan. For the past few weeks, she'd been making her final sweep through the territory she protected, starting in the Far Northern boglands where people dredged the swamps to harvest and then smelt the blooms of iron she worked with as a blacksmith.

Behind her, brittle leaves rustled. Could someone be shuffling through them?

Astrid spun, hand on the hilt of the sword at her side.

No longer swirling, brown leaves clung in patchwork to the air now facing her. She could see through empty patches here and there, but the leaves outlined the form of a man.

DiStephan's ghost.

He pointed to the side between two pine trees that flanked the path.

Astrid nodded her thanks to the ghost and withdrew her sword quietly from its sheath while she studied the trees and the space between them, covered with pine needles and leaves. The space measured the length of a horse and a half, which indicated the presence of a growing lizard experienced in killing people. They could lie still in trenches for hours, plenty of time to become camouflaged by quickly falling leaves. Astrid struggled to make out the shape of the lizard but took her best guess at which end was which. It would be impossible to sneak up on the thing.

Holding on tight to the grip of her sword, Astrid sprinted toward the trench, dead leaves crunching loudly beneath her feet, ready to face the lizard that would spring up out of it.

But nothing happened.

Astrid pulled up just short of the space between the trees. This might be an especially crafty lizard. One waiting for her to assume it wasn't there, letting her get close enough so it could grab her throat.

Astrid's heart raced, beating so hard she could feel it bang against her chest. She didn't want to die, especially not from a lizard bite. The poisons in its spit would kill its victim within a day or two. Still new to dragonslaying, she missed her early days when she had the ability to see and speak with DiStephan's ghost. She ached, still missing his touch. She missed seeing his quick smile and amused eyes. She longed to understand his thoughts just by looking at his face.

And she hated him for dying and leaving her to be her town's only hope for keeping lizards at bay. Astrid barely knew how to wield a sword, and there already had been too many times that she'd come close to losing her life. She missed her smithery. She wanted to be a blacksmith again.

Taking a quiet, deep breath, Astrid reminded herself that what others thought of as "dragon" season would end soon. But what most people called "dragons" were actually overgrown lizards, not true dragons like Taddeo and Norah.

Astrid neared her home of Guell on her final sweep through the region. In a day or so, she would confidently hang up her sword and return to her anvil for the winter, taking comfort in the heat of her blacksmithing fire during the long winter months. The lizards wouldn't return until spring.

This could be the last lizard I have to face this year, Astrid told herself. *And Guell needs more meat to get us all through winter.*

Tired of waiting for the lizard to surprise her, Astrid leapt forward, plunging her sword into its hiding place, aiming for the target most likely to be its head.

The blade sank into a pile of leaves. Nothing leapt out at her. Astrid stabbed the leaves in different places, making sure nothing lay in wait beneath them. Finally, she dragged the tip of her sword through them. This was a lizard's hiding place, all right. The shape and size of the trench seemed right, and the edges bore claw marks. She knelt by the trench, running her fingers through a set of claw marks. There—mingled with the smell of freshly turned earth—wafted the lizard scent she'd detected minutes ago. The lizard had been here not long ago.

Or maybe it waited nearby.

Something tapped her shoulder.

Astrid jumped up in surprise, still clutching her sword.

A spindly tree branch pointed first at the lizard's trench and then beyond the trees that flanked it.

DiStephan again. In the days when she'd been able to see and communicate with his ghost, he'd told her about the thinness of the veil between her world and the spirit world. It took most of his energy to make his presence known at all. He could move and manipulate lightweight things—like a tree branch. She knew she shouldn't be surprised each time he tapped her shoulder, but one never knew what else might be lurking in the woods.

Suddenly, Astrid realized where she was. Whispering, in case the lizard might be close enough to hear her, Astrid said, "That leads back to my camp. No lizard goes anywhere near a dragonslayer's camp. They're too crafty."

Again, the tree's spindly limb pointed with a sharp insistence toward the camp. Astrid smiled. She imagined she could hear the sound of DiStephan's voice in her head: *Trust me.*

For the next hour, Astrid crept through the forest silently. At the time she'd first met DiStephan in childhood, she'd been traveling through these woods with a childseller. DiStephan and his father, Guell's dragonslayer at the time, had heard them coming long before they arrived. Astrid had asked DiStephan how he'd known of their presence, and he'd laughed and said she'd been as loud as cattle. It had only been during the past few months that Astrid had come to appreciate what he meant. She'd spent her life surrounded by the loud banging of hammer against iron, the crackle of fire, and the whoosh of the bellows. Never before had she experienced such quiet, and she'd become attuned to the subtle sounds of the animals and trees.

Finally, she spotted her camp—what had once been the camp of DiStephan and his father. Beyond the abrupt line where the forest ended lay a strip of beach sheltered by sheer cliffs. Astrid's heart raced again, but this time with anticipation. She was almost home. Astrid took a deep breath, grateful for the heavy scent of salt in the air. She picked up her pace, making her way through this last stretch of forest.

But the moment she stepped out of it and onto the beach, a lizard sprang from its hiding place, jaws wide open as it lunged toward her face.

CHAPTER TWO

With a startled cry, Astrid sprang a step back while she drove the pommel of her sword into the veined jowls of the lizard's throat. Stunned, the lizard paused, taking a hesitant step back on its bowed, crablike legs. As she'd suspected, it looked to be the length of a horse and a half, looking like an enormous and well-fed snake with four legs.

Swinging her sword above her head, Astrid tried to rush toward the beast, only to be yanked back by her own hair. She glanced back quickly to find out who seized her from behind but saw that the single braid hanging down her back had snagged in a tree limb. She called out for help. "DiStephan!"

As the lizard shook off the pommel blow, invisible hands threw scoops of sand at its eyes.

Keeping one hand on her sword's grip, Astrid reached back with her free hand, wrapped her fingers around her braid, and pulled hard to free it. Her hair came free from the tree but the tree branch broke the thread keeping her dark hair braided.

Astrid darted away from the tree line, circling the lizard. Its scales were earthy and mottled, reflecting shades of brown and black and gold. Shaking its flat serpent head, the lizard backed away. A white film lowered between its eye and eyelids.

Astrid charged forward and stepped onto one of the lizard's bowed legs, using it like a ladder to climb up on its back. But the lizard jerked sideways, throwing her off. It lashed its tail, scraping the sand as it flicked its long, yellow tongue.

Rolling onto her feet, Astrid's hair now hung in the thick ribbons in which it had been braided. She charged again, running diagonally toward the lizard's head and then making a sharp turn toward its back legs, hoping to catch it off guard. Instead, the lizard turned and struck her with its tail, sending her tumbling toward the tree line again.

The ocean wind whipped the ribbons of her hair around her face, blinding her for a moment. Astrid panicked, still dizzy from the blow but regained her footing. Thrusting her sword forward with one hand, she reached back with the other, frantic at the smell of the foul, hot breath of the lizard she couldn't see.

The moment she touched bark, Astrid scrambled up the nearest tree, dragging her sword with her. Panting, she climbed high and fast, ignoring the thorny limbs that scratched her skin. The tree shook; the lizard reared on its back legs and slammed its chest against the tree in the same way Astrid had seen lizards battle each other chest-to-chest over a fresh kill. She lost her footing on the shaking tree, the lizard nipping at her heels. Realizing she had positioned herself where she wanted to be, Astrid aimed her sword point at the open jaws just below her, letting herself slide down toward the lizard. She plunged the sword into its mouth and throat, but the lizard slapped her off the tree with its leg.

Again, the thick ribbons of hair swirled around her head while she fell, keeping her blinded. In desperation, Astrid reached out, grasping for anything that could slow or break her fall. Panic seized her heart. She realized that Starlight, the sword she'd made for DiStephan so many years ago, lay no longer in her hands.

It was the last thing she remembered before she hit the ground and lost consciousness.

CHAPTER THREE

Minutes later, Astrid awoke to the sting of thrown sand against her face. She tried to protest, but she choked on her own hair, still splayed across her face. Coughing, she pushed herself to sit up, head throbbing and body aching.

A nearby grunt and foul breath made her jump to her feet, ignoring the pain as she pushed the hair away from her face.

The lizard, sword stuck in its mouth and throat, had dragged itself toward Astrid, leaving a trail of blood in the sand. Flat on its belly, it struggled to inch itself forward.

DiStephan had thrown sand to warn her, and the sting of it had startled her awake.

"Thank you," Astrid said, pulling a dagger free from where she kept it tucked under her belt. The lizard's ridged eyes seemed listless, but Astrid wasn't willing to take any chances. She approached with caution before jumping on the lizard's back and plunging the dagger into its neck.

The beast shuddered beneath her in wave after wave. After one last groan, the air left the lizard's body and it lay still beneath her.

"Are you well?" a familiar accented voice said behind her.

Pulling the dagger out of the dead lizard's neck, Astrid slid off its back and saw Taddeo. Bracing one foot against the lizard's jaw, Astrid rolled up her sleeves, took a firm grip on her sword's hilt, and began to work it loose. "How long have you been standing there?" she said. "I could have used your help."

When DiStephan had gone missing, Guell and the other villages in the region had hired Taddeo, a stranger from the Far East, to replace him. He appeared to be a light-skinned man, strong and tall, with cool green eyes. But Astrid knew him to be a dragon. Not a lizard like the ones she hunted and killed, but a true dragon with the power to take any shape he chose.

"Are you quite well?" Taddeo said. He stood at ease with his hands behind his back.

The last time they'd had a conversation like this, his thoughts had changed the shape of her body, startling her so much that she'd found herself unable to change it back for days. But that had happened before she'd become a dragonslayer. She felt different now. Solid. "I'm fine, Taddeo. Why do you ask?"

He stared, but Astrid assumed he'd never seen her dressed in her dragonslayer clothes. As a blacksmith, she'd worn trousers and a leather vest. Now, she wore pants and a tunic made of patchwork cloth: stitched-together scraps of linen dyed brown and green that helped her blend in with the woods. "I ask," Taddeo said, "because you appear to be coming apart at the seams."

Astrid laughed, now wriggling the sword to loosen it from the lizard's mouth. "That's ridiculous."

He walked toward her slowly, grabbed her wrist, and pulled her hand free from the sword. Before she could protest, he extended her arm and twisted it slightly. "Then what kind of explanation do you offer for this?" Taddeo said.

Three scars crawled like worms across the back of her forearm. Astrid yanked her wrist free from Taddeo's hold. In childhood, she'd been chewed up and spit out by a dragon, leaving her body covered in hideous scars. After reaching adulthood, she'd shapeshifted her body, hiding her scars by smoothing out her skin. But when she'd decided to become a dragonslayer, her scars had resurfaced to form the image of a sword down her spine and chest, like identical tattoos bisecting each side of her body.

Astrid stared at her arm, closing her eyes and imagining her skin clear and smooth again. The wayward scars halted as if confused before reversing direction and crawling back up her arm toward her chest and spine where they belonged. She rolled her sleeves back down to cover her skin.

"How long has this happened?"

Astrid returned her attention to the sword still stuck inside the lizard's throat. "It's nothing."

"I see."

"Why are you here, Taddeo? What do you want from me now?" Although Astrid looked at her sword, she checked from the corner of her eye for Taddeo's reaction, but he showed none.

"Along the dragonslayer's winter route, there is a place with a Dragon's Well. Drink from the water in that well, and it will restore your arm."

Astrid stiffened. Anyone who ate lizard meat or drank lizard's blood perceived her skin to be flawless and her physique normal. In truth, her skin was covered in scars; one arm was real, and the other a ghost arm that existed only by the power of her belief in it. Taddeo had come into her life and manipulated her in an effort to free his niece Norah from captivity on Tower Island, home to the Scaldings. Months ago, he had succeeded in freeing Norah, who had devoured Astrid's arm to stay alive.

"Drinking the water from Dragon's Well also has the power to seal your scars in place," Taddeo continued. "DiStephan can lead you there—he drank from the well himself when he filled his father's shoes. You are likely to travel through regions where people cannot see you as you wish, and this restoration will eliminate those problems. It is well advised to disguise your phantom arm on the way to Dragon's Well, but—"

"I'm not going on the winter route." With a loud grunt, Astrid pulled her sword free from the lizard she'd killed. "I'm staying in Guell. I'll be working at my anvil until spring. Then I'll hunt lizards again."

Taddeo took a patient tone and began to lecture. "Every dragonslayer follows lizards as they migrate."

"I've followed them out of the Far Northlands and soon out of Guell." Astrid licked the blood gingerly from her blade, grateful for the immediate warmth that coursed through her body. "I protect the people who pay me. Let the foreigners protect themselves."

Taddeo frowned. "You would willingly let harm come to others?"

Astrid continued licking her sword clean, her lips dark with blood. "You mean foreigners who would think nothing of invading Guell if we weren't protected by Dragon's Head?" She nodded toward the rocky outcrop by the sea, visible from here, a favorite breeding ground for lizards. "Foreigners who would raid our village and steal our goods?"

"DiStephan followed the winter route."

Hearing his name spoken aloud by someone else stung. Astrid had grown used to the solitude nature of dragonslaying. She thought nothing of spending most of her time walking through the woods and talking to the ghost of her lover. But hearing his name out loud from Taddeo's lips came as a harsh reminder of DiStephan's death. "DiStephan and his father came from the Southlands," Astrid said. "He followed the winter route. He went back to his first home where his own people welcomed him. I'm from the Northlands. My people are here."

"But DiStephan—"

"I'm not DiStephan."

"I see," Taddeo said again. This time, his voice weighed heavy with disappointment.

Astrid licked the last drop of blood from the sword. Removing her gloves and tucking them under her real arm, she pulled out a small square of cloth from the leather pouch attached to her belt and wiped the blade carefully before sheathing it. "I don't suppose you'd be willing to help me get this lizard to Guell."

"Put your gloves back on," Taddeo said softly. "And remember the danger of a lizard's bite, even when it's first hatched." He gazed beyond her toward her dragonslayer's camp.

She followed his gaze toward the small ring of stones encircling the cinders of a fire she'd made weeks ago. Apparently, something had dug into the sand, scattering hardened chunks of it around a pile of shells. But that didn't make any sense. Astrid had often watched gulls soar and drop clams on the hard rocks below until the shells broke open. But gulls used the rocks lining the sea's edge, not the beach itself. Clams dropped onto sand would never break open.

Something moved within the sand. Astrid walked toward it slowly, keeping one hand on the hilt of the dagger tucked into her belt. Something had dug into the sand, leaving a pile of round stones.

As she walked closer, Astrid saw that most of them had broken apart. Only three out of 20 were still intact, and those stones trembled, even though the ground beneath them did not. Suddenly, a small dark snout broke through the surface from inside the stone.

No, Astrid thought. *It's impossible. How could this happen in a dragonslayer's camp?* Turning, she said, "Taddeo..."

But he'd already vanished, leaving her alone.

Astrid sighed. She knew she couldn't count on him to help her take the lizard's carcass into Guell. At least he'd left her with good advice. Astrid put her gloves back on and walked toward a pile of lizard eggs.

Chapter Four

Astrid knelt by the lizard eggs, each one double the size of a chicken's egg. The eggshells' brown and gray exterior would make them blend in with the color of the forest floor. The three unhatched eggs bore cracks, and a filmy membrane seemed to breathe of its own accord between each crack.

What were hatching eggs doing inside a dragonslayer's camp, especially this late in autumn? Lizards left the Northlands every fall, seeking the warmth of the southern countries but not before mating and laying a clutch of eggs, usually hidden in caves. The eggs usually hatched in the spring, although some had been discovered hatching in summer. For these eggs to be hatching now, they would have had to be laid last winter. It made no sense for a lizard to remain in the Northlands during winter and even less that no one would have discovered its presence. Last winter, DiStephan was still alive and had been roaming the Southlands, keeping people safe from lizard attacks.

The infant lizard poked the rest of its head through the eggshell, wriggling until it freed its body. Unlike adult lizards, the newborn's skin had narrow horizontal stripes of black dotted with ivory. But while trying to break entirely loose of the shell, its tail remained trapped inside. The creature looked back at the egg, befuddled. It reminded Astrid of the temperamental brown smoke breathed out by a fire in the making.

Her dragonslayer duties included destroying these eggs, but it didn't feel right.

Watching the newborn's bewilderment at the problem of freeing its tail from the egg, Astrid murmured, "I would call you Smoke."

The cold sea breeze lightly slapped her face. In it, she recognized the shape of DiStephan's hand.

Astrid knew DiStephan wouldn't understand. The last time she'd seen him alive, he'd detected the scent of lizard in the air and discovered a hatchling. Horrified, she'd seen him beat it into a bloody pulp. That had made her wonder what he might do to her if she angered him. It had been a stupid, baseless fear that she now regretted. Now that she had become a dragonslayer, Astrid understood that DiStephan had lived true to the duties he'd agreed to accept.

"I know," Astrid said to DiStephan's ghost. "I understand what I'm supposed to do. A lizard is a lizard, no matter its size. But I'm not you."

The breeze died down in compliance.

What about the lizard she had just killed? Astrid turned around to verify its death. It lay sprawled where she had left its body, still and lifeless. Was it the mother? Had it been a mother protecting its young? Astrid took care not to react in front of

DiStephan's ghost, because she knew he'd be disappointed in her for thinking such things. DiStephan believed that a dragonslayer's duty meant killing all lizards, but Astrid had yet to come to grips with that mindset.

The newborn lizard struggled mightily against the eggshell holding its tail inside, wriggling in one direction after another.

Withdrawing her dagger from her belt, Astrid held the weapon in her left spirit hand, ready to protect herself if Smoke succeeded in freeing itself. After all, a lizard's bite was deadly. Even a nip from a newborn could be fatal. Using her spirit hand would keep her safe. Inching closer to the pile of eggs, she studied the nest. The claw marks of an adult surrounded the eggs. With the blade of her dagger, Astrid explored the empty eggs that had already hatched. Most of them were crushed and bloody, unlike Smoke's egg, which had one small opening the newborn had poked open with his nose. Astrid examined the sand surrounding the hatched eggs. The newly hatched lizards would have left tiny claw marks, and their tails would have left sweeping, telltale marks if they left the nest in search of food. But the only marks in the sand were the huge, deep claw marks of the adult she'd killed.

"It was feeding," Astrid said aloud, examining the other crushed eggshells. "This lizard wasn't the mother. It must have seen the sand moving once the eggs started to hatch and dug up the nest." Astrid knew adult lizards perceived young ones as food. Therefore, young lizards spent the first few years of life in trees, where the adults couldn't reach them. "It had already eaten most of the eggs by the time I arrived. I came back to camp, and I found the lizard eating them. Maybe it felt threatened by me. It wasn't protecting its young. It was protecting its supper."

With one final tug, Smoke freed himself from the egg. He circled it, collapsed with exhaustion, and curled up, holding the eggshell close.

I saved them, Astrid thought, seeing the next egg tremble, ready to hatch. *They're alive because of me.*

A new thought occurred to her. Rising to her feet, Astrid called out, "Taddeo! Are these dragons? Or are they lizards?"

The sea breeze kicked up again, swirling around her.

Astrid faced the emptiness surrounding her. "They placed me in a cage with a young dragon when I was a girl. In all that time, I only saw her as a dragon, not in any other form. Children can't control their shape until they grow up—what if the same is true for dragons? I know Norah hatched from an egg. What if she couldn't take any form other than a dragon as a child? What if these are dragons?"

The sea breeze swirled harder and faster around her. Clearly, DiStephan believed they were lizards.

"Stop!" Astrid called out. "I know what you want me to do. I know what I have to do. Dragonslayers don't take chances, not when it comes to protecting people."

Satisfied, the sea breeze died.

Chapter Five

After hiding the lizard's nest and its hatchlings, Astrid noticed rustling sounds outside her camp. She withdrew her sword then took a few steps toward the edge of the forest, squinting while she tried to read the sounds.

Until earlier this year, Astrid's world had been one of smoke and fire and smiting iron. Since first arriving in Guell in childhood, she'd spent most of her time in the smithery, finding comfort and safety in its blazing heat. She'd spent years learning to read fire, coming to understand how to start it and the meaning of smoke when it turned white or brown or black. She'd studied the nuances of flame and letting its colors talk to her. Most of all, she'd become fluent in the language of iron, sensitive to every shade it could take at the forge, from cold black to warm orange to hot cherry red to burning yellow sparked with white. The intimate world of the smithery made her feel at home. Even though she'd spent the past several months befriending the forest, she still felt like a lost stranger.

As the noise in the woods grew louder, Astrid tilted her head, trying to angle her ears to pick up the sound better. Lizards spent much of their time laying low, waiting for prey. They tended to make quick, sharp sounds of attack. But lizards also searched for carrion, in which case they'd move slowly, dragging the back of each foot before plopping it against the ground as their tails swept behind.

Concentrating, Astrid heard no sounds of attack or dragged paws or tails. Instead, she detected the crunch of brittle leaves underfoot and the snap of fallen twigs.

Men made those sounds as they traveled in the woods. And these men were bound to walk into her camp very soon.

I should have heard them much sooner, Astrid realized, angry with herself. She could forgive herself for not paying attention to the sounds of the forest because her focus had been on fighting the lizard. Any time she faced a dangerous animal, the key was to focus entirely on the fight. But she shouldn't have let herself be distracted by the nest of eggs. Astrid now realized she'd let her guard down and, even worse, let her senses down. The outside world wasn't safe like her smithery. Here, she had to constantly watch and listen and smell and taste and touch.

A new sea breeze blustered at her back, nudging her forward and lifting her thick ribbons of hair into the air. Looking up, Astrid took note of the dark clouds that had formed, standing in the sky like a fortress of boulders.

She glanced around her camp, thinking ahead in case she needed to fight the men who would arrive within moments. With the sea to her back, the slain lizard lay directly to her left and the fire pit. Her sleeping shelter, a simple lean-to of branches with a thatched roof, lay behind to her right. For the first time in months, Astrid became painfully aware that with the help of DiStephan's ghost, she'd learned to slay dragons but she knew little about wielding weapons against men. Her past luck in fighting brigands, slave owners, and her own brother came from the help she'd received from DiStephan's ghost and the dragons, Taddeo and Norah. If the men approaching her camp were reasonable, she would have no qualms about offering part of the slain lizard to them, even though it represented enough meat for Guell to survive the winter in comfort.

But if they were brigands, Astrid might have to run, leaving her bounty behind.

The sea wind behind her kicked up again, this time swirling around her. The ribbons of her hair lifted and wrapped around Astrid's face, blinding her as the men stepped out of the forest and into her camp.

CHAPTER SIX

Astrid clawed at her face with her phantom hand. She pushed her hair away from her eyes while still clinging to her dagger with her real hand, ready to protect herself from the men invading her camp.

"No troubles," a familiar voice said. "It's all friends here—no dragons."

Holding her hair back from her face, Astrid smiled, tucking her dagger back under her belt, relieved and warmed by the sight of friends.

Randim stepped out of a cart led by two of the strongest farm horses from Guell. Soot surrounded his thick eyebrows and large blue eyes, a sure sign that he'd been at the forge all day. His long dark hair pulled away from his square and serious face. Instead of a simple tieback, the hair had been braided for a finger length at the nape of his neck and then hung freely, clearly Lenore's handiwork.

One of the horses snorted and stomped in protest, and Randim patted its neck in reassurance. He grinned at the sight of the slain lizard. "The ghostie was right. That dragon will make enough meat to last until spring." Like everyone other than Astrid, Randim believed the animal to be a dragon, even though Astrid had adopted Taddeo's habit of calling them lizards. No one other than Astrid knew that Taddeo and Norah were true dragons or that dragons and lizards were different creatures, even though they sometimes looked the same.

"DiStephan?" Astrid wasn't surprised that Randim had seen him. Even now, she noticed the slight bulge in the blacksmith's cheek. Because he'd adopted the habit of chewing Night's Bane as a child, he'd slowly grown accustomed to it. Although the herb made it possible for the living to see the dead, any adult who chewed more than a handful of it would be poisoned. Astrid had already consumed her share of Night's Bane and could never chew it again without risk to her life. Because Randim had developed a resistance to the herb, he served as DiStephan's most direct contact with the living, often much to Randim's distaste.

"He told Randim you were likely to face a dragon roaming near the crops." Trep vaulted out of the cart, landing lightly on his feet. Tall and fair, he wore his fine blond hair in small braids twisted together in a long ponytail.

Astrid turned toward Randim. "When did you see DiStephan? He's been with me all day."

Randim shrugged. "Earlier. He said you were rambling on and wouldn't notice if he popped out for awhile."

Trep beamed, gesturing toward the cart. "Ain't she a beauty? We call her the Girly

Cart, after you. We made it just for hauling dragons." Trep paused. "Dead ones, that is."

Longer than most carts used on the farmland surrounding Guell, its wood was roughly hon. After all, blacksmiths made up most of Guell's population. Unsurprisingly, instead of simply nailing the cart together, they'd forged iron fittings that clung to the cart like a lover's embrace. From each corner, tendrils of iron extended from a solid corner, intertwining in intricate patterns along the cart's exterior.

Astrid stepped forward, touching the iron and taking in its beauty. Her fingers traced one path of the design, which turned and weaved among other tendrils of iron. The blacksmiths had borrowed the design used by jewelers who made broaches inspired by dragons. When she'd first come to Guell as a little girl, DiStephan had given her such a broach.

Happily, Trep nudged Randim. "Girly likes it!"

The last blacksmith, 16-year-old Donel, tied the reins he'd been holding to a nearby branch and walked to Astrid's side. "I wanted to call it Mistress Dragonslayer's Cart, but everyone says it takes too long to say."

Astrid looked at him in surprise. "You've grown!"

Donel grinned, now standing an inch taller than Astrid. "A bit."

"And you cut your hair!" Astrid ran her fingers through Donel's berry-brown hair, which had been long just months ago. Now each strand measured shorter than the length of her thumb. Previously straight, his hair now curled, like wood shavings. Astrid poked at one of the curls. "How do you make your hair do this?"

"He's become a pretty little thing, hasn't he?" Trep teased.

Embarrassed, Donel pulled away from Astrid and muttered, "It does it on its own. I can't help it."

Astrid said, "You look very handsome. And manly." Turning her attention back to the cart, she said, "Thank you. It's the most beautiful cart I've ever seen."

"Good," Randim said, clapping her back. "Let's put it to good use. Trep, grab the lizard's tail—"

The wind swooshed between them, whipping Astrid's hair across her face again. "Wait," she sputtered, fighting her own hair.

Randim continued, pretending he hadn't heard her. "Donel, guide the horses and back up the cart so we can slide the beast onto it."

"Please." Astrid raised her voice. "Someone cut my hair off."

Trep laughed. "Girly wants to look like Donel!"

Astrid gazed at Donel's new, short locks. "I need it shorter."

Trep laughed harder, while Randim gave her a disapproving look. "There is just enough light left in the day for us to load the carcass and cart it back to Guell. You can amuse everyone once we return."

Before Randim could turn away, Astrid grasped his arm. "I'm serious," she said. "I walked into camp and the lizard attacked. My braid snagged on a branch and it tore the tie. My hair came loose and blinded me. My hair nearly got me killed today. It has to come off."

"But it's pretty and womanly." Trep brightened. "I'll teach you how to braid it tiny, like mine, and twist them braids together tight. They've never caught fire. That's what happened to Donel, his hair catching fire in the smithery and all."

"Donel!" Astrid looked him up and down with concern. "Were you hurt?"

"Only his pride," Trep said, laughing.

Sighing, Donel stared at the ground and took the reins to the horses, finally following instructions while Randim walked toward the dead lizard.

Astrid withdrew her dagger and offered it to Trep. "Please cut my hair."

Trep looked at her as if she were holding a poisonous snake. "Why not just wish your hair shorter?"

Astrid had met Randim, Trep, and the other blacksmiths who now called Guell their home several months ago, and none of them had tasted lizard meat before, which meant that none of them had ever known how to shift shape. The blacksmiths were still learning the nuances, even now as they made their muscles larger so they could lift the lizard onto the cart. "Color is one thing," Astrid said. After all, she had naturally blond hair, but after she'd grown old enough to master shapeshifting skills, she'd changed the color of everything about her: her blond hair to dark brown, her light eyes to black, and her skin from scarred and pale white to smooth and brown. "But changing anything else about hair is tricky. I've tried, and it's always gone wrong." Astrid hesitated, remembering how her changed feelings about her lifelong friend Mauri had turned the woman's hair dry and stiff like hay. When Mauri had shaken her head, her hair had cracked and bits of it had broken off. "It has to be cut." Astrid raised the dagger to her head. If no one would help her, she'd do the deed herself.

"Girly!" Trep protested. He pried the dagger from her hand, sighing heavily. With his free hand, he held Astrid's chin, tilting her head one way, then the other. Grasping one small strand at a time, he carefully sliced off her hair.

As Donel guided the horses and Randim lined the cart up next to the lizard, Randim called out, "Trep! Stop wasting time and get over here!"

Trep hesitated and called over his shoulder. "No girly who can twist iron into a dragonish sword should cut her own hair. She can't walk around looking like a barbarian." Quietly, to Astrid, he said, "Just because your hair is short doesn't mean you can't be stylish and beautiful." He paused and studied his handiwork. "It might look quite nice if we left it a bit long in back."

"No!" Astrid tempered her rejection when Trep's expression sank. "Thank you. I need it short all over. I don't want to take any chances."

Trep returned to slicing off her hair. Nodding, he said, "I understand. That dragon spooked you. We'll see to it that none of this misbehaving hair troubles you again."

"Trep!" A frustrated Randim stormed to his side, then paused and stared in dismay at Astrid. "What are you doing to her?"

Frantic, Astrid reached for her head, feeling that the hair on one side had been cropped, while the other side hadn't been touched yet. Running her fingers through the cropped side, she smiled at Trep. "It feels perfect."

Randim gazed in horror at her. "Have you gone mad?"

Trep waved the back of his dagger hand at Randim to shoo him away. "It's only half done. Give us a moment. I'll be hauling dragon carcass with you soon enough."

Open-mouthed, Randim stared from Astrid's half-cropped head to Trep and back to Astrid again. Shaking his head, he walked back to the cart in defeat.

Minutes later, Trep finished the job, handed the dagger back to Astrid, and ran both hands through her short hair, admiring his work. Giggling, he said, "Now everyone will call you Girly just to tell you apart from the boys." He patted her back as he joined Randim and Donel to load the lizard onto the cart.

Astrid marveled at the way she felt, cool and clean and light, running her own fingers through her freshly cut hair. She'd never realized its weight until she found herself free of it.

But when she looked down and saw the mass of her long, dark hair on the ground, surrounding her like seaweed that had washed up on the beach, someone might as well have stolen her dagger and driven it through her heart. Her hair had always been a part of her, an announcement to all the world of her womanhood. Her crowning glory. Every woman cherished her own hair as a source of pride and beauty, and Astrid had rid herself of it willingly.

"Oh, no," Astrid whispered, her blood pounding against her skin. "What have I done?"

CHAPTER SEVEN

Sitting by Randim's side at the front of the cart, Donel drove the horses, while Trep and Astrid rode in back next to the dead lizard. Absent-absentmindedly, Astrid pulled at her newly shorn hair, shorter than the length of her thumb.

"Stop playing with it," Trep said. "What's done is done—and you're the one who asked for it."

Astrid nodded and put her hands in her lap. Trep's words were true. She'd begged for someone to chop her hair off, and she didn't want him to regret helping her.

They arrived at the outskirts of Guell in time to see the sun sink to the treetops, casting long shadows and deepening the chill in the air. Randim and Trep jumped out of the cart, striding toward the village gate.

Astrid remembered when Guell had no gate, leaving itself open to anyone who wished to enter, even though other villages were digging trenches around their borders to discourage attacks. Guell's proximity to Dragon's Head and the dragons it attracted once provided all the safety its residents needed.

As Randim and Trep unlocked the gate and swung it open, Astrid gazed at the masterpiece created by the blacksmiths who now lived in Guell. First, they'd forged long iron pikes to set into the ground, shackled close together in a row to form a fence encompassing the village. Next, they'd fashioned thin ribbons of iron to wrap around hundreds of broken bones and twist onto a pike or shackle.

Although intended only to protect Guell, the fence provided a constant reminder of where she came from and why most of its past villagers had been murdered: her brother Drageen had planned the raid to create the circumstances and ingredients needed to conjure valuable bloodstones from Astrid's body. He'd intended to use them to protect himself, never imagining that Astrid would stop him. She'd never wanted to harm any living thing, but she'd killed her brother and his alchemist by letting them be consumed by the fires on Dragon's Head, and their deaths haunted her. Fighting back guilt, she stared at the dead lizard next to her, ignoring the fence while Donel drove the cart through the gate and Randim locked them inside.

❧❧

The sight of the village Guell startled Astrid even though it was her home. In some ways, it seemed the same. In other ways, it had become something entirely different.

Years ago, no trenches or barricades surrounded Guell. Now an iron fence bearing the bones of its former residents protected the village. Situated on a peninsula just beyond the forest, a stretch of trees had divided the crops from a half-moon of cottages. Oak and pine trees formed a towering canopy over the village, letting the sun dapple through. Their roots gnarled up through the ground like the toes of giant birds, covered with old, brown pine needles and cones. The trunks looked like the skinny legs of monstrous cranes or storks.

Some cottages looked like thatched roofs sitting on the ground, because the houses were hidden underneath. The wealthy, like Astrid, lived under large thatch roofs covering thick stone walls, dividing each cottage into one main room and two alcoves between the walls and the place where the roof sloped down to meet the ground. The less fortunate had no walls: a smaller thatched roof covered a single room dug into the ground. Day and night, smoke rose from the hole in the peak of each roof.

The others were wattle-and-daub houses built by the blacksmiths' wives. The former symmetry of Guell had been replaced with a new blend of homes and faces.

Donel backed the cart up to a long iron table covered by a thatched roof. Trep lowered the back of the cart, and the men dragged the lizard onto the outdoor table.

Her interest peaked, Astrid hopped around them, content to let them do all the work. She'd killed the thing, after all. "This is new," she said, running her fingertips across the tabletop.

Trep grinned. "I figured we should have an easy way for Donel to butcher—"

"I told you!" Donel scrunched his face up, pulling mightily on one of the lizard's legs. "I'm a blacksmith now, just like you. Someone else is going to have to learn how to butcher."

With a mischievous twinkle in his eye, Trep continued as if he hadn't heard Donel speak. "Considering the boy's expertise, his father being a true butcher and all—"

"And he wasn't my real father." Donel beaded with sweat, struggling with his grip on the lizard, despite the cool autumn air. "He bought me from a childseller, just like Blacksmith Temple bought Mistress Dragonslayer."

Holding back his laughter, Trep said, "I figured stone wouldn't do, because all the dragon blood would fall between the stones and be soaked up by the ground, which is troublesome because we all know Girly needs to drink it, not to mention that this ground's seen too many troubles already. Wood ain't useful for the same kinds of reasons. So I says, let's forge a table top, and we'll cover it with sheep's wool in the winter to protect it, just like the wool inside the sheath that protects the blade of a sword." Trep winked at Astrid. "It was my idea and all, and you'd think the butcher's boy would show some thankfulness."

With one final heave, the men dragged the lizard's corpse onto the iron table, a simple tabletop with raised edges and supported by blocks of stone. Astrid recognized them. They were the stones that had formed the supporting walls of finer houses like hers. Those other houses had burned to the ground, leaving nothing behind but the blackened walls.

Trep and Randim stood back, looking expectantly at Donel. With a burdened sigh, he picked up a cleaver from the tabletop and began the work he'd learned from his adopted father.

"Where is she?" Lenore called out from the throng of women and children who emerged from the village to gather around the butchering table. Lenore raced toward Randim, her long skirt brushing through the brittle fallen leaves. Normally braided tightly down her back, today Lenore's hair was unbound and free. She caught her breath in surprise, taking in the sight of the slain lizard and Donel cutting it up into meat for the villagers.

Astrid smiled at Lenore's approach, but Lenore's gaze swept past her. *She doesn't recognize me*, Astrid realized.

No one seemed to notice Lenore. Instead, they swarmed with excitement around the new supply of meat that would help them survive the winter.

Lenore raised her voice and both fists toward the sky to command attention. Although tears welled in her eyes, her voice was strong. "Where is she? Did that thing kill her?"

Everyone paused and looked at Lenore in surprise.

A sudden gust swirled around her feet, spinning slowly around her body until it swirled her hair high into the air, rippling like the highest branches of a tree.

Astrid felt struck by the sight, thinking this is how Lenore must have looked in the old days when she'd begged a blacksmith for help in a life she needed to reclaim. Astrid took in Lenore's wide and steady stance, her raised arms, her determined jaw, and the freeness with which her hair whipped in the air.

Randim laughed, and Lenore's eyes blazed with anger.

"No troubles," Randim said, still smiling. "She's standing right next to you."

Baffled, Lenore spun, glancing briefly at Astrid and then scanning the throng of villagers surrounding Donel and offering their unwanted advice to him while he carved up the lizard. "Where?"

Astrid reached out and took Lenore's hands. "I'm fine."

Lenore stared at Astrid until she recognized her friend. "Your face—you look so different without your hair." Lenore tried to blink back her tears, but they spilled down her face. She held on tight to Astrid's hands. "I didn't know it was you." Suddenly, Lenore stopped, studying Astrid closely. The expression fell away from her face, and her eyes filled with dread. "What happened?" She let go of Astrid's hands and touched her cropped hair gingerly, as if it might break. "Who did this to you?"

Trep stepped up and clapped Astrid heartily on the back. "I'm the one to blame," he said happily.

Lenore turned to Trep, enraged. "What's wrong with you?" Her face flushed with anger, Lenore slapped him.

"No!" Astrid stepped between the still enraged Lenore and a devastated Trep. "I asked him to cut my hair off. Trep did nothing wrong."

Tears glistened on Lenore's face again, as she stared at Astrid's hair in disbelief. "Why?"

"I had braided my hair, like you often do. When this lizard attacked, my hair snagged in a tree. I had to fight the lizard while trying to free myself from the tree. My hair almost got me killed today." Lowering her voice, Astrid took a step closer to Lenore so only her friend could hear her words. "I thought about you and how you asked a blacksmith to cut off your feet so you could keep on living. I know it's not the same, but I thought of you."

Astrid glanced down at the hem of Lenore's long skirt where the toes of the silver shoes she'd made for her friend peeked out from the hem. Astrid's closest friends had been DiStephan and Mauri. She treasured the presence of DiStephan's spirit, but Mauri was lost forever. Astrid appreciated the irony of having made a new friend with a woman who walked on the spirit feet that existed because she believed in them.

Astrid looked back up to see a seriousness in Lenore's gaze that she'd never seen before. Lenore was the most confident woman Astrid had ever met as well as the only woman who laughed and kept the shape she desired whenever men looked at her with the kind of longing that had the power to change her body against her will. Lenore spoke, and her voice had a gritty undertone laced with fear. "You're not leaving Guell this winter? You're staying in your own smithery and becoming a blacksmith again?"

"Of course." Astrid blinked in surprise. Everyone in Guell knew her plan.

Lenore studied Astrid's face and then sank her fingers through her cropped hair until Astrid noticed her sharp fingernails scratch her scalp. "Promise me."

Astrid felt startled by Lenore's insistent touch. For the past several months, Astrid had embraced the life of a hermit while she followed DiStephan's spirit through the Northlands, tracing the established route of the dragonslayer. She'd introduced herself to each village as his successor. Welcomed everywhere she went, she'd been touched and delighted by the invitations to feasts where people told their stories about DiStephan and what he'd done for them.

And yet such respect meant people rarely touched her, usually nothing more than a brief hand on her arm. However much she loved DiStephan in her travels, she missed his physical presence. Now she realized the solace brought by the simple touch of a friend. "Of course." Astrid smiled, looking straight into Lenore's eyes to make sure she saw her intent. "I promise. I'll spend the winter in Guell."

Casting one last worried glance at Astrid's short hair, Lenore nodded her understanding, pulled her hands back to herself, and wrung them for a moment.

"There you are!" A booming voice called out from the throng surrounding the slain lizard. A hefty man stepped toward them, his long free-flowing hair the color of a rusty setting sun. His broad face sported a bushy beard lighter in shade, and his small blue eyes were as piercing as the truth. He smelled of old sweat and dust.

Astrid recognized the scent immediately. It stank with the tang of someone who had traveled for weeks or months without the chance to bathe. A merchant from the Lower Northlands who traveled throughout the Southlands, Sigurthor brought unusual dried meats and fruits to trade at the end of every dragon season.

Sigurthor clapped a hearty hand on Donel's back while the boy butchered the lizard. "Don't you go and bother saving any of that for me. Your father always tried, but I'll have none of that ghastly stuff. But where is the dragonslayer? You said you'd be bringing him back with you."

His forehead creased with concern, Donel glanced at Astrid. "That's our new dragonslayer."

Sigurthor followed his gaze. "A boy?" Sigurthor bellowed in disbelief. "You've hired a boy?"

Astrid realized Sigurthor meant her. "A boy?" she said with equal disbelief.

"It's your hair," Lenore whispered. "At first glance, I thought you were a boy, too."

Anger flared inside Astrid at the insult. "I'm not a boy!" she said. "I'm a woman!"

Sigurthor squinted as if that might help him see better. He stepped toward Astrid slowly, looking up and down. "I'm looking for the dragonslayer who calls Guell home. The successor who fills the shoes of DiStephan and his father before him."

"You know me," Astrid said patiently. He'd never paid much attention to her in the past, but surely Sigurthor remembered her. "I'm Astrid."

Sigurthor stopped suddenly, his face slack with dismay. Then his pale skin flushed with anger. "Law breaker!" he shouted, pointing at Astrid. "Pay the price for your crime!"

CHAPTER EIGHT

"Law breaker?" Astrid replied in disbelief. "When has slaying lizards become a crime?"

"Any woman who pretends to be a man insults all men." Sigurthor's color continued to rise while he glared at her. "It is a crime to dress like a man. It is a crime to wear your hair like a boy. And it should be a crime to pretend to do a man's job." Sigurthor paused, seeming to make a mental note. "I'll take that up with my chieftain. We need a new law for that."

DiStephan had told Astrid and everyone else in Guell how the Northlands had been changing over the years. Not only had villages begun to dig ditches on their outskirts to discourage attacks from brigands, but villages had chosen chieftains to be their lawmakers in regions throughout the Northlands outside of Scalding territory. Chieftains memorized all laws and settled disputes, keeping the peace among villages. And if someone committed a crime, making amends typically boiled down to paying for the crime with an acceptable offer to the offended party.

Like most men, Sigurthor wore his wealth on his body in the form of silver armbands and rings. Wealth took many forms in addition to silver: land, livestock, butter, cheese, and homespun cloth. Sigurthor typically came to Guell each year with goods from the southern part of the Northlands and the Southlands and then left with a cart loaded with cloth and cheese. But now he eyed the sword at Astrid's side. Because of the value of iron and the amount required—not to mention the craftsmanship—one sword had the kind of value that could feed and clothe a man for a year. Other than a chest full of silver or a vast stretch of farmland, Astrid knew of nothing more valuable than a dragonslayer's sword.

"You're in Guell," Astrid said, standing her ground. "We have no such laws."

Sigurthor paused, then scoffed. He turned his attention from Astrid, ignoring her. To Randim and Trep, Sigurthor said, "Surely you don't condone women making a mockery of men. Everything about her ridicules us."

Randim ignored him.

Astrid spoke louder. "Guell is part of Scalding territory. Your laws have no meaning here."

Paying no attention to her, Sigurthor's eyes widened at Randim's refusal to speak. "Are you a woman? Is Guell nothing but a village full of women?"

Astrid became aware of a stillness that surrounded them all. Randim and Trep stood nearby, each suddenly tense. At the butchering table, Donel had stopped his work, his face taut and grim. The dozens of villagers in Guell had gathered to take their share of lizard meat, but now they all stared at Sigurthor and Astrid. One of the blacksmiths clenched his fists and his teeth, and his wife held him back with a gentle touch on his shoulder.

"I'm a dragonslayer and a blacksmith," Astrid said. "I belong in Guell. I have nothing to do with you or your laws."

Sigurthor's face darkened. "DiStephan was my friend. Each year we traveled together from Guell, and he killed every dragon that crossed our path." He cast a bitter look at Astrid. "If any ill befalls me, my blood is on your hands."

A sense of unease seeped into Astrid's bones. She watched Sigurthor blend back in among the villagers who watched Donel butcher the lizard. Guell meant safety, surrounded by her friends and neighbors. But something in her bones told her to be careful.

She sensed danger as surely as she had the ability to smell the scent of lizards in the air.

Chapter Nine

That evening, with bellies full of bread and roasted lizard meat, Astrid and Donel strolled down the narrow spit of land that separated the village of Guell from her smithery. A sea breeze chilled her face and filled her nose with the tang of salt. In the distance, waves boomed against Dragon Head, the rocky outcrop near Astrid's cottage. Donel carried a torch even though the full moon hovered near the horizon, filling their path with light. Astrid smiled. "How do you like being rich and successful and prominent now that you're a blacksmith?"

Donel snorted. "In a village full of blacksmiths with years more experience than me? You might as well ask how I like being poor and struggling." He paused and grinned. "But it's a far cry better than being elbow-deep in guts and blood all day." Donel looked over his shoulder to make sure no one could overhear. "I don't mind cutting up a dragon, but I'm happy the blacksmiths' women do their own butchering when it comes to pigs and cattle."

"Are people settling in? Getting along?"

"You mean with the blacksmiths and their families? It seems fine." Donel shrugged. "It's odd with the village being smaller and with more people blacksmithing than farming, but that's likely to turn around soon enough."

Astrid nodded. She'd met the blacksmiths at a time that they'd worked mostly for Drageen, shoring up Tower Island by surrounding it with a fence of iron to keep dragons out. Like most villages, Guell survived by farming, which required most of its people to tend crops and livestock. A village would typically have one blacksmith—like Astrid—to forge and mend iron for farming tools. In exchange for helping Astrid buy the survivors of Guell out of slavery, the blacksmiths had accepted her offer to share ownership of its land, even though it meant working the land themselves.

"Will it bother you?" Astrid said. "Spending more time farming than blacksmithing?"

"I'd spend every minute of the day at the anvil if I could," Donel said wistfully. "But we all need to spend our fair share of time in the fields. And after all my years of knocking at your door and begging to be your apprentice, I'm happy something's finally come of it!"

Astrid laughed. "Is it anything like you imagined?"

Donel sighed in content, gazing at the bright moon ahead of them. "Who in his right mind wouldn't prefer creating something useful and beautiful out of a raw piece of iron to killing?" He stopped suddenly, his eyes wide with horror. "I'm sorry,

Mistress Dragonslayer! I didn't mean-"

"I feel the same, Donel," Astrid said quietly. "I don't like killing any more than you." She draped her arm across the boy's shoulders and hugged him briefly. "I'm looking forward to a long winter working in my smithery. I miss the fire and the heat."

As they approached her cottage, he led her into the smithery, lit by his torch. "I've tried to keep it exactly as you left it," Donel said, brushing a stray bit of slag off the top of the anvil.

Astrid breathed in the scent of iron and lingering smoke, gazing at the long forging table and the neat row of blacksmithing tools: hammers and fire rakes and tongs, all forged by her own hand or by Temple, the blacksmith who had bought her from the childseller and made her his apprentice many years ago. The smithery appeared alien and familiar at the same time, like a long lost friend from childhood.

"Here's a place for your weapons," Donel said, beaming with pride. "I figured since DiStephan always took his with him when he went to the Southlands each winter, yours should have a safe place by your side." He gestured to a corner of the smithery that had once stood empty. Now, several elaborate bars with double hooks had been forged and nailed to the wall. A spare ax and a few daggers hung neatly on either side of the largest hooked bar in the center. The design reminded Astrid of the ironwork of the Girly Cart they'd made for hauling dead lizards back to Guell: thin threads of iron wove in and out and among other tendrils of iron, curling and twisting together while forming the shape of a dragon, and the hook on each end looked like a crooked leg. The image of a large star rose at the center of the dragon's back, rays of light attaching it to the animal.

"Starlight," Astrid whispered.

"Yes, Ma'am," Donel said, clearly pleased with himself as he stood straighter, throwing his shoulders back and resting his hands on his waist. He looked expectantly from Astrid to the hook he'd made for her dragonslaying sword—the first sword she'd ever made and the sword DiStephan had kept by his side since the day of its creation.

Astrid hesitated. During the past months, she'd grown used to Starlight's weight at her side with every step she took. At night, she slept with her arms around the sheathed sword. Leaving it alone in the smithery seemed like a cold and heartless thing to do.

But Donel had spoken the truth. All her weapons had been forged in the smithery. Keeping them in the smithery meant they'd remain in her sight and at her side throughout the winter. She untied the sheath from her belt and eased Starlight's crossguard into the hooks, the blade centered between them. The sword's grip hid the star, but its rays streamed behind it, and the dragon seemed to be resting upon the crossguard. The effect dazzled Astrid. "It's beautiful."

"Oh," Donel said, excitement rising in his voice. "I also made this for you." He removed a dagger from a hooked bar next to Starlight and handed it to her. Grinning, he said, "I figured our Mistress Dragonslayer can never have too many daggers."

Astrid wrapped her fingers around the leather grip, studying the dagger's blade. Donel's torchlight illuminated the patterned design, like tiny dragon scales running down the blade's center. Those scales shone faintly blue next to the edges, polished mirror bright. "You made it like Starlight," Astrid said in wonder. Her eyes shone as brightly as its edges and she smiled at Donel. "You made this dagger the same way we make dragonslayer swords!"

"I remember DiStephan always needed new daggers because his bent or broke, so I thought, why not make a dagger like a sword? Why not twist different pieces of iron together to make it stronger?" Bubbling with excitement, Donel pointed at the blade. "And see how pretty the patterns came out? Trep and Randim made it, but I helped. It was my idea, and I took the blooms of iron and forged them into those long rods—"

"The billets," Astrid said, enjoying Donel's enthusiasm.

"Right. The billets. I made a couple of billets, and then we cut them short, into dagger-size billets. Then we hammered them thinner than usual because we didn't want you to end up with a blade as wide as a sword." Donel paused, breathless from talking. "It's Starlight's little sister."

The name came to Astrid immediately, and she remembered the same had happened to DiStephan when he'd seen Starlight for the first time. She raised the dagger above her head and brought it down in a slashing motion. "Falling Star," she said.

Delighted, Donel clapped his hands together. "That's a very threatening name! You can say, 'Beware or my star shall fall upon you!'"

Astrid laughed. "I may do just that." Carefully, she returned Falling Star back to its hooks. "But for now I'm ready to sleep in my own bed."

"Right," Donel said, casting one last look around the smithery before they left.

Astrid recognized that look. It's what every blacksmith did to make sure everything was in its place, tidy and neat.

"You've been sleeping on the ground for months, haven't you?" Donel said. "I've kept your cottage the way you like, and mine's been built in Guell, so I'm just a stone's throw away if you need anything."

"Good night, Donel. Thank you for taking care of everything while I was gone."

Donel nodded his head, unsuccessful at his attempt to hide his smile. "And all those years you told me you didn't want an apprentice. 'I don't want one. Never have, never will.' That's what you always said." He waved, walking back toward Guell. "Like I said, you couldn't resist me."

Laughing, Astrid walked into her cottage, dimly lit by a smoldering fire in its central hearth. Like her smithery, it felt strangely familiar and alien at the same time, but she found comfort in sitting by the fire, adding wood, and tending it until it blazed. Fire had been her friend since childhood, and she basked in its company. Finally, she crawled into bed and slept the deep sleep of gratitude at having come home at last.

⁂

Astrid cried out the next morning, sitting up in bed with a start. It took her several moments to wake up and get her bearings: she'd returned to Guell and spent the night in her own home. But her heart raced and sweat beaded her forehead.

Had she heard brigands in her sleep? Could Guell be under attack?

Astrid bolted out of her cottage, straining her eyes as she looked across the spit of land that separated her cottage and smithery from the village. In the distance, steady columns of smoke rose from cottages, and cows lowed contentedly. She heard the murmur of conversation and women's laughter.

The ocean wind slammed the cottage door shut behind her. Astrid turned to look, and dust swirled to form the faint outline of a man pointing at her smithery.

"DiStephan," she said.

Astrid burst into her smithery, her heart pounding harder. She saw the problem at once, racing to the wall and slamming her hands against the empty spot below the waiting hooks.

Starlight had disappeared.

CHAPTER TEN

Astrid stared in disbelief at the hooked bar on which she had hung the dragon-slayer's sword just last night. All her other weapons surrounded the empty space: the ax and daggers—and Falling Star, the dagger forged in the same manner as her swords.

But why had Starlight vanished? Who could have taken it? Why would anyone who lived in Guell—?

Astrid clenched her teeth, realizing what must have happened. Sigurthor had stolen it, angry that she'd refused to escort him back to his home like DiStephan had done every year.

When Astrid left her smithery, her wall of weapons held nothing but empty hooks.

⁊⁊

"Sigurthor!" Astrid shouted, storming into Guell. She'd tucked each dagger under her belt, and she carried the ax in hand.

The dirt streets were empty, even though thin streams of smoke rose through the center of every thatched roof in the village. Astrid paused, spinning slowly while she tried to gain her bearings. It had been months since she'd last been in Guell, and her neighbors had built several new cottages, changing the look of the village. She remembered where Sigurthor had planned to sleep last night, but she couldn't find the right cottage. "Randim!" Astrid shouted. "Lenore!"

"They've gone to the fields."

Astrid noticed the wife of a blacksmith sitting in the doorway of a cottage. She'd wrapped a strip of cloth, dyed blue with woad, around her head but her curly red hair flowed freely through its open end and down her back. "Who?" Astrid said.

"Everyone." The blacksmith's wife had draped a long length of the same blue cloth across her lap and placed her baby in its center. Now, the woman methodically wrapped the cloth around the infant. "Today could be the last good day we get for harvesting."

The sky domed clear and bright, and the sun warmed Astrid's face as she gazed up, but the autumn chill pierced the air with a warning that winter would soon be upon them.

A little girl crept slowly from the shadows inside the cottage with her hands raised menacingly above her head. She jumped forward, wrapping her pudgy arms around the woman's neck while she shouted, "Boo!"

Without flinching, the woman continued her meticulous swaddling of the infant in her lap. She said, "Oh, that was quite frightening."

The little girl giggled in delight.

"Now, back inside with you. You know the rule: children must be heard and not seen."

Still giggling, the girl skipped back inside.

For a moment, Astrid remembered her own childhood, tucked safely inside Temple's smithery, now hers. It took many years of practice to hold back one's thoughts so that they wouldn't change others, and children were kept out of the way of adults until they'd mastered that skill.

Astrid watched the woman tie the ends of the same cloth swaddling her infant around herself, binding the baby to her chest. "Where do Randim and Lenore live?"

Finally, the woman looked up and froze at the sight of the ax in Astrid's hand. Wide-eyed, the blacksmith's wife placed each hand on the doorway as if blocking the entrance to her home with her body. Calmly, she said, "Are there dragons about?"

Astrid shook her head. "Just a thief."

Heaving a sigh of relief, the blacksmith's wife pointed to a cottage across from her own.

Tightening her grip on the ax, Astrid stomped toward it, not caring if he heard her coming. No one could escape the wrath of a dragonslayer.

But she opened the door and found the cottage empty.

CHAPTER ELEVEN

Astrid's gaze swept the empty cottage, searching for any sign of Sigurthor's presence. Although the odor of the hearth fire and smoke permeated the cottage, her nose twitched at the scent of old sweat and dust common to traveling merchants. If he wasn't here, why could she still smell him?

A blanket lay in a puddle next to the hearth. Astrid raised a handful of it to her face and inhaled. It reeked with the awful stink of the merchant who must have stolen her sword.

Most everyone in Guell already toiled in the fields to bring in the last harvest, which meant Sigurthor had left the village. But he was much older than Astrid, heavier, and slower. If she hurried, Astrid could probably catch up with him by afternoon. Only one dirt road led from Guell, and it eventually forked in three directions. Sigurthor might take any one of them.

Outside, the infant's sharp cry pierced the air. Looking through the open doorway, Astrid saw the blacksmith's wife walk back and forth, the swaddled baby still wrapped close against her chest, until the cry dissolved into contented gurgles.

Of course.

Still holding onto her ax, Astrid picked up the blanket with her free hand before she left the cottage where Sigurthor had spent the night.

❧❧

By the time Astrid entered the dragonslayer's camp outside of Guell at mid-morning, the sun had barely climbed above the treetops, casting long shadows onto the open ground beyond the forest's edge. The sky appeared cloudless and the sun warmed the back of her neck despite the icy ocean breeze sweeping through the camp.

Guilt gnawed at Astrid. She knelt by the small stones encircling the remains of past fires, now littered with broken eggshells. Putting down the folded blanket and ax, she freed the leather gloves tucked into her belt and slipped them on. She picked up only the blanket. She stood and headed toward her sleeping shelter. Kneeling outside it, she gazed into the shelter and said, "There you are."

A tiny lizard scampered from the shelter, jumped up, and clamped its jaws around one of her gloved fingers. The pressure of his bite felt like a slight pinch, and his teeth were too small to pierce the leather.

"No," Astrid said firmly. She recognized the lizard immediately: she'd named it after watching it hatch. "Let go, Smoke. You must not bite people. It will kill them."

Smoke's eyes brightened, seemingly in recognition, while he continued to dangle from her finger.

Before she could react, a second tiny lizard darted up her bent leg, flung itself up onto her arm, and sped to her hand, where it nosed her gloved fingertips before clamping onto one with its mouth. The second lizard's eyes were pale amber.

Astrid smiled. "Where there's Smoke, there's Fire."

As she eased the hand with two lizards dangling from it to the ground, she reached into the folds of the blanket with her other hand and withdrew a chunk of lizard meat. She suspected the hatchlings smelled the scent of it on her gloves, and now she would lure them with the real thing.

Sure enough, Smoke and Fire quickly released her fingertips and pounced on the meat the moment she tossed it toward them.

Unease crept into her belly. Her dragonslayer duties meant killing lizards, not feeding them. But if Taddeo had pointed them out to her, didn't that mean they were more likely to be dragons than lizards? Astrid's family had betrayed and harmed her. Her own brother had tried to murder her. Dragons had taken her in and accepted her as one of their own. How could she take the chance of harming the newborns of those who had come to her aid and saved her life? Lizards were just animals. Astrid didn't understand exactly what dragons were, but she experienced more of an allegiance to them than to most people she'd met.

Astrid turned her attention toward the blanket, shaking out the folds and thinking back to the way she'd seen the blacksmith's wife swaddle her infant. Astrid wouldn't be able to use the same technique, but it inspired her to create a small pouch by tying strategic knots and wrapping the rest of the blanket around her chest. Once finished, she looked up to see Smoke and Fire dragging the chunk of meat back into her sleeping shelter. Crawling into the shelter in pursuit, Astrid saw one more hatchling curled up around its broken eggshell.

Letting go of the meat, Smoke nudged the third lizard until its sibling stretched its jaws open in a lazy yawn. Unlike Smoke and Fire, whose coloring consisted of narrow horizontal stripes of black dotted with ivory, the last lizard sported solid pale gray skin, the same color as slag, the gray flakes that magically emerged from the iron during hammering.

Gingerly, Astrid reached for the meat and picked it up before Fire could attack her hand. Smoke and Fire darted toward her, transfixed on the meat even though it disappeared into the blanket pouch on her belly. Leaning forward, she opened the mouth of the pouch, letting them see the meat inside.

In unison, the two hatchlings stared steadily at Astrid.

"I'm not going to hurt you," she said. "I need your help."

Fire took a tentative step forward and looked at Smoke for approval. Smoke sped into the pouch with Fire on its heels.

The last lizard had rolled onto its back, still under the sleeping shelter, its jaws opening wide in another yawn.

"You, too, Slag," Astrid said, picking the hatchling up by the tip of its tail and dropping it into the pouch. "There's a merchant we need to find."

Picking up her ax, Astrid cast one last look before leaving the dragonslayer's camp with three lizard hatchlings rustling inside the blanket against her belly.

≈≈

"Which way did he go?" Astrid said, sitting on the ground at the place where the path from Guell forked in three different directions. After removing Smoke, Fire, and Slag from the blanket pouch, she'd placed them at the fork. But instead of following Sigurthor's scent, they looked longingly at the meat they'd been chewing on for the past few hours, now in Astrid's hand.

When they'd first arrived at the fork, she'd tried asking DiStephan's ghost but received no response. She assumed he was angry with her for keeping the baby lizards instead of killing them.

Years ago, DiStephan had told her of tracking dogs in the Southern lands that were trained to hunt animals by detecting their scent in the woods. Astrid suspected these lizards had the same capability. She had to figure out how to let them know what she needed from them.

She closed her fingers to hide the meat while she used her other hand to withdraw one of the daggers tucked under her belt to cut off a small corner of the blanket. She returned the dagger to her belt and slipped the meat back inside the blanket pouch.

She showed the blanket scrap to the hatchlings. "This blanket has the scent of a bad man who stole my weapon," Astrid said, looking into each lizard's eyes. She held it close to her nose and breathed deeply, flinching at the faint stink of many weeks worth of the man's sweat. "Now—which way did he go?" On her hands and knees, Astrid crawled toward the path branching off to the left. "This way?" She backtracked and crawled toward the center road. "This way?" She backtracked again and crawled toward the path on the right. "Or this way?"

Smoke looked at her blankly. Fire stared at the pouch where she'd hidden the meat. Slag curled up, resting its head on its own tail. Slag's eyes closed sleepily.

Astrid sat on the ground again, placing the piece of blanket between the hatchlings. Smoke poked at the blanket piece with one foot. Fire took a few tentative steps toward Astrid, still fixated on the blanket pouch that held the meat.

On this windless day, dirt swirled in the center of the path on the left.

Astrid decided to make one final attempt at communicating with DiStephan's ghost. Maybe he'd cooled off enough to listen. "Do you know where Sigurthor went?" Astrid said. "He stole Starlight, didn't he?"

The dirt swirled steadily then blew itself at the lizards.

"I couldn't leave them to fend for themselves," she explained to the ghost. "They might be dragons."

While Astrid respected all living things, she'd learned that lizards and dragons were entirely different creatures. Lizards were animals whose opinions of themselves had inflated their bodies to a gigantic size. But they were nothing more than animals. Dragons could take the shape of lizards or people or water. She didn't understand what dragons were or what they wanted with her, but her instinct told her to protect anything that might be one. And right now that meant protecting Smoke, Fire, and Slag.

Astrid sighed as she watched Smoke chew on the piece of blanket she'd cut off to provide Sigurthor's scent. Fire crept toward her. Slag rolled onto his back and stretched. She shouldn't have expected so much from them. They'd only hatched yesterday.

She scooped each hatchling up by its tail, dropped them inside the blanket pouch, and took her ax in hand, following the swirling dust caused by DiStephan's ghost onto the left fork in the road. She could catch up with Sigurthor soon and hoped he'd have the good sense to give Starlight back to her. Astrid dreaded the thought of using the ax against him, but she had already decided to take whatever steps were necessary to regain the sword she loved.

CHAPTER TWELVE

Astrid traveled all day on foot through the forest, pausing to gather autumn berries every time she stumbled upon them. Every so often she thought she could smell the heavy musk of an animal nearby, but the brittle, fallen leaves blanketing her path made it impossible to walk without crunching through them. Other than occasional chirps of squirrels in the trees above, Astrid heard nothing other than her own explosive footsteps.

The forest hosted a mixture of pine and leafy trees, and the latter were now bare trunks and branches. All around her, seemingly for miles, trees stood like sentinels, quietly keeping the secrets of the forest to themselves. The sun had traveled low on the horizon all day, casting soft beams of pale light among the black tree skeletons. Finally, the path led out of the forest and alongside a field of wheat waving like ocean waves in the wind.

Astrid paused. The forest rose slightly above the field, nestled in a narrow valley between the forest and the mountains leading to the interior of the Northlands. Men cut down the stalks with scythes while women bundled up the wheat into sheaves and shouldered them onto carts. If Sigurthor had come this way, which DiStephan's ghost seemed to indicate, surely they had seen him.

She gazed at the path ahead that paralleled the field and led into the mountains. The journey appeared bleak and long. Sigurthor could have stopped here to rest. He could be here even now.

Astrid made her way carefully down the gentle slope into the valley, but the people working the fields seemed too intent on their work to notice her presence. She walked toward the sea of wheat and sensed the wind moving through it, giving the rustling stalks of grain the same life and spirit as any other creature. The closer she stepped, the harder her heart beat. She couldn't help but fear that if she let herself drift too close, the crops would sweep her into their depths, covering her mouth and nose with grain until she drowned in it.

She paused and looked back at the path she'd traveled from Guell. Enough time remained to continue forward on that path, trusting she'd catch up with Sigurthor somewhere in the mountains. Or she could turn back and return to Guell.

Astrid clenched her jaw in determination. Months ago her friends and neighbors had been taken captive and sold into slavery, and she hadn't given up on them. Starlight was her friend and ally, and the thought of her best blade in the merchant's hands sickened her.

Keeping a good arm's length from the edge of the crop, just in case something might reach out and pull her into it, Astrid paced its length until she reached an opening where the wheat had been harvested and the stalks were flattened to the ground, creating a path into the crop. The stalks crackled and popped like fire beneath her feet, and their unevenness gave her pause. "Hello?" she called out, but her voice sank among the chopping sounds of the scythes, the bustle of sheaves being gathered, and the wind whipping through the still-standing stalks towering above her head. Nervously walking between pulsing walls of wheat, Astrid stumbled upon a crossroad inside the crop. Looking to her right, she saw a cart and a woman heaving a bundle of wheat onto it. "Hello!" Astrid called out, striding forward.

Finished with her bundle, the woman looked up.

"I've come from Guell," Astrid shouted, walking toward the cart and the woman. "I'm looking for a merchant traveling through this region. He took something of mine that doesn't belong to him."

As Astrid drew near, the woman froze, her face pale with fear. She pointed at Astrid and screamed, "Monster!"

CHAPTER THIRTEEN

The woman screamed, frozen in place.

Astrid shuddered at being called a monster. When she'd first come to Guell, she saw herself as a monster because of the scars covering her body. Her greatest wish had been answered the moment the blacksmith Temple had told her that one day she'd learn how to choose the way she appeared to others. Much later in life she learned only those who ate lizard meat would see the shape she chose for herself. People who had no lizard meat to eat—or who refused it—saw her for what she truly was.

She'd never wanted anyone to be afraid of her, and her heart ached after the woman screamed and her pointing finger trembled in horror.

"Please," Astrid said softly and taking a slow step forward. "I'm not a monster. I'm a dragonslayer."

The woman screamed as if being tortured and dropped to her knees, folding her hands in a pleading gesture. "Don't kill me!"

The walls of wheat surrounding Astrid thrashed and churned as a dozen men and women emerged from the crop behind the pleading woman, who cried out, "There she is! The monster!" She wept in terror.

Two men forged ahead of the crowd, taking a few cautious steps beyond the crumpled woman, pausing when they came close enough to get a good look at Astrid. Their eyes widened in surprise. One man's nose looked misshapen, long and crooked, from having been broken. The other's large forehead seemed slightly dented in one corner and his hair had receded around it. She clearly remembered the day they'd stormed her cottage and she'd fought back by using her hammers for weapons. "Lumpy," she said, remembering what she'd called them on the day their paths had crossed and she'd witnessed the damage they'd earned from fighting with Astrid. "Broken Nose."

As Astrid walked toward them, the men and women behind them uttered a collective gasp of horror, and a few gathered the weeping woman in their arms and dragged her back out of harm's way. Lumpy and Broken Nose stood their ground.

"She be no joke," Lumpy called back to the crowd behind him. "This monster be the task we been give. Stand back."

"Monster?" Astrid said in disbelief. With every step she took toward Lumpy and Broken Nose, the men and women behind them took two steps back. "You're calling me a monster?"

Lumpy tilted his head, studying her closely. "Your hair be chopped off. What happened? Did it catch fire in the smiting camp?"

Broken Nose straightened his stance and raised his chin. "We sold you in a square deal to Randim and warned him to keep you locked up. If you tried your tricks and got away, ain't our problem and no one can hold us accountable."

Lumpy brightened and gestured to the crop surrounding them. "All this be ours now. We was riding along, planning on sailing far away from Scalding territory, but then we heard you murdered your own brother—"

"He died in a fair fight," Astrid said, her throat tightening with emotion.

"We bought this land, and it's ours now," Broken Nose said, ruffled like an animal defending its territory.

"I have no quarrel with that," Astrid said. "And neither will Randim. I'm not his property any more—I struck a deal and earned my freedom. He's my friend—Randim and the other blacksmiths. We've rebuilt Guell."

Lumpy brightened. "She be like a sweet pony now, not a barbarian girl." He patted her cropped hair.

"I never have been and never will be a barbarian. Stop calling me that." Astrid shrugged away from his touch and eyed the brigands with suspicion. "Have you told these people that I'm a monster? Are you planning to hurt them?"

"No!" Lumpy withdrew his hand from her head as if she'd stung him. "We be farmers now. These be our workers." He hesitated. "We might be mentioning we could protect them from the Scalding monster that roams the countryside looking to rip people's innards out and eat them alive."

"Because we used to be brigands," Broken Nose added. "And we conquered the monster before."

"And I'm the monster you conquered?" Astrid pressed her lips together, willing herself to quell the anger that threatened to rise up inside her. Quietly, she said, "I'm disappointed in both of you."

"It was his idea and all," Lumpy said. "How was we to know you be showing up again?"

The villagers talked behind them, straining their necks to watch the confrontation.

Broken Nose turned to face them. "No need to fear. The monster will be leaving soon." Turning back to Astrid, he said, "Why don't you give them a good growl? Give them a bit of a start, at least."

Astrid suppressed a smile as inspiration struck. "Do any of your people eat dragon meat?"

Lumpy shuddered. "Everyone be saying dragon meat's enchanted, and no good comes from enchantment. We have none of that mischief here!"

Astrid considered her options. If Lumpy, Broken Nose, and their people rejected the notion of eating lizard meat, then they all saw Astrid's true form: a one-armed woman covered with scars. No matter what Astrid did to change her shape, none of them would see it.

But there were other ways to impress them.

Rolling up the sleeve of one arm to expose bare skin, she pulled Falling Star from her belt and waved it slowly above her head. "Behold!" Astrid cried out in the most menacing voice she could muster. "My magical dagger!"

The crowd looked at the dagger questioningly then at Astrid as if waiting for something to happen.

Lumpy squinted. "What be magical about it?"

Astrid's heart sank, realizing she'd forgotten she had both a real arm and a spirit arm. She'd meant to make the dagger seem to float in mid-air, but she obviously held it with her flesh-and-blood arm, not her spirit arm. Thinking quickly, Astrid handed it slowly to Lumpy. "See how it bears the same qualities of a dragonslayer's sword."

Lumpy gasped in delight. "So it does!

"Like a snake," Broken Nose murmured, looking over Lumpy's shoulder and pointing at the dagger's blade. "Crawling right down the middle."

Lumpy gazed at the blade with admiration. "Like a pretty blue snake hidden inside! Like magic!"

The people behind them crept up to catch a glimpse of Falling Star.

At the same time, Astrid rolled up the sleeve of her spirit arm and snatched Falling Star out of Lumpy's hands with a hand that would appear invisible to everyone else. "And I control the magic—because I am a monster!"

The women shrieked, and one of the men fainted. The others pointed at the dagger Astrid held high above her head. "It's an enchanted dagger!"

Lumpy's eyes welled with tears and he sank to his knees, looking at Astrid in wonder. "My pretty pony girl be an enchantress!"

But Broken Nose crossed his arms, unimpressed.

The villagers screamed, shielding themselves with their arms and stumbling away from Astrid.

"She's turning into a dragon!" one of the village men shouted, wide-eyed in horror. He stepped bravely in front of the women.

"By the gods," Broken Nose murmured, paling as he stared at Astrid's chest. "What have you gone and done to yourself?"

Baffled, Astrid looked down to see the baby lizard Slag poke its head sleepily from the makeshift cloth pouch she'd tied around her chest. Slag struggled to free its front legs and let them dangle over the edge of the cloth while he yawned, opening his jaw impossibly wide.

"That's a dragon." Lumpy's voice trembled. He clung to Broken Nose's arm. "Why there be a dragon poking out of your chest?"

Determined, Astrid addressed the villagers cowering behind the brigands. "Behold my power to transform into a dragon! This is only the beginning. If you refuse to help me, I'll complete my transformation and breathe fire on you and your harvest!"

One of the villagers dropped to his knees. "Please, no! Tell us what you need and we'll help you!"

"Monsters need food!" she shouted to the villagers. Quietly, to Broken Nose and Lumpy, she said, "I'm tracking a merchant named Sigurthor."

"Big man?" Lumpy said. "Red hair? Stinky?"

Astrid nodded. "Yes. That's him."

Lumpy rose back on his feet and shrugged his shoulders. "Haven't seen him."

"The idea is to get rid of her so we prove our value as landowners who can protect their workers," Broken Nose said softly through his clenched teeth. To Astrid, he said, "He stopped by earlier today. We traded, he left." Broken Nose looked her up and down slowly. "Shameless woman."

Astrid ignored him, letting her spirit hand and Falling Star drift down to her side. She tucked the still-sleepy Slag back inside the cloth pouch. "Which way?"

Broken Nose pointed toward the mountains. "We can give you food," he said loudly, glancing back at the villagers behind him. "If you agree not to devour any of our babies!"

One of the women began to weep.

Astrid didn't care. She needed to find Sigurthor, reclaim Starlight, and go back home to Guell. If anyone could be stupid enough to see Astrid as a baby-eating monster, then so be it.

"Agreed," Astrid called out. "Provided you give me a horse."

"You can have his horse," Lumpy said.

Broken Nose groaned.

Cheerfully, Lumpy added, "But it could be days before you catch up with Sigurthor, and your horse needs to eat—you should take a cart, too."

Annoyed, Broken Nose turned to Lumpy and said, "Why don't we just give her the entire crop we harvested?"

Lumpy looked at him blankly. "I don't think it can all fit in the cart."

A short time later, despite an invitation from Lumpy to stay and get a good night's rest, Astrid left their settlement, driving a cart led by Broken Nose's small but sturdy horse. Any brigand riding the horse would have his feet dragging the ground. Astrid stopped the cart when she heard Lumpy calling her name.

Breathless, he raced to catch up with her, leaving the others behind in the wheat field. He ran down the dirt road. "Wait!" he called, pulling up to stop alongside her cart, resting his hands against its side panel.

Astrid stared at the brigand struggling to catch his breath.

"You ever been outside Scalding territory?" Lumpy's chest heaved. He placed one hand over his heart, as if that might help slow his labored breath.

Astrid shook her head.

Lumpy's brow furrowed with worry. "Could be days before you catch up with Sigurthor—maybe weeks. That means you be heading toward danger." He pointed at her breasts. "It be best to bind up your ladies. You already got your hair chopped short. If people mistake you for a boy, let them. You be safer that way."

A chill ran down Astrid's arms, flesh and spirit alike. "Why do you care what happens to me? You and your friend helped destroy my home and my people."

Lumpy looked at her for a long moment. The moment he spoke, his voice softened. "We killed no one in Guell. We was told to take you and keep you safe. It be no good excuse, but no one told us folks would be murdered."

Astrid's voice came out hard and cold. It hadn't been long since she'd witnessed the destruction of what Guell used to be before the blacksmiths rebuilt it. Most of its original villagers had been killed that day. "And neither of you has killed before?"

Lumpy looked down, studying the side of the cart and ran his fingers alongside it. "This be the first real home I ever had. I got a nice woman and we be having a baby soon. And some nights I can't sleep for wondering what I'd do if someone took my woman or the baby away and did them harm." He shook his head slowly, unable to speak.

Astrid sighed. Like dozens of other brigands, Lumpy and Broken Nose had been paid by her brother Drageen to destroy Guell, but she had to admit she hadn't seen either man kill any of her neighbors. Lumpy had extended a certain degree of kindness to her since they'd captured her. Despite everything, she had a soft spot in her heart for him. But that didn't change the fact he was a brigand and therefore a potential threat. "And you expect me to believe you've changed your ways? That you're just a simple farmer now?"

Lumpy looked up again, wiping his eyes as if the wind had blown dust into them. "Just be careful, is all. The world out there—it ain't nothing like what you ever known before."

As he walked back toward the wheat field, Astrid drove forward toward the mountains into which Sigurthor had disappeared.

Somehow, they loomed even larger as the brigand's warning haunted her.

Chapter Fourteen

For the next few days, Astrid drove the horse and cart along a dirt road through mountains that rose sharply on either side. It looked as if a god had dragged a giant plow through the ground, forcing the dirt up into mounds now hardened into rock, towering toward the sky. Gray clouds hung so low that they brushed across mountaintops while they drifted by. White fog and mist clung to the mountains like smoke. Astrid shivered, trying to shrug off the clammy chill that seemed determined to penetrate her bones. Even her teeth ached with the cold.

As the road elevated and dipped, Astrid spotted a thin strip of grassland forming a valley in the distance below. The road wound around an upcoming corner and then slowly descended toward the valley.

The horse hesitated, snorting as if worried about what lay ahead.

In the distance, Astrid noticed something move. Squinting, she tried to get a better look, but the distance proved too great. Something indeed moved, but she could make out nothing that looked clearer than specks.

Astrid murmured, "DiStephan?" even though she expected no answer. She hadn't sensed his presence since she'd encountered the brigands harvesting their wheat. She'd heard tales of animals sensing ghosts easier than humans could, and she suspected that DiStephan didn't want to spook the horse. A frightened horse could overturn a cart and hurt its driver.

She placed a hand on each weapon tucked under her belt, just to make sure they were still in place, before urging the horse to continue their journey toward the valley below.

❧ ❧

Later that day, the horse whinnied in protest while Astrid coaxed it into the narrow valley. She kept a close eye on her surroundings, gazing from the road to the mountains to the grassy valley as the cart bumped along the road. Finally, she noticed a figure lying in the grass up ahead.

The horse stopped suddenly, and no amount of coaxing made a difference. Astrid called out and signaled it with the reins, but the horse ignored her. It edged toward the side of the road and nibbled on grass instead.

Astrid hopped out of the cart, faced the horse with the reins in hand, and tried to reason with it. "I'm right here with you," she said to the horse, running one hand over the coarse mane that draped along one side of the horse's neck and poked stiffly across its forehead like the haircut of a rakish boy.

She'd forgotten to ask the horse's name, and the brigands hadn't told her. She assumed it had a name because she remembered hearing the brigands talk about their horses before. She struggled to remember the name Lumpy had given to his favorite horse.

"We haven't been properly introduced," Astrid said, glancing nervously at the motionless figure up ahead before returning her attention to the horse. "My name is Astrid, and I'll call you Blossom, because that might be your name, even though you belonged to Broken Nose, and Blossom is a name that Lumpy gives to his horses."

Blossom paused before yanking a mouthful of grass free from its roots.

"Stay here. I will find out who—or what—that thing is and then we can be on our way. But you must stay here and wait for me." Astrid patted the horse's neck.

Blossom shook its head and took a step away from Astrid, continuing to feed on the grass.

Taking a deep breath, Astrid kept a steady but cautious pace down the center of the road, still glancing from side to side as she approached the motionless figure. At the moment she grew close enough to recognize him, she ran, forgetting her caution.

"Sigurthor!" she said, kneeling next to the man lying on his back and staring vacantly at the sky above. She touched his face but withdrew her hand quickly. His skin seemed as gray as the clouds and as chilled as the air. She could do nothing to help him—he'd been dead for hours.

Panic seized Astrid, and she struggled to push him onto his side and then onto his front. She'd assumed his body had been lying on top of it. However, no weapon lay beneath him.

Starlight had been stolen from Sigurthor.

CHAPTER FIFTEEN

Norah loved being alone.

Until several months ago, she'd spent her entire life inside a cage on top of Tower Island, the stronghold and home of the Scaldings.

Evil people.

Norah snorted and shook her long black hair in disgust at the thought of them. Keeping her locked up, feeding her just enough to keep her alive, and leaving her caged on top of the island's tower even when the bitter winds of winter ripped through its bars. She shivered at the memory, chest heaving and eyes watering.

Their negligence left her struggling to learn language, even now. "Safe now," she whispered to herself. "Safe here."

She curled up on the stone floor of her nook inside the ocean-side cave carved by the clan of dragons to which she belonged. Despite enough room to stretch out, she rarely did. In varying shades of brown, the stone felt smooth to the touch. She found comfort in the distant lapping of the sea against the shore and the heaviness of the warm salt air.

Dim light danced through the arched entrance to her nook. Twisting passage-ways filled the rest of the cave and intertwined into a multi-tiered catacomb. Norah listened closely, and she could make out the granular sound of the fall of sand below, thin sheets of sand sliding over a stone wall like a waterfall and slipping into a pool infested with snaking tree trunks. She liked the way the trees rose above and sank beneath the rippling water, even though she rarely ventured down to see it.

Norah preferred to stay alone in her nook. Here, she could count on being warm and dry and well fed by those who brought fish to her. Among her own kind at last, Norah still flinched at the thought of letting any of them near. She understood herself to be a dragon, like them, but she didn't understand what that meant. If she was a dragon, why did she prefer to look like a woman?

A dark shadow rippled through the light dancing in the archway.

Instinctively, Norah scuttled on all fours across the stone floor, backing into a corner and hissing through bared teeth at the shadow.

"I believe you have healed enough," the shadow said. Slowly, Taddeo stepped through the archway into her nook.

Heart racing, Norah sank onto her haunches, nestling her back against the safety of the stone wall. Taddeo had freed her from the tyranny of the Scaldings. He'd pried open the bars of her cage, even though the iron burned his hands, which still bore the scars. He'd pulled her from the cage and leapt with her from the tower, plummeting into the ocean below, ultimately bringing her here to their clan's secret cavern. She trusted Taddeo, even though his presence always startled her.

Taddeo hesitated, seemingly thinking better of taking a step forward. Instead, he sank to his knees, looking straight across the room at Norah instead of down at her. "We are dragons of the water, not of the earth. This is a place of rest and refuge for us, but our true strength lies in the sea and the rivers and the rain. Not here."

Norah shook her head slightly. "Safe here."

"Yes," Taddeo said patiently. "But there is more to life than being safe."

Norah shook her head again, pushing herself deeper into the corner.

"Do you remember the dragon we freed from Dragon's Head?"

Norah frowned.

"It is the place where the Scalding girl fought her brother. One of our kind was trapped in the rock by a Scalding many years ago..."

"Scalding." Norah hissed, her eyes narrowed with anger.

"But now the Scalding brother is trapped in the rock, and the dragon is free of it." Taddeo gazed at Norah, and his tone softened. "It would be a great service if you were to help this dragon."

Norah frowned. How could she possibly help anyone?

"He spent many years trapped inside the rock—far, far longer than you were trapped inside the Scaldings' cage."

Norah felt something soften inside her. Someone else had been caged, too, inside a rock instead of behind iron bars. Did that mean he couldn't move within the rock? Had it been impossible for him to eat? For all their wicked ways, the Scaldings had shown some decency and given Norah enough food to keep her alive.

Taddeo sighed heavily. "There is a Dragon's Well in the Southlands. Any dragon that drinks from it will be healed in whatever way is most needed. It would be of the greatest help if you traveled with him and make sure he drinks from it."

Norah didn't understand where the Southlands were and was too embarrassed to show her ignorance. Could the Southlands be the place at the bottom of the cave where the sand fell into the pool of snaking tree trunks? Norah liked it there. "Here?" she said hopefully. "Below?"

Taddeo pondered her question for a moment. "No," he said quietly. "I have sent Astrid to find it, as well. The ghost of the last dragonslayer has drunk from the well and can show her the way."

Horrified, Norah wrapped her arms around herself. "No."

"You know Astrid's scent as well as you know your own. Simply follow her trail. There is no need for her to see you or be aware of your presence."

Norah shook her head in refusal, glaring at Taddeo. She pointed at the entrance to her nook, gesturing toward the depths of the cave. "Others!"

"No one else can succeed in performing this task. No one knows the girl's scent better than you. Anyone else—including myself—would lose her scent too easily."

Norah wasn't convinced that Taddeo told the truth. She shook her head again.

"The fate of all dragons depends on you. I promise the dragon you help will keep you safe. Now that you're free of the Scaldings, we will make sure no one lays an unwelcome hand on you again."

Norah pondered Taddeo's words. Ever since he'd set her free, no one had harmed her. Instead, they'd helped her. "Safe as here?"

"Yes," Taddeo said warmly. "Wherever you go, we will always do everything within our power to make sure you are as safe as you are here."

Norah took a deep breath. She didn't like leaving her nook, but she remembered her relief and joy on the day Taddeo had set her free. She would very much like it if she could help another dragon feel free, too.

~~~

Leaving Norah behind in her niche, Taddeo strode through the twisting walkways of the cave, its walls open and airy, made of stone strands interwoven like vines. He caught a faint scent of fish that grew stronger while he wound his way down to the lowest level where shallow pools of water dotted the cave floor. Stripping off his clothes, Taddeo transformed himself into a dragon and slid to the bottom of a pool, resting below the water.

He never relished lying, especially not to his own kind. Although he could have sent Astrid with Norah, Taddeo planned a better time for their paths to cross again. Norah despised all Scaldings, including Astrid. These things had to be handled delicately.

After many fruitless attempts, Taddeo had lied to Norah as a last resort. It had become clear that Norah didn't care whether she lived or died, but she had to make her way to Dragon's Well. She was tied to Astrid in the same way that Taddeo was tied to DiStephan, dragon to dragonslayer. While Taddeo had the strength to survive DiStephan's death, Norah had been weakened by years of imprisonment on Tower Island. If anything happened to Astrid, Norah would die. Likewise, if Norah were to die first, her death would make it impossible for Astrid to survive.

All promises led to consequences, and these conditions were the consequences of a promise made generations ago.

And now that Drageen and his alchemist were safely locked inside Dragon's Head, Astrid's survival became critical. Taddeo imagined the howls of the Scaldings who would soon be chased from Tower Island.

CHAPTER SIXTEEN

Astrid knelt by Sigurthor's prone body, ignoring the stench of his death while she studied everything surrounding him. Already, his gray skin had paled to a faint blue. She stared in fascination at the indentations her fingertips had left behind.

"What happened here?" Astrid whispered to the ground surrounding the merchant's body. "Who killed Sigurthor? And what happened to Starlight?"

She struggled to tap into the new skills she'd learned as a dragonslayer. In childhood, she'd been Temple's apprentice in his smithery, learning the language of fire and iron. She'd first mastered the art of starting and maintaining a good flame, paying attention to what the different colors and types of smoke conveyed. She'd witnessed how long it takes for iron to heat before it can be smited or welded, each requiring a different amount of time in the fire. She'd learned the different colors of iron—black and brown, red and orange, yellow and white—and what those colors indicate with regard to how the iron could be shaped and for how long. She'd spent many years working at her trade in the smithery, and the knowledge had come to her slowly but surely.

But being a dragonslayer meant something entirely different.

No master had trained Astrid. DiStephan's ghost helped where he could, but it didn't compare to serving an apprenticeship. Instead of working along the side of an expert and watching how he worked, Astrid had jumped headfirst into the work of a dragonslayer, stumbling to learn quickly. She learned mostly from her own mistakes, and she'd been lucky that no mistake had been severe enough to cost her life. Although DiStephan had given her some guidance, she'd had no real training with weapons—mostly, she followed her instincts every time she used a sword, dagger, or ax.

And she'd realized on her own that the world had the power to talk to her in its own language—she just had to learn how to speak and understand that language.

The patch of grass between Astrid and the body suddenly lit up. Looking up, she saw a narrow beam of sunlight spilling between a break in the cloudy skies above and landing near her feet. Not knowing whether it might be the influence of DiStephan or the gods, Astrid smiled her thanks and turned to study the sunlight patch of grass. It wasn't where she'd found him lying on his back, nor was it where she'd flipped him over on his stomach. But she recognized this to be a place where he or someone else had laid, maybe earlier today.

Unlike the rest of the ground, covered with frost-crisp brown grass, this must have been where Sigurthor had fallen to die. His body would have been warm at the time it fell, and that warmth had melted away any frost, leaving the ground softer and more receptive to holding the imprint of anything that touched it, like the fingerprint indentions now left by Astrid's touch on Sigurthor's bluish skin.

No. Astrid frowned. That couldn't be right. The ground would have warmed after Sigurthor's body had laid there, so the only imprint would have come after he'd been dead, which was impossible.

Unless someone had turned his body over *after* it had warmed and softened the ground beneath him.

Sitting cross-legged, Astrid propped an elbow on her knee and rested her chin in her hand, letting her gaze drift across the sunlit patch of grass. What could she be looking at?

Slowly, as if standing out of bed and stretching toward the sky to begin a new day, a blade of grass unkinked itself and straightened, revealing an indentation in the ground.

Astrid leaned forward, twisting her head to get a better look while keeping her hands free of the grass. The indentation looked smaller than the palm of her hand. It rounded smoothly into the dirt underneath the grass, wide at one end and narrowing to a point at the other.

It had the same shape and size as Starlight's pommel.

Instantly, the sunlit patch of grass made sense. Astrid could see where Sigurthor had fallen onto his chest. If he'd worn Starlight in its sheath by his side, the pommel could have slipped easily in front of his belly, and the weight of his body would have pressed it into the softening ground. Scanning the patch, she could make out where his elbows, knees, face, and feet had landed.

But why had he been killed?

Astrid shrugged at her own question. A better question might be, why ask why? Merchants often told stories of wars breaking out across the territories they traveled, and no one walking or riding the roads could count on staying safe from attack by brigands. Having just ended one leg of his trading route, Sigurthor would have left Guell weighed down with wealth and goods, used to traveling this leg of his annual journey with DiStephan at his side for protection.

Of course. Taking another look, Astrid saw none of Sigurthor's goods or any of the silver he'd worn.

Astrid's heart sank with a new realization, remembering how upset Sigurthor had become when he learned she'd replaced DiStephan and refused to accompany Sigurthor back to his homeland, which DiStephan had always done. "Sigurthor was more afraid of brigands than dragons," Astrid said softly.

She took her time studying the ground and finding subtle new clues in the twist of a grass blade and a scrape in the dirt below it, as wide as a sheath. She read the ground and whispered, "They left him here for awhile. Maybe his horse ran free and they chased it down."

At the thought of such a possibility, Astrid looked up and sighed in relief because she saw Blossom where she'd left him, still grazing by the road.

Returning her attention to the task at hand, Astrid kept talking through what she saw before her eyes. "When they were ready to go, they took one last look at Sigurthor. Maybe to make sure he was dead. Or maybe to make sure they'd taken everything worth taking. If he'd been wearing his cape and if Starlight had laid flat on the ground, they wouldn't have known he had it until they turned him over."

Brigands probably would have grabbed the sword without unsheathing it, not even realizing they had stolen a dragonslayer's sword, something far more valuable than an ordinary one because of its unusual size and durability.

Astrid covered her face with her hands, not knowing what to do next. She'd promised everyone in Guell she'd spend the winter in the village and perform black-smithing work until the next dragon season began. Lenore and Donel and even Trep must be worried—she'd vanished early this morning from the village although they were expecting her to be there. She'd made a promise, and she needed to keep it.

But how could she let Starlight go? Temple had guided her while she made it, and it had become DiStephan's favorite weapon. Starlight helped her remember their voices and faces and the way they smiled and frowned and laughed. It represented the last connection she had to the two men she'd loved most, and without it she feared forgetting them. She loved Starlight as much as she loved any living person.

Pressing her fingertips against her eyes and forcing them to stay dry, Astrid choked back her tears, refusing to let them well. "Blacksmiths don't cry," she whispered to herself. Glancing back at the path she'd traveled, she said out loud, "I'll come back to Guell as soon as I can."

Taking a deep breath, she returned her attention to the body and looked for more indications of how Sigurthor had been killed. Other than matted and bloody hair, there seemed to be no wounds elsewhere on his body. Following a few spots of blood, Astrid found a rock nearby and discovered blood on its underside. She pursed her lips, wondering if they'd intended to kill Sigurthor or simply knock him out so they could rob him. The signs were unclear.

She circled the body slowly, studying the ground in front of her many times before taking a new step onto it. She froze at the sight of an odd footprint.

Astrid knelt by a soft patch of wet ground near Sigurthor's head in which a strange impression had been left. At first glance, it looked like the print a man's leather shoe would leave behind: a single impression several inches long and a few inches wide. Astrid noticed a small crescent of ground left unchanged, suggesting the arch of a foot.

But the impression of claw marks startled her most: five at the end where a man's toes would be and one at the other end where one would expect to see his heel. No lizard had left this mark. Lizards dragged the tops of their feet along the ground every time they walked and then plopped them back into place, leaving long trails of claw marks.

There were no indications of dragging feet, only remnants of sharp tips digging hard enough in the ground to leave cone-like holes as big as Astrid's fingertips. She kept staring at the strange footprint, trying to make sense of it. For months now, she'd learned to read the tracks of lizards, deer, bear, wolves, and all of the smaller animals in the woods. The hooves of deer were pointed like a small plow. Wolves left prints illustrating the group of round pads on which they walked. Although bear feet were more similar to those of men, they were enormous by comparison and clawed.

Astrid jumped at the cawing sound of a crow flying overhead, its outstretched wings looking tattered as it soared above her. Cautiously, she gazed all around, wondering if whatever had left this print could be watching her from the cover of a copse of trees on the nearby mountainside. Gingerly, she ran her fingertips across the footprint, trying to understand it with her touch. She could find no other footprint.

No man or bear or wolf or deer or even lizard had left this behind. Not even a dragon could have made this footprint.

It had been made by an unknown, undiscovered monster. And for some reason that Astrid found impossible to fathom, that monster had stolen Starlight.

CHAPTER SEVENTEEN

For the next few weeks, Astrid drove Blossom and the cart through the mountain pass. She'd left Sigurthor where she'd found him but piled stones on top of his body to keep lizards or any other animals from making a meal of him. Even though he'd stolen Starlight and lost it to the monster that killed him, at least she should give the man a decent burial. Despite her disappointment, she saw him as a fellow country-man. Astrid believed it her duty to treat any countryman with respect and honor. The Northlands had been fortunate to keep its own peace, but these were turbulent times in other parts of the world. And no one could predict when that turbulence might travel and threaten all Northlanders.

Astrid had hesitated to keep traveling through the mountains instead of going back to Guell. It seemed like an impossible task: if a monster had stolen Starlight, how could she ever hope to find that monster? A footprint in the muddy ground indicated a creature made up of part man and part beast. She didn't know what the monster looked like. But clearly that monster had taken Starlight, even though she couldn't imagine what use a monster could have for a sword.

Astrid cast a backward glance over her shoulder at the sound of a thump break-ing the solitude of Blossom's clopping steps. As she suspected, Fire fidgeted in his sleep, curled up between his brothers.

Among the food and water Lumpy had packed into the cart, Astrid had found a neatly folded cape made of black wool and fur along with two simple wool cloaks, apparently making sure she wouldn't freeze to death in case winter arrived with a vengeance. Climbing higher in the mountains, she wore the wool-and-fur cape every day and used the two spare cloaks in the cart to create a small nest for Smoke, Fire, and Slag. The young lizards had grown, even though they still spent most of their time asleep. Astrid had discovered more than one adult lizard stretched out and sunning itself on a large rock. She imagined lizards migrated South because the Northern winters were too cold for their taste, and she suspected cool air made them sluggish and sleepy.

Although recognizing the lack of wisdom in taking care of the young lizards, Astrid still suspected they might be dragons. Taddeo had tested her before—what if he now tested her by putting baby dragons in front of her to learn what she would do with them? After all, he'd been the one to point them out to her in the dragonslayer's camp. She didn't know what she would do with them yet, but leaving them alone in the mountains to die would be heartless.

One day, the road eased down gradually while the mountains cascaded into foothills. Astrid cried out for joy at the sound of seabirds screaming in the distance and the thick scent of saltwater. She traveled through a stretch of farmland, already harvested and resting as if hibernating in anticipation of the approaching winter. Finally, the road led to a coastal town below.

Astrid paused, studying the view of the bustling village. A long and wide walkway of wooden boards ran parallel to the sea. On the port side of the walkway, ships bobbed where they were tethered to the dock like cattle feeding from a trough. Crates were set up on the dock in front of each ship, apparently selling goods brought by sea. On the other side of the walkway, rows of wooden houses jammed next to each other. Even from Astrid's vantage point on the mountain road behind and above the town, she could hear the voices of hundreds of people crowding the walkway, bartering for goods.

The monster that stole Starlight from Sigurthor wouldn't have come to a town like this. Even though Astrid had spotted more of its tracks along the mountain pass during her travels, she suspected the monster had left the road and taken refuge somewhere along the way, maybe in these low-lying hills behind the town.

The thought sickened her. Winter crept closer every day, and hunting a monster in these hills and mountains would be an impossible task. It was one thing to hunt lizards: often, she simply kept her eyes on the skies for the carrion birds that quickly found kills made by lizards. The birds typically showed up in time to scoop the bones stripped clean by the lizards, fly high and drop those bones on rocks below to break them open in order to eat the marrow inside. Even if Astrid arrived after the lizards had left the scene of the kill, tracking them came easily. Other times, Astrid visited villages, heard accounts of recent lizard sightings, and had no problems picking up the trail.

But lizards were so large and cumbersome that they could go nowhere without leaving plenty of evidence. Broken branches and trees made it easy for Astrid to imagine the lizard that had done the damage. And lizards always dug trenches to lie in wait for prey to come along—those trenches yielded plenty of information. Not to mention the deep, scarring claw marks left in the ground, as obvious as furrows dug by a plow in a field.

But the monster that had stolen Starlight must be different, appearing far smaller than a lizard and leaving little evidence behind. In fact, Astrid had already wondered if the monster might be a dragon that had taken the shape of a man. Like Taddeo.

But Astrid had sniffed every track of the monster she'd found, and it didn't smell like Taddeo or any other dragon she'd ever encountered.

She suspected it to be an unfamiliar monster, which meant she probably wouldn't recognize the monster when she saw it. How could she track a monster if she didn't know what to look for?

"What now?" Astrid said quietly, looking up at the cold and clouded sky. Winter threatened to begin soon. Maybe she should turn around and head back to Guell before the onslaught of the first snowstorm.

Astrid shuddered at the sensation of Smoke pouncing upon her shoulder. The tiny lizard crawled underneath her shirt and poked his head out at the end of the sleeve. Lately, the lizards had become more active for a short time each afternoon, crawling from their nest in the back of the cart to sit next to Astrid and eventually crawl into her lap and sleep. Sometimes they crawled on her, exploring the terrain of her body and keeping balance by wrapping tails around her neck or arm. It surprised Astrid that she didn't mind, even though she suspected they only wanted to soak up the heat from her body.

She shook Smoke gently from her sleeve into her hand and dropped him next to his brothers in the nest behind her. "I should go into town and get supplies for the return journey." Her ax, Falling Star, and other daggers were the only items she could trade, and she hated to part with any of them. But food and water mattered most.

However, Smoke jumped out of the nest and onto her arm, and the other lizards followed suit. More and more, they sought warmth, and Astrid decided they'd be safer with her than exploring on their own. She wrapped cloth around her chest, tightly enough to stay in place but loosely enough to create folds in which the lizards could nestle out of sight while drawing upon the heat of her body. Happily, the lizards slipped into the folds of the cloth and safely out of sight.

Astrid left the cart hidden in a thicket of trees behind a hill near the village. After unhitching Blossom from the cart, she rode the horse to a small house on the edge of the village and made arrangements to have Blossom watered and fed.

Entering the crowded marketplace in the village, Astrid hugged the black wool and fur cape around her, remembering Lumpy's advice to let people see her as a boy, along with Sigurthor's warning that in the rest of the Northlands a woman who dressed like a man or cut her hair short had committed a crime. And Astrid had done both.

But Astrid noticed a new bounce in her step as the wooden floorboards squeaked beneath her feet and she breathed in the ocean air spiced with the scent of the marketplace. Squeezing her way through the crowd, she caught glimpses of merchants selling bright yellow, blue, and green wools and linens by the arm length, potatoes and rye, cloves and saffron. Most women wore traditional linen sheathes and overdresses, held in place with large silver broaches shaped like dragons and other animals. Clearly, they were women of the Northlands. Astrid recognized her male countrymen by the breeches they wore gathered at the knee and the cloaks they wore, similar to hers.

But others in the crowd wore strange and exotic clothes from other lands, speaking tongues Astrid had never heard before. She recognized a few people wearing the styles she'd seen on the islands to the west of the Northlands, but most were completely foreign to her. She imagined from their dark and peculiar looks that they were visitors from the Southlands and perhaps even the Far Eastern lands.

"Weapons!" a merchant called from dockside. "Fine weapons!"

Astrid rose to the balls of her feet, straining to peer over the crowd to discover the merchant's location. A man selling weapons would most likely buy her spare daggers.

Through the briefly parting crowd, she glimpsed him displaying all manner of weapons on top of a few wooden crates stacked up to chest height. The weapons merchant looked to be slightly older than Astrid, and his shoulder-length straight black hair fell like sheets of rain around his head from beneath a simple forest green hat. At first glance, he seemed to be the sort of man who would use any excuse to sleep in a sunny field instead of working it. He called out to potential customers, his manner light and carefree. Whenever a woman walked past, the merchant eyed her as if she were for sale. But Astrid suspected him to be more in the market for temporary companionship than a wife.

In the water behind the merchant floated a long and sleek wooden boat with the masthead of a dragon.

"Here be dragons," Astrid murmured to herself, remembering another time that she'd sailed on such a ship. That kind of ship most likely belonged to a Northlander or to someone in league with one. So perhaps the weapons merchant could be trusted to some degree.

Astrid threaded her way through the busy crowd until she reached the edge of the weapons merchant's crates. She noticed the sun glint off a small iron pin in the shape of a dagger attached to his hat. She'd heard of guilds for merchants and the pins identifying them. The dagger pin must be one that identified him as a member of the weapons guild. He glanced at her for a moment and frowned before catching sight of a woman walking behind Astrid.

"Dear lady," he said to the other woman, who walked past without acknowledging him. Still hopeful, he called out, "Won't you pause for a look?"

Astrid's eyes widened with anger. There, from the belt around the merchant's waist, hung Starlight in its sheath.

CHAPTER EIGHTEEN

Astrid leaned forward, reaching for the grip with the intent of pulling Starlight from its sheath, hanging from the weapons merchant's waist.

Just as quickly, he sidestepped her reach and withdrew Starlight into his own hands, pointing the tip between her eyes.

"What are you doing with my sword?"

The merchant locked his unblinking gaze on her. "I made a fair trade for the sword," he said, raising his voice and succeeding in getting attention from the surrounding crowd. Men and women turned to watch Astrid and the merchant. "And I doubt the sword is yours—what need does a boy have for a sword? Especially a cripple."

"I'm not—" Astrid bit her lip before she could finish her sentence. While she wandered outside of Guell and the far Northlands where no such laws existed about how a woman could dress or do with her time, she would take Lumpy's advice and let people think what they would about her. And if this merchant saw her as a cripple, it meant he didn't drink the lizard's blood that would make it possible for him to see the phantom arm she'd created from her own belief. "I'm not just any boy," Astrid said. "I'm the dragonslayer from Guell."

"I know the dragonslayer, and you're not him."

"DiStephan is dead," Astrid said softly. "Killed by a dragon months ago." She paused, remembering that even though DiStephan's ghost had been able to talk to her, he'd never mentioned how he died. She realized she'd always assumed a lizard had killed him. "And that sword is mine now."

"He can't be dead," the merchant said. Shaking his head, the man's eyes watered. "I know DiStephan." He put Starlight back in its sheath then sat on an empty crate, staring into space. "We're friends. He must have mentioned me. I'm Vinchi. We've known each other since we were boys."

Because she'd traveled throughout the far Northlands during the past few months to perform her dragonslayer duties, she'd met many people who claimed to have befriended DiStephan but knew nothing about him. People commonly tried to gain favor from others by insisting they had a dragonslayer for a friend.

Suddenly, a petite woman with neatly coiffed auburn hair yelled from the deck of a nearby ship, waving a pair of brown trousers above her head. Screaming with anger in a language Astrid didn't understand, the woman stormed off the ship and down its plank toward the crowd.

"Oh, no," Vinchi said, his voice trembling. He stared at the woman waving the trousers. "This time she's gone too far."

CHAPTER NINETEEN

Astrid stared at the petite woman who marched down the wooden plank connecting her ship to the dock. With every step, the plank shuddered beneath her feet as if in fear.

"No, Margreet," Vinchi whispered to himself. "Go back to the ship and be silent."

Although Margreet wore her reddish hair tucked into a neat bun at the nape of her neck, a few tendrils hung free to frame her face. Her eyes blazed with anger and her shouts pierced the air while she waved her hands for emphasis. She held the trousers in one hand, and its legs flew about like a flag on a ship's mast.

When her feet hit the wooden boards of the town's walkway, Margreet hesitated, turning to face a fur trader near Astrid and Vinchi. Clenching her jaw, Margreet strode toward the fur merchant with clenched fists and a face flushed with anger.

The crowd fell silent in waves. No one on the walkway spoke a word except for Margreet.

Astrid strained to understand until she realized Margreet was a foreigner speaking in another tongue that everyone else seemed to know. Only Astrid failed to recognize Margreet's words.

Everyone parted to give her a clear path toward the fur trader.

Astrid watched a woman in the crowd cling to a man who appeared to be her husband, close her eyes, and press her face against his shoulder. Others in the crowd paled and stepped back with faces drawn with fear while staying close enough to watch.

Glancing at Vinchi, Astrid felt startled to see his eyes fill with tears even though he clenched his own fists. She pushed her way to the front of the crowd.

A broad and tall man sporting an unkempt yellow beard and a shaved head sorted through his pile of furs on the crates in front of him. He had the large, meaty hands of a butcher.

Astrid recognized the pelts of wolves, bears, and smaller animals. She noted that he had no lizard skins and questioned his courage. Lizards were larger and faster than bears and more wily than wolves.

Margreet thrust the trousers at the fur trader like throwing a punch. The trousers looked new and finely made. Astrid would have guessed they'd never been worn had it not been for a stain near the crotch.

The kind of stain a man would leave after the throes of sex.

As the crowd shifted around her, Astrid turned to see Vinchi join her side. "Are they married?" Astrid whispered to him.

Vinchi nodded, keeping his gaze on Margreet.

But it looks like that stain is a surprise to her, Astrid thought. *Margreet wasn't there when it happened.*

Tears streamed down Margreet's face but she stood strong and firm.

The fur trader folded his arms and took a casual stance, but color began to rise slowly up his throat while his eyes darkened.

Margreet pointed at the trousers with her free hand. Astrid didn't understand the language, but Margreet screamed what sounded like accusations. She pounded her own chest, wiped the tears from her face, and stood straighter.

The fur trader laughed, but his laughter darkened to match his eyes.

Margreet's jaw slackened. She gazed at the fur trader—her husband—in disbelief. Speaking slowly, she asked him a question.

Despite the foreign language, Astrid clearly heard the edge in Margreet's voice, as sharp as Starlight's edges.

The fur trader's face flushed deep to match his wife's. Putting his hands on his hips, he asked what sounded like the same question with the same edge in his voice.

"No," Vinchi said softly to himself. "Don't let him bait you."

Margreet tilted her head to one side, looking her husband up and down. Then she held the trousers up to her own waist as if measuring their fit against her body. Clearly, they were sized to fit her husband—if so inclined, Margreet could probably cut them up and make at least one entire dress out of them, possibly two. And yet she held them in a way that indicated she planned to wear them herself. She smiled sweetly at the fur trader but spoke firmly.

The crowd gasped in response and cowered back.

Vinchi sniffed. He quickly wiped away the tears that spilled from his eyes.

The fur trader shoved his crates aside. Men and women alike winced as wooden boxes clattered and furs tumbled onto the walkway. The fur trader shouted and pointed toward the crowd. His finger scanned everyone circling Margreet, seeming to identify witnesses.

Margreet hugged the trousers to her chest, obviously claiming ownership of them. Her voice laced with contempt, she glanced down at her husband's feet and back up at his face.

Smirking with contempt, the fur trader walked toward his wife slowly, reaching one hand toward her. He spoke briefly and quietly.

Margreet shook her head, still clutching the trousers.

The fur trader lunged at her, ripping the trousers from her grasp and holding them high above his head, too high for her to reach. Circling in place, he addressed the crowd, letting his voice rise in questions as he waved the trousers above his head.

Margreet raised her voice above his as she pointed at his crotch.

Furious, the fur trader balled up the trousers and slammed them onto the ground between them. He pointed at the trousers, yelling at Margreet.

Pulling her small frame up even taller, Margreet slapped her hands together and shouted her response.

The fur trader hesitated, his face relaxing with surprise. Laughing, he gestured for Margreet to come to him.

Balling her hands into fists, Margreet jumped over the trousers and swung at her husband's gut.

The fur trader simply extended one hand and braced it against her forehead, keeping his wife easily away at arm's distance where she couldn't touch him.

Someone in the crowd giggled.

The fur trader waved a friendly gesture at the crowd with his free hand and then slammed a fist up into Margreet's jaw, the force throwing her up into the air before she landed hard on her back. As quickly as a lizard, the fur trader threw a punch at her eyes, kicked her hard in the belly and raised another fist high, aiming at the top of his wife's head.

Before she realized it, Astrid darted between them, pulling the ax from her belt with her first step and placing it against the fur trader's neck. "Lower your fist," she said calmly, not caring whether the man could understand her words.

She had every faith that he understood the intention of a sharp blade, even when it belonged to the lowly head of an ax.

CHAPTER TWENTY

Gershon froze at the sharp touch of the iron blade against his neck and stared at the boy holding the ax handle.

The boy stood no higher than Gershon's shoulders, slender and with one sleeve of his shirt hanging loosely at his side. The boy's hair was badly cut, looking like someone had chopped it off with an ax. Worse, scars criss-crossed his face and every inch of exposed skin. Whatever kind of fight had left such souvenirs had also cost the boy one of his arms. Gershon couldn't help but wonder, *How does a scarred cripple like that convince a woman to climb into his bed?*

Maybe that could explain the boy's obvious anger.

A fur trader from the Midlands, Gershon knew enough of the Northland languages to succeed in the marketplace, his approach to every land in which he traveled. Unlike a gifted few, he had neither the ear nor the patience to become fluent in any language other than his own. Who needed more than a smattering of foreign words? Even now, he doubted he needed many words to educate this youngster.

Gershon smiled as he raised one hand slowly to push the ax blade away from his neck.

But the boy held the handle firm and fast, fire blazing in his eyes as his voice became low and guttural and too fast for Gershon to understand. Gershon knew little about iron weapons. His big, meaty fists were usually the only weapons he needed. But Gershon knew enough to understand that with a sharp edge resting on his own neck, the boy had the physical advantage. Heaving a reluctant sigh, Gershon realized he'd have to reason with the child.

Still smiling, Gershon pointed slowly and gently at the woman near his feet, her face now covered in blood. "She," Gershon said in the foreign Northland tongue, "my wife."

The boy called out to the potential customers surrounding them on the wooden walkway, and this time Gershon understood when the boy said, "Help her."

But no one in the crowd moved. Why would they? Gershon had known many of these people for years. He had no conflict with them.

He's just a boy, Gershon reminded himself. *He has yet to comprehend the way of the world. Perhaps his father is dead or incompetent.*

Gershon often met boys like this in his travels, and he was honored to give them the wisdom of a man. He would speak to them with great care, slowly and gently. After all, they would someday be his colleagues—over the years, some of these boys had grown up to become some of his best customers. At the same time, Gershon knew he provided a service to all people by doing his part to educate these wayward sons.

The boy called out to the crowd again, but Gershon didn't follow the words. Surprised, he watched Vinchi hurry to Margreet's side.

Gershon started at the grip of many strong hands on his own arms and shoulders. Stunned, he turned his head from side to side, blurting in his own language, "Why are you doing this to me?"

Vinchi stood, holding Margreet's limp body in his arms. "Because you nearly killed her this time," he answered in Gershon's language.

"But she's mine," Gershon whispered. "Why is this any of your concern?" He watched in horror, startled by a tear that rolled down Vinchi's face.

"Some things," Vinchi said, "are too beautiful to kill." He then spoke to the boy in the Northlander language, and the boy nodded his agreement. Vinchi strode toward the plank of his own ship, still carrying Margreet in his arms.

A wave of terror washed through Gershon. "No!" he called out, struggling in the arms of those who held him back. "You can't steal from me! She is my greatest treasure!"

The boy gained Gershon's attention by pressing the sharp edge harder against his neck, pricking his skin with it.

Gershon started at the horrific sight of a young dragon poking its head out of the boy's chest. Screaming, Gershon cried out, "Dragon!"

The tiny thing spat at him, and Gershon thought he felt the dragon's spit land on his neck where the boy's ax had nicked him.

The men holding him in place spun their heads to look for the dragon, but Gershon saw the boy tuck the tiny dragon back inside his body before they had a chance to see it.

Gershon panted in fear. Just as his neighbors had warned him, the Northlands had become infested with monsters and sorcerers.

And now a dreaded monster had infected him.

The large man fainted, but he became vaguely aware of the clatter of footsteps along the plank leading to Vinchi's ship.

CHAPTER TWENTY-ONE

Damn him! Astrid thought. *What do I have to do to get Starlight back from Vinchi? He should have given it back to me the moment I told him it belongs to me!*

Vinchi had haphazardly thrown his best weapons into a bag and raced on board ship. Astrid followed. She'd let Starlight get away from her once when Sigurthor had stolen it, and she'd never let that happen again. She'd demanded that Vinchi return Starlight to her, but he'd refused, repeating his claim that he'd come by it rightfully.

And now he'd locked her below deck with the troublemaker who'd caused this mess while he sorted out his makeshift crew and set a course unknown to Astrid.

Sitting on a wooden bench below the deck of the ship, she steadied herself as the ship rolled through the waves. Astrid felt queasy because she wasn't on deck to watch the horizon and let her body gain its bearings. This Northlander ship, long and narrow, had been designed for sailing across oceans and rowing upon rivers. On deck, sailing was like gliding, smooth and effortless. But down here, the ride became a bit bumpier.

The shipbuilders had painstakingly curved long wooden planks to form the sides of the ship. But it creaked and cracked and moaned while the men above scampered like rats, manning the oars and unfurling the enormous square sail. Sometimes Astrid thought she saw the planks move slightly in and out, as if the ship were breathing. She gripped the edge of her bench, closing her eyes briefly. She willed herself not to be sick.

Near Astrid's feet, Margreet whimpered softly, curled up on the floor with her arms wrapped around her knees.

During the past few weeks, Astrid had learned how to tell when the baby lizards, still tucked inside the cloth wrapped around her chest, were sleeping. Fortunately, they slept most of the time. She could feel the steady rhythmic breath of each one and sank slowly to her knees to keep from waking them.

Astrid's anger bubbled equally at Margreet and Vinchi. If it hadn't been for Margreet, Astrid might have already convinced Vinchi to give Starlight back to her, and she'd be on her way home to Guell right now. "Quiet," Astrid said. "You're not making this pleasant for either of us." Margreet didn't answer, so Astrid touched her shoulder.

Jerking away from Astrid's hand, Margreet looked up. Her eyelids had turned blue from bruising, her cheeks flushed, and her lips were red with blood. She held her hands up between herself and Astrid, ready to protect herself from another beating.

Astrid's heart sank. How could any man treat a woman this way? How could Margreet's husband love her and lay anything but a tender hand upon her?

Astrid lowered herself to the floor. The handle of her ax tucked back under her belt clattered.

Again, Margreet jerked, scooting away from Astrid.

Determined to calm the woman, Astrid pulled her new dagger, Falling Star, from her belt. "See how pretty it is?" Astrid breathed on the blade, smiling to see its pattern emerge.

Margreet caught her breath, leaning forward a bit to stare at the dagger. She spoke, and her voice rose as if asking a question. She pointed at Astrid.

Taking her best guess at what Margreet might be asking, Astrid said, "I stopped your husband from killing you."

Margreet sat up straighter, talking more rapidly and pointing to herself.

Astrid squinted as if that might help her understand this foreign language, but it only made her head hurt. "I don't know what you're saying."

Placing her hands on her hips, Margreet took on the same fiery tone she'd used with her husband, spouting what seemed like an endless argument.

Astrid froze, sensing the baby lizards stir within the cloth bound around her chest. Margreet's raised voice had stirred them from their slumber.

Astrid realized her cloak had fallen behind the bench. If she could grab it in time, she might be able to keep them hidden.

Smoke poked his head out, yawning happily.

Margreet stopped in mid-sentence, her mouth hanging open as she gawked at the lizard.

Fire wriggled out of his hiding place, flopping his tiny feet over the edge of the cloth and snapping at the air.

Astrid recognized the same word Margreet's husband had uttered before passing out. "Dragone!" Margreet shouted, pointing at Smoke and Fire.

Then she began screaming like a woman being murdered.

Chapter Twenty-Two

Leaning forward with the thought of calming Margreet's screams, Astrid's cloth, circled around her body in one long strip, loosened enough so that all three of the baby lizards tumbled onto the floor. Above, hurried footsteps pounded across the deck and down the stairs.

Shaking in terror, Margreet shrieked louder. She hopped on top of the bench, kneeling and splaying her hands on its surface to steady herself against the ship's pitch.

The lizards scampered for the nearest hiding place, disappearing behind the wide barrels lining the sides of the ship.

Vinchi ran down the stairs, his eyebrows drawn together in worry. He shouted a question to Margreet, rushing to her side.

In response, Margreet pointed first at Astrid and then at the barrels, spouting her answer.

Astrid tensed, recognizing the one word of Margreet's language that she'd already come to understand.

Vinchi stood still for a moment, his eyes glazed in confusion. He asked another question, shorter this time.

Margreet sat up on her knees and pounded a fist into the open palm of her other hand. Her voice rang strong and defiant.

Crossing his arms, Vinchi turned toward Astrid. "Tiny dragons?"

Astrid laughed, feigning surprise.

Margreet's eyes blazed. She uttered an angry rant, jabbing an accusing finger at Astrid.

Astrid shrugged, keeping her attention on Vinchi. "Do you see any dragons?" she said.

Vinchi interrupted the still ranting Margreet.

Margreet caught her breath, inhaling quickly and holding it, while she listened to Vinchi. Shaking her head insistently, she gestured toward the barrels. Margreet stood on the floor and illustrated her point by lying on the floor and repeating everything she'd done once she'd seen the baby lizards, from pointing and screaming at Astrid to jumping on top of the bench.

Margreet and Vinchi turned to Astrid, seemingly waiting for an explanation.

Astrid shrugged again. "If you can find a dragon on this ship, I'd be very interested in seeing it." She spoke with the same tone she'd use to calm a frightened child.

Margreet tossed her hands up toward the ceiling and rolled her eyes in disbelief.

Vinchi walked a thorough sweep, approaching each barrel with caution and jumping every time a wooden floorboard creaked under his feet. Finally, he spoke to Margreet with an apologetic tone.

Margreet shook her head, her lips pressed together in disappointment. She cast an accusing glance at Astrid.

"Don't forget she was struck in the head," Astrid said helpfully. "Sometimes people get confused after they get hit in the head."

Margreet turned to Vinchi, tapping her foot expectantly.

He closed his eyes and shook his head.

Margreet cleared her throat.

Vinchi took a deep breath and then spoke to Margreet, gesturing toward her with one hand and Astrid with the other.

Margreet responded by brushing past him and stomping up the stairs toward the deck.

"What did you say?" Astrid asked, surprised at how timid her own voice sounded.

"I told her it's between the two of you to resolve your differences."

Astrid nodded, relieved that the baby lizards—or baby dragons—had found safety. Once Vinchi followed Margreet up to the deck, Astrid might have the opportunity to coax them back to her.

"Thank you for helping her," Vinchi said. He gazed at the stairs for a long moment before turning back to Astrid. "Most of the men I'd hired came with us, and we'll plan our next step once we land at a Midland port." He hesitated. "Say, what's your name?"

Astrid's thoughts raced. She wore man's clothes as well as cropped hair, and Lumpy had advised her to let people assume she was a boy. "I'm Ran—" No! *Randim might be well enough known in the Northlands that I shouldn't use his name.* "...Donel."

"Ran...Donel?" Vinchi said slowly, sounding as surprised as if she'd told him she could dance on the moon.

"Yes," Astrid said, drawing herself to stand tall in confidence. "My name is Randonel."

Vinchi smiled. "I think not. I recognize you from everything I've been told. You are Astrid, the Iron Maiden."

Chapter Twenty-Three

"Tired," Norah said with a heavy sigh. She sank into the dried brown grass, crunchy with early morning frost. She gazed up at the sun that skimmed the mountaintops surrounding them.

Winter approached, and daylight grew shorter every day along with the sun's path. Before long, the days would be full of night, and the sun would only dare to skim above the southern horizon for a short time each day.

Wendill had been walking well ahead of her on the path snaking through the mountains, full of unending energy. Norah supposed that at the time he'd been trapped inside the rocky outcrop of Dragon's Head his energy had wound up tight and now he finally had a chance to use it. When he chose to take the form of a man, Wendill adopted a small stature that made him barely taller than Norah and almost as slender. His close-cropped hair was as black as fertile soil. His nose and cheekbones and chin were so sharp that Norah wondered if he'd kept the same rocky shape his face had since he'd been entrapped on Dragon's Head.

But what surprised Norah most was the strangeness of his skin, which looked like pale brown leaves after they'd fallen and been worn thin and brittle by the harshness of winter. Norah didn't dare touch him for fear his skin might fall apart.

"You and Taddeo—you come from the realm of water," Wendill stated. "It would be easier for you if we traveled by sea rather than across land."

Norah shrugged. Months ago, she assumed she had rid herself of the Scaldings forever, but Taddeo had swooped her out into the sea. Without thinking, she'd changed into her dragon form, following Taddeo's lead and swimming next to him. What happened after that baffled Norah. Her body had burst, transforming from the body of a dragon into drops of water, somehow separate from all the other water in the sea. Again, following Taddeo's lead, she remembered rising like mist above a ship that bore the Scalding sister and brother and carrying it to Dragon's Head, where the Scalding brother had been sacrificed, therefore setting Wendill free to emerge from the rock and dive into the ocean below.

"You swim," Norah said. "I saw."

"That's right. I can swim, although not as well as you."

Wendill spoke with a soft and gentle voice, even more so than Taddeo. Although they'd been traveling together for only a few days, Norah noticed her new boldness. She drew up her courage and asked the question she'd been pondering from the beginning of their journey. "Why walk?"

"Although I can swim, I'm not of the water, like you and Taddeo." Wendill ran his hand through the crunchy brown grass between them as if running his hand through his own hair. "My kin is of the earth. I accepted entrapment in the rock because it was no more painful than being entrapped in a lover's arms." He paused and gazed up at the low-hanging sun. "But I missed the sky. It is time for us both to stretch our legs and remember who we are."

Norah didn't dare tell him that she'd never known who she was, leaving her nothing to remember. Taddeo had entrusted her with an important mission, emphasizing that this dragon Wendill represented the key to their kind. As Taddeo had explained, if Wendill didn't drink from Dragon's Well and heal from his entrapment, then all dragons would suffer.

Wendill wore a cloth pouch on his belt, and he now reached into it, withdrawing a handful of berries.

He offered a handful to Norah, but she shook her head to refuse them. She'd happily eaten fish given to her by dragons, but guilt had gnawed at her since she'd left the dragon stronghold. Eating now seemed wrong, so she'd stopped doing it. She'd grown used to ignoring the hunger that ate away at her belly. Norah had already caused too much harm to too many living things. Berries were living things and deserved to stay alive. She would not contribute to the death of any more living things, even if they were nothing but berries.

"It is important to eat," Wendill said. "It is how we stay alive." Norah ignored him, so Wendill ate the berries himself. "It is part of who we are and why we are here among other living things."

Norah looked away. If being alive meant harming other creatures, then she wanted none of it.

"I need you to stay strong," Wendill said. "How else can you guide me to our destination? How can I drink from the Dragon's Well if you don't lead me to it?"

Norah felt the weight of the survival of all dragons depending upon her every decision. And Wendill spoke the truth. She had to keep herself strong and alive until she had fulfilled her duty of delivering him to Dragon's Well and watching him drink his fill from it.

Reluctantly, Norah accepted the berries into her own hands, silently apologizing to each individual fruit as she consumed it.

CHAPTER TWENTY-FOUR

"The Iron Maiden?" Astrid said, her eyes unfocused as she looked at Vinchi.

He smiled, casting a knowing glance down the length of Astrid's body and up again. "I knew it was you!" He paused. "But no one told me about your scars or that you lost an arm." Vinchi reached for her cropped hair. "Or about you being punished. What did you do to deserve this?"

Astrid smacked his hand away before he could touch her.

Vinchi pulled his hand back. His eyebrows arched in surprise. "I retract the question."

"Keep your hands to yourself." Astrid's voice rang sharp and clear. The man who had bought her and taken her as his apprentice—Temple—had warned Astrid about men who dared to become familiar with women too easily and too quickly. Temple had taught her that in the same way she needed to treat others with kindness and respect, she deserved to be treated the same way—especially by men. Astrid took Vinchi's casual attempt to touch her hair as even more proof that his intentions were no good when it came to women.

Vinchi shrugged. "I merely meant to help."

Astrid shook her head and crossed her arms in disbelief. Honestly. This man acted more brash and bold than anyone she'd met in quite a long time. "Why did you call me the Iron Maiden?"

"Merchants talk. DiStephan traveled with many of us during the time that dragons migrate. Everyone knows you as the maker of Starlight and his other weapons. You're a blacksmith. An ironworker. What better name to call you than the Iron Maiden?"

"'Astrid' is fine," she said dryly.

"But 'the Iron Maiden' has spark and fire. It strikes fear into the hearts of anyone who might be foolish enough to stand in the way of a dragonslayer. From the way DiStephan always spoke of you, it fits."

"Then you should honor what he would want and give Starlight back to me."

Vinchi frowned and acted offended. "How do you know he wouldn't want me to have it?"

"Because I'm the dragonslayer. If you won't give it back to me like an honorable man, I should take it from you."

"Steal like a common brigand? Or would you prefer to murder me in my sleep like a barbarian?"

Astrid felt as if she'd been slapped. "Of course not. I'm neither a thief nor a murderer."

"Fine. Then you will accept that Starlight is mine."

Astrid took a long look at Vinchi. He spoke rapidly, like a child caught in a naughty act. She suspected he told lies the moment they came to mind.

But she did like the idea of striking fear into the hearts of dangerous people. Especially someone like Margreet's husband. "Why did they fight?" Astrid nodded at the stairs Margreet had climbed to the deck above.

Vinchi looked down and his voice softened. "Margreet accused Gershon of being with another woman. He denied it. Margreet claimed that she herself would make a better husband, so she should be the one to wear the pants in the family."

Astrid smiled. Good for Margreet. Astrid liked people who spoke their minds.

"He challenged her to a fight—whoever won would be the husband in their marriage and wear the pants." Vinchi took a deep breath, but when he spoke again, his voice cracked. "And she was foolish enough to take him up on his challenge."

He cared for the woman. Despite his mischievous ways toward women, Vinchi seemed to have genuine feelings for Margreet.

"Is she your sister?"

Vinchi shook his head. "I only met her after they married, several years ago. Everyone knew this day would come. Margreet and Gershon fight all the time. No one likes the way he treats her, but—" Vinchi shrugged again. "What can you do?"

"What you've already done. Take her away from him."

Trembling, Vinchi sank to the bench before his legs gave out beneath him. "He'll come after us," he said, staring into empty space. "He'll kill us—and her, too."

"I've faced worse," Astrid said, touching the handle of the ax tucked under her belt. "Dragons are bigger and stronger and faster than Gershon."

"But he's right to come after us. And I was wrong to take her."

Astonished, Astrid said, "Why?"

Vinchi looked up at her. "Because Margreet is his wife. And being his wife means that she is his property. I've stolen Gershon's property away from him, which makes me a common thief."

"Nonsense," Astrid snorted. "No man should treat his wife that way. Not unless he bought her as a slave. And that still makes no sense—if a man marries a slave, she becomes a free woman. And no man has the right to treat a free woman that way."

"You don't understand. This isn't Scalding territory. Different territories and countries have different customs."

Astrid laughed with a chilly undertone. "Tower Island is the harshest, cruelest place in the world. Don't you know what they did to me?"

"Yes," Vinchi said quietly. "DiStephan told me. He admired your courage. But the Scaldings control much of the Northlands, including the Far North and Guell, and all of them are known to be the best and safest places for women to live."

"Guell?" Astrid said. "Guell isn't Scalding territory. It's—" She paused, realizing she'd always assumed Guell stood alone because of its proximity to Dragon's Head. She considered Guell home, but most people perceived it as one of the most dangerous places in the world. She'd always assumed everyone who had lived there owned the land equally—but now she recognized she'd made the wrong assumption.

The Scaldings owned Guell.

CHAPTER TWENTY-FIVE

"How can Guell be Scalding territory?" Astrid sat on the bench next to Vinchi, watching every shift in the expression on his face and hoping to discern the truth from it.

"I know they manipulated you," Vinchi said quietly. "I'm sorry they did that to you."

Astrid became aware of her heart racing. For a moment, she felt like a child again, terrified by the world and everything in it. "What do you know?"

"They put you in a cage with a young dragon that chewed you up and spit you out. No one knows why it didn't—why it *couldn't*—kill you. The Scaldings gave you to a child seller, who sold you to a blacksmith in Guell. But it was all a ploy. Nothing but trickery. Last year, the Scalding leader captured you after destroying Guell and everyone in it. They say there was magic involved, and that you're at the heart of it."

"There's no such thing as magic," Astrid said. Although she'd believed this all her life, she silently questioned her own belief.

"They're a strange lot, the Scaldings," Vinchi said. "Every woman I've ever met from Scalding territory told me she had the freedom to live however she pleased because the Scaldings made it possible. I know some of the Northern lands outside of Scalding territory try to put women in their place, but I've never heard of one laying a harmful hand on his wife or daughter. It's just not done in the North."

Suddenly dizzy, Astrid rubbed her face with both hands. None of this made any sense. She'd known DiStephan since they'd met in childhood, and he'd never told her such stories. Astrid had always assumed that the rest of the world was like Guell.

She jumped at the sensation of something crawling between her face and hands. Crying out, she sat up sharply, staring at the palms of her hands. Her scars crawled across them like worms.

This had happened weeks ago when she saw Taddeo. He'd noticed the scars that had loosened themselves from the pattern they'd formed down her spine and chest, observing that Astrid appeared to be coming apart at the seams. He'd advised her to take the winter route and drink from the Dragon's Well to lock her scars into place and restore the arm she'd lost to Norah.

For the first time, Astrid considered taking his advice.

"Is something wrong?" Vinchi sounded genuinely concerned.

He looked squarely at her face, unable to see the scars crawling across her hands. Because he'd obviously eaten no lizard meat recently. That meant he saw the true

Astrid, not the one she wanted others to see.

"No," Astrid said softly, rubbing her palms together. She concentrated to force the scars to migrate back where they belonged. "Nothing's wrong."

If she were to drink from the Dragon's Well, that would change. No one would be able to see her scars any more, except where they'd welded together like the pattern on a dragonslayer's sword—and they'd hold in place instead of wandering across her skin. The rest of her skin would be smooth and perfect. And her phantom arm would become real and solid.

At least, that's what Taddeo claimed.

Astrid thought about everyone she'd left at home in Guell: Lenore and Randim, Donel and Trep, and all the others. Guilt still nagged at her for failing to let them know that she'd left Guell, even though she hadn't expected to be gone for longer than several hours. Even worse, she had no way to inform them she'd be taking the winter route after all. What must they be thinking? That a lizard had killed her?

Resting her elbows on her thighs, Astrid leaned forward and covered her face with her hands, closing her eyes to shut out the world. A new thought occurred to her. If Scalding territory provided the best and safest place for women to live, that must have been her brother Drageen's doing. The brother whom she'd fought. The brother whom she'd watched die at the moment he became encased in the rocky folds of Dragon's Head.

What if that's why he manipulated me? Astrid thought. *What if he protected women but doing so required him to harm me? What if I've endangered all the women in Scalding territory for the sake of protecting myself?*

For the first time, Astrid regretted fighting her brother. She wondered if she should have allowed him to use and torture her so that he could continue keeping other women safe. She remembered arguing with him on Tower Island. He'd mentioned an attack on Limru, a sacred place in the Midlands. Drageen had also claimed he needed to scare bloodstones out of Astrid to make himself invincible in case the same marauders who attacked Limru came to the Northlands. And now she realized Drageen had wanted to defend Scalding territory not just for the sake of its men, but equally for its women. She'd destroyed a man who might have been a champion if he'd only had the chance to live and fight.

A sudden shriek pierced the silence between them, and Astrid and Vinchi jumped. Startled, they stared at each other for a brief moment before racing up the stairs.

CHAPTER TWENTY-SIX

As their feet hit the wooden deck, the ship rolled slightly. Astrid and Vinchi paused, gaining their footing. They faced a bracing ocean wind that pushed the air back into their mouths if they tried to speak.

The cool sea spray stung Vinchi's face, and he shivered. The air smelled clean and tangy with salt. Wispy clouds threaded the bright blue sky, and the ship's enormous square sail snapped loud as thunder in the wind. Vinchi saw nothing but the horizon of the ocean meeting the sky surrounding them.

Margreet stood at the railing. She jumped and waved her arms wildly, shrieking at the open water. The wind had tousled her carefully coiffed hair into a fine mess: tendrils had flown free of the bun at the back of her neck and were now plastered across her face, wet with sea spray.

"What is she doing?" Astrid asked.

Anxious to answer that question himself, Vinchi wove his way between the handful of seamen now struggling to control the ship in the high winds. "Margreet!" he called out. "What's wrong?"

She spun to face him, her eyes blazing with anger. She jammed her fists onto her waist.

Vinchi sensed his heart skip a beat. Even though angry, Margreet radiated beauty. "Please," he said. "How can I help?"

Margreet nearly spit her response at him. "Get me back to my husband. Now!"

Vinchi's jaw dropped open in astonishment. "The man who might have killed you?"

The wind loosened some of the tendrils plastered against her forehead, and Margreet impatiently pushed them out of her eyes. "He loves me."

Vinchi stared at her in disbelief.

The Iron Maiden sidled up next to him. "What did she say?"

To Margreet, Vinchi said, "Any man who truly loved you would never harm you." His voice rising in anger, he added, "He wouldn't strike you. Not ever!"

Vinchi froze as Margreet's gaze traveled slowly up and down his body. She had never looked at him like this before. At least, not in any place beyond his dreams.

"A man...like you?" Margreet said.

Vinchi felt as if he'd been bound by ropes squeezing the air from his chest. He wanted to run and escape this embarrassment, to jump over the ship's railing and swim to the horizon, but his feet would not move. He'd always known he had no right to long for another man's wife, but his heart could understand the language of his mind no better than the Iron Maiden could understand Margreet's words. And he'd never dreamed Margreet would speak to him so directly, even though she spoke that way to everyone else. Vinchi thought she didn't notice him.

Of course, stealing her away had made it much easier.

Vinchi's throat grew dry. Margreet took a step forward and repeated her question. "A man—like you—would never lay a harmful hand upon me?"

"That's right," Vinchi said, mustering his courage.

"Then you must be inexperienced in the ways of love," Margreet said, crossing her arms.

The Iron Maiden nudged her elbow into his ribs. "What's she saying?"

Switching to the language of the Northlands, Vinchi said, "She wants to go back to her husband."

"What?" the Iron Maiden said. Turning to Margreet, she said, "What is wrong with you?"

Margreet gave the Iron Maiden a fleeting glance, raising her eyebrows at Astrid's tone, even though she didn't understand her words.

"The boy," Vinchi said, referring to Astrid, "wants to know what is wrong with you." Maybe he could reason with Margreet by proving he wasn't the only one who questioned her demand.

Margreet waved one hand toward the Iron Maiden as if brushing a fly away from her face. "Why should I care what a one-armed boy thinks?" Margreet then stared pointedly at Vinchi. "Why should I care what two boys think?"

"I am your elder," Vinchi said, standing straighter. "I'm a good merchant. I make a good living."

"And my husband is a strong, powerful man who protects me from the likes of you."

Vinchi doubled over, feeling like he'd been punched in the stomach. "How can you say that? What makes you think I could ever hurt you, while that beast nearly beat you to a bloody pulp?"

The Iron Maiden took a cautious step toward Margreet. "Translate!" Astrid said to Vinchi.

"Margreet is stubborn," Vinchi said, keeping his gaze on both women. "She thinks her husband protects her from other men."

The Iron Maiden mirrored Margreet's earlier stance, planting her feet firmly on deck and her fists on her waist while shaking her head in disbelief. To Margreet, the Iron Maiden said, "Has your mind fallen out of your ears and into the sea? Are you empty headed?"

Before Vinchi could open his mouth, Margreet held up a cautionary hand, then brushed it toward Astrid. "I do not need to know what the boy says," Margreet said.

Vinchi looked at the Iron Maiden and repeated Margreet's words.

Astrid looked at him blankly.

Margreet cleared her throat. "The boy expects you to speak his language, not mine."

Confused for a moment, Vinchi realized he'd been translating so quickly that he forgot which language he spoke.

The Iron Maiden held up her own hand. "Don't bother translating. Tell Margreet that this dragonslayer will not let her commit suicide by returning to a man so quick to kill her. Tell her we will now tie her up and keep her below deck—and gag her, if need be."

Vinchi hesitated, then spoke in a firm tone that the Iron Maiden would expect from him. But instead of repeating her words, he spoke for himself. "Margreet," he said. "We will honor your wishes and return you to the man you love."

CHAPTER TWENTY-SEVEN

At first, Gershon believed he was floating up from the bottom of a murky lake, the air in his lungs making his body buoyant enough to drift to the sun-speckled surface high above. His body went limp and relaxed, and his thoughts became muddled and distant. He couldn't recognize his location or if he even cared. Drifting up through the lake was a pleasant experience.

The sudden memory of a small dragon head emerging from the chest of a boy startled Gershon into consciousness. "Dragon!" he shrieked, bolting upright, eyes wide with terror.

"There, there," a soft but familiar female voice murmured in his ear. The voice turned away and called out, "He's awake!"

Gershon winced. He became aware of the throbbing reverberating through his head like a beating drum. Someone must have punched him from behind. Gershon rarely lost a fight and even more rarely lost consciousness. "What happened?" he said, squinting at the harsh light surrounding him. "Who hit me?"

"Nobody," the familiar voice said softly and sweetly. "You fainted."

Gershon decided he must have misheard her. He squinted harder until the fuzzy shape came into focus. A young woman with long blond hair sat next to him, holding a ladle of some concoction or another. After a few moments, he recognized her as Frieda, a Northlander whose farmer father had tried to broker a marriage deal with Gershon years ago, before he'd met Margreet.

"Here," Frieda said. "I spent the morning making soup. It will clear your head."

Gershon grunted his appreciation and took a mouthful of soup, thick with chopped potatoes and purple carrots, a Northern delicacy. He always forgot Frieda's talent as a cook until he took a bite of one of her meals. As promised, the aroma, fragrant with herbs, cleared his head quickly. The taste was satisfying and welcome.

He ran an inquisitive hand through his scalp and paused, discovering a raised, tender bump on the back of his head. Frowning, he growled at Frieda, "Who hit me?"

Gershon sat on the wooden planks covering the market street, and Frieda knelt by his side. The rest of the marketplace bustled around them. Speaking so softly that only he could hear, Frieda said, "You truly fainted, dear sir. You hit your head when you fell, because everyone felt such surprise that no one could move quickly enough to break your fall." She slipped her hand through the crook of his arm. "It happens to everyone from time to time."

Had it not been for his throbbing head, Gershon would have struck the woman down to put her in her place. But the pain in his head made the simple act of lifting a hand an impossible task. Instead, he simply yelled at her. "Wretched woman! How dare you question me?"

Frieda raised an eyebrow and whispered, "My brothers are here in the marketplace with me. Unlike the rest of the world, Northlanders protect their women."

Her brothers. Gershon remembered them from the fight that broke out because he refused the marriage deal. Frieda's tall, strong brothers threatened him if he didn't accept Frieda and expand her family's trading reach into the territories through which Gershon traveled. Frieda had been the one to calm troubled waters by suggesting they strike a trading agreement that required no marriage. Ever since, Gershon had bought sacks filled with their purple carrots to sell across the seas.

But accusing Gershon of fainting! How dare anyone go so far? "I did not faint. Never have fainted. Never will."

Frieda's smile laced her voice. "Of course. My mistake."

A cloth merchant from a Midland country rushed toward them, his shoes clattering along the wooden planks. The cloth merchant wore a simple linen gown belted at the waist, and his wispy gray hair stood up in tufts like feathers on an owl's head. His large dark eyes watered with fear. "Gershon!" the cloth merchant said as he extended a hand. Leaning forward, the cloth merchant whispered, "I saw the magic that boy cast upon you!"

Normally, Gershon would have scowled at the offered hand and popped to his feet without accepting assistance from anyone. But his head still throbbed and Gershon now wondered if the boy had done something to knock him out without having to throw a punch. Some kind of trickery, perhaps.

Gershon took the cloth merchant's hand and let him pull Gershon to his feet. "What did you see?"

The cloth merchant's face had gone red from the strain of helping the larger man stand up. He dabbed at the sweat beading between his eyebrows with his sleeve. "One minute the boy pulled a dragon out of his chest, and the next minute that same dragon vanished into nothingness!" The cloth merchant's eyes remained wide. He raised one hand to illustrate, fingers spread wide and taut. "And the dragon did something to you. Fire came out of its mouth and a strange light shined out of its eyes—straight at you!" He paused and his eyes lost focus as he rethought his words. He shook his hand at Gershon. "That light—it could have been a poison!"

Frieda giggled, standing up next to the men. "That's impossible. How can poison take the form of light?"

The cloth merchant inhaled sharply like a man so insulted that it took his breath away. "Heathen!"

"I'm a Northlander," Frieda said coolly, correcting him.

The cloth merchant shook a trembling finger at her, his face flushing scarlet as sweat popped up along his hairline. "The one true Krystr says your gods are false! And you will suffer for worshipping the wrong gods."

"The White Krystr," Frieda hissed.

Gershon stepped between them when the cloth merchant's color faded in response to Frieda's insult. Even Midlanders knew that here in the North, the color white identified cowards and women. "Go back to your brothers," Gershon said to Frieda. "Feed them the fine soup you gave to me." *That should be enough to placate the woman*, he thought.

Ignoring the heathen woman, the cloth merchant led Gershon down the street. "There is someone here you should meet," the cloth merchant said. "Someone who can help."

Gershon frowned. "Help with what?"

"Finding your wife. Vinchi and the boy sailed off with her."

Stunned, Gershon stopped, oblivious to the crowd brushing past him. The throbbing in his head intensified, and his vision blacked out for a moment as he swayed where he stood.

Impossible! How could his most prized possession have been stolen?

Chapter Twenty-Eight

"This is peculiar," Wendill said, kneeling in a patch of grass and staring keenly at it.

Norah sat on a nearby rock, clutching her stomach. After eating the few berries that Wendill had given to her, she felt nauseated and light-headed.

What if Wendill had poisoned her?

Norah struggled to think and instead opted to sink into her feelings, a dark and comfortable place. She'd spent all her life in a cage on top of Tower Island. She'd never imagined a world existed beyond that place of stone and steel surrounded by a vast expanse of sky. She'd stayed alive by chewing into the Scalding girl for the first several years of her life, inhaling the girl's blood to ease Norah's own savage hunger while sickened at the thought of devouring the girl. Whenever Norah had looked into the Scalding girl's eyes, she'd seen herself and couldn't help but think how she'd feel if she were the weak one and the Scalding girl had the power to consume Norah. No matter how much she hated the wicked, wicked Scaldings, Norah couldn't bear to kill the girl, even if it meant starvation.

For the past several months, Norah had healed inside the cave occupied by Taddeo and other dragons. They'd kept her safe and fed her what little Norah would eat, but no one revealed any information about her other than simply recognizing her as a dragon.

But what did being a dragon mean? Norah knew she'd hatched inside the cage. She'd been startled the first time she'd transformed into a dragon and even more so when, in the womanly shape she held now, she'd begun to become part of the cave itself, as if the stone had seeped into her blood and therefore made her something hard and heartless. Inexplicably, the Scalding girl had reached out to Norah, who repaid her by devouring her arm.

Still spinning, Norah's head dropped in shame. How could she have had the strength to resist such a thing for so many years only to give in at a time of crisis? Consuming the Scalding girl's arm had revived Norah and made it possible for her to heal, but to what end? Still shocked by the vastness of the world, Norah shuddered at the sight of the mountains rising on either side of this valley, feeling as if the world clutched her firmly in its jaws, ready to revive itself by consuming her the way she'd consumed the Scalding girl's arm months ago.

Maybe she should trust her first instinct—maybe Wendill had poisoned her. Maybe he acted as Taddeo's agent. Maybe Taddeo had lied about being Norah's uncle.

Or maybe Wendill wasn't who he claimed to be.

"Come look at this," Wendill called as he studied the ground.

Norah doubled over. "Sick," she murmured.

Moments later, she gasped at the sharp fingertip pressure against her skull. The nausea vanished and the world came back into focus. Astonished, she gazed at Wendill, now at her side with one hand on her head. "Better," she said.

Wendill released his healing grip on her head. Frustration laced his voice. "It's been so long since you've had a real meal that your body can't remember how to digest food." He reached into his pouch and handed a few more berries to her. "Eat more—that should help."

Willing to do anything to keep from feeling sick again, Norah took the berries and nibbled on them.

"Come look at what I found." Wendill led her to the patch of grass. "What do you make of this?"

Norah frowned at the impression in wet dirt surrounded by grass. "Footprint?"

"Yes. But what kind of footprint is it?"

Norah touched it gingerly, careful not to disturb the imprint. "Don't know."

"Stand next to it for a moment."

Like other dragons, Norah walked in bare feet. Obeying Wendill, she placed her own foot parallel to the imprint, a few inches away from it. Wendill nodded, and she withdrew, leaving her own footprint behind.

By comparison, Norah's footprint looked shorter and slightly narrower, but the impressions were similar in shape. "Man?"

Wendill paused. "Male. But not necessarily a man."

"Then what?"

Wendill pointed at the pebble-like impression each of Norah's toes had left in the mud. He then pointed to the long and narrow marks extending from the ball of the other footprint.

Norah frowned, then leaned over the foreign footprint until her nose touched the ground. She inhaled deeply, taking in the sweetness of the grass, the tangy earthiness beneath it, and a faint, peculiar scent that puzzled her.

She examined the long, narrow marks and the tiny points that had dug deeper into the ground than the rest of the print. "Talons?"

"Or claws," Wendill said softly. "Like the claws we have when we take the shape of a dragon."

Norah became light-headed again, but the berries she'd eaten seemed to settle in her stomach safely. "Not dragon." She sat up slowly, frowning at Wendill. "Not man."

Wendill looked at her steadily, but Norah thought she saw fear in his eyes. "Exactly."

Chapter Twenty-Nine

Margreet paced the ship's narrow deck, losing patience every time the seamen, bustling to lower the square sail and tie it down, crossed her path. Vinchi worked among them, calling out orders, while the annoying boy stayed out of the way, clutching the ax in his only hand while his other shirt sleeve hung empty and useless. Margreet caught Vinchi's gaze, and she shouted, "Hurry!"

Vinchi looked away, acting as if he hadn't heard her.

Men. Stupid, stupid men.

Gershon would tan their hides for stealing Margreet away. He was her husband. Her protector. The man who let her share his safe and warm bed.

Out of breath from pacing, Margreet slipped to the side of the ship where she gazed at the nearby shore of the Midlands. She recognized this major port of Gershon's home country in the Upper Midlands. A handful of ships nestled next to each other by the simple dock where ropes tethered them to fat posts. A delta opened up adjacent to the dock, where a river poured itself into the sea. Hills jagged with rocky spines surrounded the port village, casting ominous shadows upon its streets. The first time Margreet had seen them, she had clutched her husband's arm in terror, believing it to be the shadow of a dragon ready to attack.

Margreet had been born and raised in a more pastoral country in the Lower Midlands, where one could count on the weather being more kind and gentle throughout the year. Here, like the Northlands, winter came early and took its time to depart. A sudden icy gust made her shiver. At times like this, she missed her homeland.

Don't think that, Margreet told herself. *It's dangerous.*

Once upon a time, the Lower Midlands had been safe, but no place could be perceived as safe anymore. Not with the infiltration of the armies of the Krystr. The world constantly changed, and not in a good way. Margreet had already learned her lesson. She'd witnessed the mistake of her mother, who believed in standing up for the sake of a just cause. On the day of her mother's murder, Margreet had been lucky to save herself by finding a hiding place in a thicket of trees. After the attack ended, Margreet stayed in her hiding place until thirst and hunger drove her out. Although she hadn't seen the destruction itself, looking at the aftermath changed Margreet. She'd been a bright and happy child. Approaching adulthood, she'd been quick to make jokes and laugh. But after she'd understood what the Krystr's men were willing to do for the sake of their new god, Margreet's lightheartedness escaped like the dying breath of an old man.

Before, she'd enjoyed life and perceived it as an adventure. Now, she saw life being little more than a test of endurance. Her one and only mission focused on survival. She cared about nothing else.

And Gershon was her best bet for survival.

Finally, Vinchi and his seamen unfurled and secured the sail. They removed a dozen oars hanging on the ship's outer hull, threaded them through the holes just below the railing on each side of the ship, and sat down to row.

Margreet turned away from them, looking out to sea. That might be Gershon's ship in the distance, although to Margreet it looked like little more than a speck on the horizon. Surely, someone would have told Gershon where to find Vinchi. Pausing, she thought she remembered Vinchi mentioning this port days ago. Of course. Gershon already knew where to find her, and he'd be here soon to reclaim her as his own.

Her eyes filled with tears for a moment, thinking of the day she'd met Gershon. She'd wandered the roads alone, always a bad idea. Brigands scoured roads looking for victims to rob. Armies marched everywhere, whether they were soldiers of Krystr or a small band of men defending their own territory or trying to steal away new land from its rightful owner. And then, of course, there were dragons that hid by roadsides, patiently waiting to devour the next unwitting animal or traveler. One day, Gershon had driven his cart up behind a walking Margreet and offered a ride. Margreet had been weak from hunger and still faced many more days of walking, so she'd accepted the offer. Gershon had been respectful and kept his hands to himself on the journey, but once they arrived at a village, he paid the local clerk to marry them.

Margreet had been surprised but grateful. Since the destruction caused by the armies of the Krystr, she'd felt alone and hopeless. Marrying a merchant such as Gershon meant she would have food and shelter for the rest of her life. Margreet didn't hesitate to marry him.

Oddly enough, she began to grow in confidence, knowing she could depend on her husband to make her life right. Although Margreet recognized her responsibility to run their household in the Upper Midlands, she soon became bored and turned her attention to how her husband ran his business. Margreet had many ideas for improving the business that Gershon not only used but claimed as his own ideas. At first, Margreet didn't mind—after all, as long as Gershon's business thrived, her life would be fine.

But people began to compliment Gershon on his prowess for business, and she began a habit of losing her temper. Instead of having an occasional argument like most married couples, they bickered daily. Margreet was happy for his success, but she longed for his recognition of her contribution to it.

Instead, Gershon yelled at her until he reached his breaking point. Once that point broke, he used his fists.

Margreet knew she should keep her mouth shut. They could be happy if only she were willing to let him take credit for her ideas. If only she could accept her place as a dutiful wife who accepted her mission to take care of her husband and do everything within her power to make his life easier. If only she were willing to accept the Krystr's lies that women were evil creatures that caused all the pain and suffering in the world—and therefore had to be kept in their place.

If only, if only, if only.

Run away now, a voice whispered inside Margreet's head. *These people can help you. Let them!*

Margreet knew the voice well. It had told her to hide, saving her from the attack by the Krystr's army of dedicated and dangerous men. It had been her closest ally for as long as she could remember. As a child, Margreet had been scared every time she heard it speak, but her mother had assured Margreet it was nothing more than a spark of intelligence and wisdom that served to guide her through life.

But Margreet's mother had the same kind of voice within her, and it had failed her on the day of the attack. It had led her astray. Therefore, these voices could no longer be trusted.

She shook her head, still gazing out to sea. Margreet would learn to be dutiful, and Gershon would be kind to her again. Their lives could be like their happier, earlier years of marriage. It was her fault he hit her—he'd told her so many times. She provoked him. She angered him to a point beyond reason.

And besides, he apologized so prettily and promised it would never happen again.

He always promised it would never happen again. Every time.

If you don't leave now, he will kill you!

Margreet shook the voice out of her head. It spoke the same kind of nonsense as the boy with the ax.

"Hold on," Vinchi called out.

Spinning toward his voice, Margreet noticed their ship prepared to dock. She sank to her knees, closing her eyes and hoping for a safe landing.

CHAPTER THIRTY

Feigning seasickness, Astrid raced downstairs, looking for the three baby lizards she'd brought on board.

"Smoke!" she whispered fiercely. "Fire! Slag!"

Astrid squinted as her eyes adjusted to the dim light. The sky had thickened with dark clouds, leaving little light to filter down the stairs leading below the ship's deck. She thought she saw something move in the dimness. "Smoke?"

Tiny, clawed feet skittered across the wooden floor like a smattering of raindrops striking a cloth sail.

Astrid sank to her hands and knees, hoping her new proximity to the floor would help her see better. She drummed her fingernails against the wooden surface, imitating what she'd just heard with the wish that she could attract the lizards to her.

Silence.

Vinchi's shouts to the seamen drifted down the stairs, along with the scraping of the oars and the crashing of waves against the side of the ship. Convinced they couldn't hear her, Astrid raised her voice slightly. "Smoke! Come here!" She reached an open hand on the floor, willing the lizards to step into her palm. "We're landing soon, and this ship is no place for any of you to live. If you haven't already had a run-in with them, there's usually lots of rats that hide inside ships. They could be terribly dangerous for you. I have no idea where this ship will sail next, but it could be a very long voyage and I don't know if there's anything on board that's good for young lizards to eat. And never mind the men who sail it. If they discover you, that will be the end of you."

As Astrid's eyes began to adjust to the dim light, she stifled a shriek as something sniffed her hand. A few tiny footsteps skittered away.

She noticed something on the floor next to her hand, too tiny to be a lizard. It looked like a very small stick. Astrid picked it up, surprised by the feel of its leathery, scratchy surface. It didn't feel like wood. It felt like...

The tail of a rat. Just the tail.

Astrid cried out, dropping the horrible thing and scrambling up to her knees.

Tiny eyes flashed for a moment in the dark, reflecting the small amount of light coming down the stairs.

"Smoke?"

As Astrid began to see more and more in the dim light, she thought she saw the lizard sitting on its haunches and chewing on something round clutched between its front feet.

"I'm quite serious," Astrid said. "We have to go now."

Two other shapes skittered to Smoke's side, knocking the object out of his feet and batting it across the floor toward Astrid.

Even in the dim light, she recognized it as the decapitated head of a rat.

Screaming, she jumped to her feet and ran back toward the stairs. "Stop that!" she yelled. "Smoke! Fire! Slag!"

As the ship rolled slightly with the ocean waves, the rat's head tumbled toward Astrid's feet. Screaming again, she hopped up on the stairs just as Vinchi came running down them with a pail of water in hand. Colliding, the pail flew out of Vinchi's hands, water spilling onto the floor as Vinchi and Astrid fell onto the wet surface.

Rising slowly, Vinchi squinted. He rubbed his elbow gingerly and winced in pain. "There's no fire down here. Why did you say there was?"

Astrid opened her mouth to protest and then realized what had just happened. She'd called out just loud enough for those above deck to hear her. "I apologize," she said. "I thought I saw something, but I was wrong."

Swearing, Vinchi limped back up the stairs. "Get yourself ready to land. We'll be docking soon."

Realizing she sat on a small, round object, Astrid fought back the urge to vomit. "Don't think about it," she told herself as she rose slowly and shook the legs of her pants, hoping to shake off whatever she'd landed upon. She imagined the three young lizards hiding and smiling at the result of their antics. "Well," Astrid said as she climbed up the stairs. "At least I know they're not going to starve."

Chapter Thirty-One

After Astrid climbed back up to the ship's deck, she hurried to catch up with Margreet and Vinchi. He shouldered a sack of weapons, and they walked across the wooden plank to dry ground.

"What do we do next?" Astrid said, joining Vinchi's side. "Where can we go to make sure Gershon can't find us?"

Running ahead of them, Margreet hopped from the plank onto land and darted to the edge of the small dock. The village looked much smaller than the town in the Northlands where Astrid had met Vinchi and Margreet. A handful of tall Northlanders dressed in woolen pants and cloaks carried barrels onto and off of a nearby docked ship similar to Vinchi's, like ants hurrying about their business. A local woman shivered, pulling her own cloak tighter as she zigzagged through the small crowd with a basket full of fresh fish in hand.

Astrid squeezed her eyes shut against a sudden burst of frozen rain that splattered into her face. Wiping the tiny hail pellets from her eyes, she looked up to see Margreet pacing the dock, arms crossed, staring out to sea. She didn't look like a woman eager to escape her husband.

Quite the opposite.

And now Vinchi had made his way halfway through the crowd, shielding his eyes from the hail while he asked for directions, nodding as he followed a Northlander's arm pointing toward a nearby cluster of simple wattle-and-daub houses.

Astrid caught up with him again. "What's happening? Why is Margreet waiting for Gershon?"

Vinchi glanced nervously at Astrid. "Because she wants to."

Aghast, Astrid walked quickly to keep up with Vinchi's pace. "But we brought Margreet here to protect her from him!"

Vinchi kept walking, seeming to not hear her.

"If he finds her, Gershon will kill her," Astrid said. "And her blood will be on our hands because we didn't protect her. It's the same as murder."

Vinchi stopped briefly to shift the bag he carried from one shoulder to another. The bag muffled the sound of clanging metal inside. "I never should have interfered. She's his property, not mine."

"Why can't we buy her?" Astrid said. "If she's our property, we can set her free. Then she'll be nobody's property."

"You don't know Gershon," Vinchi said softly, unable to meet Astrid's gaze.

"Once he claims ownership, he never lets go. There is nothing you could offer that would tempt him. Besides, Margreet wants to go back to him."

They walked side by side for a few moments in silence.

"Or worse," Vinchi finally said, "Gershon is the type of man to strike a deal without living up to his end. Even if we convince her not to leave and we give him something he wants, I see no way that he would let Margreet go."

"Then why are we waiting for him to get here?"

Vinchi nodded toward Margreet, still pacing anxiously while she scanned the horizon. "She wants him." His voice cracked. He sounded like a man with a broken heart.

Astrid looked from Vinchi to Margreet and back to Vinchi again. Of course. Why hadn't she noticed sooner?

"You wish Margreet had met you before she met Gershon."

Vinchi's face flushed and he hurried his pace.

"You think you could have wooed her. You think she could be waiting at home for you right now, pacing and wanting you home with her. You think she could have loved you instead of him."

"At least she'd be safe," Vinchi muttered.

"Or would she simply be your property instead of his?"

Vinchi stopped suddenly and spun to face her. The look in his eyes flared with rage and he spoke quietly through clenched teeth. "Watch your tongue, woman. We're in Daneland. In all the world, this is the one kingdom where the law says I can challenge you to combat and you must defend yourself instead of asking a man to do it for you. You may know how to slaughter dragons, but I know for a fact that you have no training in defending yourself against a man."

Startled, Astrid sensed the fine hairs on the back of her neck rise, and her skin turned to goose flesh. Vinchi spoke the truth, and she saw no evidence that he might bluff. Astrid took a deep breath, determined to use Vinchi's feelings against him. "So you would be quick to kill me for questioning your feelings but you hesitate to take Margreet to a safe place where she might learn to love you in time?"

Hope flickered faintly across Vinchi's face like a lit candle in a drafty room. "She wouldn't..."

"We don't know that," Astrid said. "How can we know until we try?"

Vinchi let his gaze wander to Margreet. His voice weakened. "We'd be breaking the law. It's theft."

"And which is the worse crime? Committing theft or allowing a woman to be murdered?"

Vinchi shook his head. "She won't let us. Once she sets her mind to something, she's too strong willed for anyone to reason with her."

"There are two of us."

Tiny hail pounded hard against Vinchi's face, making it look covered in icy tears.

"How are you going to feel," Astrid said softly, "when it's too late? What will your life be like when she's dead?"

Vinchi turned and looked toward his ship.

Astrid followed his gaze. His hired seamen were drawing the plank on board, getting ready to sail out of this harbor and on to the next.

"I told them to sail it back to my home port," Vinchi murmured. "I told them I'd meet up with them there after we give Margreet back to Gershon."

Astrid laid a gentle hand on his arm, and Vinchi started at her touch. "Wouldn't that be the same as letting Margreet commit suicide?" she whispered. "We could sail to your home port now."

Vinchi shook his head. "Gershon will look there first."

"But isn't there a whole wide world between here and your home port? Some other place we could go where Gershon wouldn't think to look? Can't we get back on the ship and sail to a place where he can't find us?"

"We would have to force Margreet on board."

Astrid withdrew Falling Star from her belt. "We have weapons. Margreet doesn't."

Astrid followed Vinchi's gaze through the crowd to Margreet. "I do know a place," he said. "And a quick way to get there."

CHAPTER THIRTY-TWO

Norah huddled by the wheel of the cart, scrunching herself to hide behind it while Wendill searched its contents. They'd found it abandoned in a thicket of trees near the village below. Norah found comfort in hiding. If anyone surprised them, she'd be able to scramble into the forest standing next to the hill.

A pile of heavy cloth plummeted to the ground next to her.

"It's a cloak," Wendill said, still searching the cart. "And plenty of food, plus a cloth I can use for a sack."

Norah buried her face in the cloak that had landed at her feet, but she withdrew and hissed. "Scalding!"

Wendill jumped from the cart, landing neatly on his feet. He carried another cloak in his arms. Extending them, he said, "What do you make of this? Does it smell like her, too?"

Rising to her feet, Norah leaned forward cautiously, careful to keep her distance. A quick sniff told enough. Wrinkling her nose, Norah nodded confirmation. The scent of the Scalding girl lingered on what would be Wendill's cloak, as well.

"Hmm," he said, sticking his own nose into the folds of the cloak. "Is that all? Just her? Or is there more?"

More? Hadn't she already tortured herself by inhaling a scent she wished she'd never known? Norah squeezed her eyes nearly shut, pursed her lips, and looked angrily at Wendill. When caged on Tower Island by the evil Scaldings and any of them dared to venture close to the bars, this very look sent them screaming away in terror every time: Norah's Death Look.

Wendill didn't seem to notice. Instead of waiting for Norah to lean forward, he stuck the cloak right under her nose.

Screeching in surprise, Norah hurried to escape, only to back into the cart, wincing as she struck an elbow against the wood.

"Well?" Wendill said.

Norah considered turning her back to him and slithering to hide under the cart, but then she realized he was right. The cloak held more scent than she'd first noticed. "Man," she said in surprise.

"The scent of a man in addition to the Scalding girl's scent?"

Norah took a tentative step forward to catch another whiff. She detected a male odor underlying the familiar one. Looking up at Wendill, she nodded.

"Which one is stronger?"

Norah answered with hesitation. "Scalding."

"Did they both wear this cloak?"

"Not Scalding."

Wendill picked up the other cloak from where it had landed on the ground. "And this one?"

A gentle breeze brought its scent to Norah. "Same."

"It has the scent of the Scalding girl and of the man?"

Norah nodded. "Different man."

Wendill took a good sniff of each cloak. "I see what you mean. A different man wore each cloak, but each has her scent on it, too."

A stronger breeze carried information that startled Norah. Wide-eyed, she took a step back, pointing at the cloaks. "Lizard!"

Wendill froze. Quietly and with purposeful calm, he said, "Could this be something the monster wore? The footstep we found? The creature that is not a man but not a dragon?"

Norah considered the question, thinking back to what she'd gleaned from smelling the footstep. She'd detected the sour sweat of a man along with the distinctive briny smell of lizard. They'd been intermingled and entwined with each other like a fish ensnared in seaweed, unable to escape.

The smell of each cloak differed greatly. The scent of man was faint and stale with age, as if months had passed since the cloaks had been worn. The scent of lizard came across as strong and fresh as that of the Scalding girl. In fact, the scent of lizard smelled far stronger.

How puzzling. Why would a lizard wear a cloak?

Answering Wendill's question, Norah shook her head. "Not monster."

Wendill smiled and relaxed. "Curious. But I imagine these are safe to wear. Even though we're bound South, the weather will turn colder with every day. Use this to stay warm." He shook out one cloak and draped it around Norah's shoulders, fastening the simple clasp. He then donned the other cloak and scanned the landscape surrounding them.

The wind reversed direction, and a strong gust blew in from the sea.

Norah cried out, sinking to huddle and hide by the wheel of the cart again.

Kneeling next to her, Wendill gazed at her in concern. "What's wrong?"

Norah pointed toward the village. The sea wind had carried dozens of scents including many from the town below, but one smell had stood out from the rest. Tears welled in Norah's eyes as she whispered, "Monster!"

CHAPTER THIRTY-THREE

"Can you detect the Scalding girl?" Wendill's brow creased with concern.

Norah closed her eyes, focusing her full attention of the scents carried by the shifting wind. Blowing from the direction of the forest, the wind carried the dankness of mud from a creek going dry, the paleness of fallen pine needles, and the musky fur of animals settling into their dens to sleep through the winter. The wind kicked up from the ocean, rich with the tang of seaweed, the taste of salt, and the distinctive briny odors of the creatures that lived in its waters.

But the breeze coming from the direction of the village made Norah shudder in fear. The scents were too varied and confusing. Smelling so many different people made her feel like she was back in her cage on Tower Island. They smelled of their own bodies mixed with the dead animal skin and tortured flax they wore. Then there were the smells of roasting meat and baking bread, filling her with unwanted desire to eat things that had once been alive.

Then she ferreted out the other scents: the monster and the Scalding.

Norah choked back tears as she opened her eyes. "Village."

"The Scalding girl is in the village? Along with the monster?"

Norah took a deep breath to reconsider the information of scent, and what she learned calmed her. "Not now."

"But they were there recently." Wendill took a deep breath, clearly relieved. "Were they in the village at the same time?"

Norah shrugged.

"Can you still follow her scent? Can she lead us to the Dragon's Well?"

Testing Wendill's question, Norah sniffed the air, inhaled deeply, and nodded.

He gazed toward the village. "Most likely we'll be fine. But if there's any sign of trouble, we'll head for the ocean and dive in. As soon as we go under water, we can change shape. That makes it easier for us to blend in with the sea and for anyone else to lose sight of us. Understand?"

Norah nodded again. At first, the thought of infiltrating the village had terrified her because she wanted to stay among her own kind.

But knowing Wendill would stay close by her side gave Norah a growing confidence.

Within a short time they entered the village. People crowded its wooden walkway so tightly that no one seemed to notice their presence. Norah sighed with relief until a new scent in the air startled her.

She tugged on Wendill's cloak, and he turned with eyebrows raised in surprise, his gaze drifting to Norah's hand, still clutching the edge of his cloak.

Norah jerked her hand back, grimacing with self-disgust. Because she'd spent her life locked inside a cage, she wasn't used to being touched or touching others. The act of touch felt like an invasion. A threat. She hated herself for taking the lowly action of touching Wendill's cloak, but she'd seen no other way to get his attention.

Shockingly, Wendill touched her arm, and concern laced his voice. "What's wrong?"

Norah automatically jerked away from him and cradled her arm where he'd made contact, as if he'd injured her. Feeling safe again, she raised her nose slightly and took a delicate whiff. "Scalding."

"I thought you said she left the village."

Norah nodded, rocking one arm inside the other like an infant. She breathed deeply, inhaling an interesting mix of smells, something she'd never quite encountered before. It spawned an irresistible urge inside her. Norah followed the scent, winding her way through the crowd to keep it close to her before the wind carried it away.

She stopped abruptly at the moment the breeze shifted toward the ocean.

Norah cried out as someone bumped into her back.

"Watch yourself!" a tall wiry woman said. Even though she'd tied her hair in a bun, fine strands had fuzzed up, making it look like a baby bird covered with fluffy down. She knelt by a basket and picked up a few raw potatoes that had spilled out of it. "If you must stand in the middle of the market, you could at least give some warning." The woman clucked to herself as she righted herself and brushed imaginary dirt from her dress. "Too many foreigners coming in these days," she muttered. "But what can you do about it?"

"Norah." Wendill caught up with her as the potato woman hurried away. He reached out but then drew his hand back, thinking better of it.

Ignoring him, Norah followed her nose to a simple wooden house at the end of the market street.

"I don't understand," Wendill said. He sniffed mightily. "I don't smell anything special."

Norah pointed at the house. "Scalding."

"I thought you said she's already left the village." Wendill pushed ahead, striding up to the house just as its door opened.

A man with the large, sad eyes of a hunting dog stepped over the threshold and looked up in surprise at Wendill and Norah. Sighing, he said, "I never knew a man to have so many friends. If you've come to visit, be forewarned that no one's been able to wake him up. On the other hand, if you're here because you think you can collect his goods, think again—he ain't dead yet."

Ah, Norah thought. *The scent is so obvious now. And tells such a strange story!*

The man standing in the doorway to the house braced his arms against the frame, but Norah easily dashed under his arms and into the house.

Sighing, the man gave up on blocking the doorway, lowering his arms and gesturing for Wendill to come in.

Norah immediately noticed the hearth in the center of the room, where a woman tended the fire and a cooking pot hung over it. Next to the hearth, a large sleeping man stretched out on blankets. His head was shiny and bare, but yellow hair grew over most of his face and hung down to his chest. His hands were enormous and thick.

Norah leaned closer and sniffed the man's gigantic hands. They smelled of the pelts of wolves and bears, foxes and badgers, rabbits and shore cats.

She also detected the acrid odor of fear—not his, but the fear of others. The scent of the Scalding intertwined with the aromas of other people, illuminating a difference about the Scalding scent that Norah couldn't pinpoint.

"What is it?" Wendill stood by her side now and spoke quietly so the others wouldn't hear. "Who is he?"

Instead of answering, Norah placed her nose so close to his skin that she almost touched him, shivering at the thought. But there, information embedded itself in the man's skin. Tantalizing information.

Norah considered the situation. The man with the hands of a giant slept. Judging from his own gamy odor, he had been sleeping for a few days. The man with the sad eyes said no one expected him to wake up. Pausing, she breathed deeply, sensing no danger in this house. Curiosity gnawed at her. The more she tried to inhale the mystery of the information withheld by this man's skin, the more she was tempted.

She'd learned long ago that the sense of smell tied strongly to the sense of taste. Whenever she had trouble understanding odors, she could take one step to gain a deeper understanding.

Just this once, Norah told herself. *Just once and never again.*

Steeling herself for the most unpleasant thing she'd ever chosen to do, Norah touched the tip of her tongue to the sleeping man's temple for a brief moment.

She found it, clear and crisp and interesting.

Ah, Norah thought as she pulled away from the sleeping man. *I am surprised and not surprised.*

"Norah?" Wendill said, shocked by her action. "Are you all right?"

The sleeping man's eyelids fluttered like moths trapped in honey. Finally, his eyes opened and he gazed groggily at Norah.

"Scalding," Norah said to him, "fears nothing."

As the man who used to sleep stared in wide-eyed wonder at Norah, she smiled. Despite the disgust of touching and tasting his skin, doing so had been worth it. Norah delighted at the new knowledge dancing across her tongue.

For the first time, she felt glad she'd ventured outside the dragons' cave where she had been safe and protected.

CHAPTER THIRTY-FOUR

At first the voices were faint and distant, and the darkness enveloping him convinced Gershon that he'd somehow lost his way on a moonless, cloudy night outside a village. But then he realized his feet weren't moving.

In fact, no part of his body moved at all.

"If you've come to visit, be forewarned that no one's been able to wake him up." The voice sounded familiar to Gershon, but he couldn't identify it. "On the other hand, if you're here because you think you can collect his goods, think again—he ain't dead yet."

Dead?

A stark and sudden chill passed through Gershon's body, but he couldn't shiver it off. How could he be dead?

No, wait—the familiar voice had said Gershon had not died. Not yet. It also had said no one had been able to wake him up. Could he be sleeping?

The chill ran through his body again, colder and darker this time. Why did he sleep and why couldn't anyone wake him up?

"What is it?" an unfamiliar male voice whispered. "Who is he?"

Who are you? Gershon tried to say, but his voice didn't work. He tried to open his eyes to no avail. *What is it?* Gershon thought, panicking. *Why can't I move? Am I paralyzed?*

The dragon, he realized. *This is the fault of the very small dragon that emerged from the boy's chest and spit on me!*

Of course. How obvious. Everyone knew that dragons killed by biting their prey. Soon after, the victim would be so stunned by the bite that he often froze in place, where the dragon would make a meal of him. Gershon had once heard of a man who'd been bitten by a dragon that attacked his village. That village's dragonslayer arrived in time to slay the dragon and prevent it from killing anyone, but the man who had already been bitten died a few days later.

It was surefire proof that a dragon's bite is poisonous.

I'm dying, Gershon thought. *How can this be happening to me? I'm strong and well and mighty of sword. I capture wild animals and skin them. I should have died on the battlefield defending my territory or my trade or my possessions. Not like this.*

Still enveloped in darkness, Gershon's foggy head cleared just enough for him to realize his eyes were shut. He tried to open his eyes, but nothing happened.

Terror struck him like lightning. *No*, Gershon thought, sinking deeper into panic.

I can't lose control. I have to be in control!

He'd learned at a young age to recognize the world as a wild and dangerous place. Survival required being in control of every situation at all times. His own father had been murdered while traveling to sell furs. Another merchant had discovered the body and a dull dagger clutched in the dead man's hand. Clearly, Gershon's father had failed to take the time to use a whetstone on his blade after skinning a catch, and the lack of a sharp edge had meant he'd had no control during the attack.

Always carry a sharpened blade. That was Gershon's motto. But now he found himself in a situation where no number of sharp weapons could help him because he'd lost control over his own body.

It made him feel betrayed by his own skin.

If he could have moved, Gershon would have jumped in surprise at the touch of a wet tongue that barely touched his temple.

The dragon, he thought. *It's come back to eat me!*

But whatever licked his face didn't bite.

Even though Gershon couldn't move a single muscle, he sensed a new tension tightening up throughout his body. Why would a dragon lick him without biting him? It made no sense.

The unfamiliar male voice spoke again, sounding as surprised as Gershon felt. "Norah? Are you all right?"

Who is Norah? Gershon wanted to shout. *And why do you ask if she's the one who's all right? I'm the one who's being attacked by a dragon!*

A strange and calming warmth spread throughout Gershon's body, the same sensation as coming home on a wintry day and sitting down to eat a bowl of hearty stew after working from sun-up 'til sundown. Gershon recognized the sensation of being wrapped inside a cozy, soft blanket.

The tongue left his skin, but the wetness it left behind lingered. Now Gershon noticed a new lightness, the same lightness that came after hauling a heavy load of furs on his shoulders and putting them down on a table. As if someone had lifted a tremendous weight off of him.

Without giving it a single thought, Gershon opened his eyes, too surprised to rejoice as the force paralyzing his body dissolved. The world shone far too bright, and he squeezed his eyes shut again to keep all the light out. Although Gershon felt as though he were moving through molasses, his eyelids fluttered rapidly while his eyes adjusted to the dim light inside the house. After the minute or so it took for his vision to settle, Gershon stared wide-eyed at the woman standing above him.

She looked like a small and slight thing, with her long black hair wild and un-kempt, looking like she'd just walked in from a windstorm. He saw the same wildness in her eyes, a look he knew all too well from his work killing and skinning animals for their fur.

This was no woman—she could be nothing but a creature of the wild.

"Scalding," she said to him, "fears nothing." She smiled a knowing smile. A smile with power behind it, the power of holding information that no one else can possibly know.

"Gershon!" One of his longtime colleagues rushed to the bedside. "We thought you was lost to us for good. You slept for days!"

A new understanding hit Gershon with the certainty of sunrise. He gazed at the woman, finally seeing the wildness in her as a thing of great beauty. "She lifted the poison out of me," Gershon said softly. "She saved my life." He lifted one hand weakly toward Norah, wanting to touch her arm.

Norah hissed at him, stepping back.

"Apologies," Gershon said, jerking his hand back. Of course. It all made sense now. She had to be a wild creature. A divine creature. An agent of the new god Krystr. Only a saintly messenger could have saved him from the dragon's bite.

Looking at him with suspicion etched across her face, the woman said, "Scalding fears nothing."

"I know you fear nothing," Gershon said. "I recognize you."

"Not Scalding!" the woman cried out.

The small man standing by the god's messenger spoke up. "This is Norah. She's not a Scalding, but we're looking for one by the name of Astrid, and we believe you know her."

Baffled, Gershon shook his head.

The man continued, "She's a young woman who carries a dragonslayer's sword."

"I've only seen a merchant with such a sword." Finally, a true shudder raced through Gershon's skin, giving him relief at last. "A boy with an ax and dagger accompanied him."

The ends of Norah's mouth curled up. "Not boy," she said. "Scalding."

"Astrid is a woman," her man said helpfully.

Gershon's head spun. None of this made sense. Unless—

He'd assumed the boy was a boy because he wore men's clothes. If that were how Astrid Scalding chose to dress, of course she'd be punished for having the audacity to sport male clothing. And the most likely punishment for her crime would be cutting off her hair.

Suddenly, everything made sense.

If she persisted in this crime and conspired not to be caught again, she would pretend to be a boy.

In that case, Astrid Scalding's dragon had done this to Gershon. It must be her fault he'd been paralyzed and nearly died.

"Yes, a woman," Gershon said. "I believe I do know her."

The man brightened. "Can you lead us to her?"

"To kill her?"

"No!" The man paled with horror. "Of course not!"

Norah looked squarely at Gershon. "Not kill," she explained.

Gershon sighed. He was disappointed that his heavenly savior chose not to avenge him. But he understood. He accepted his manly duty to avenge any wrong done against him with his own hands. To expect someone else to seek revenge—even an agent of the god Krystr—would be a womanly act. A cowardly act. Ignoble and without grace.

"Yes," Gershon said. "I can find Astrid Scalding."

CHAPTER THIRTY-FIVE

Furious, Margreet paced the ship's deck until Vinchi ordered her to sit in a corner out of the way. "How dare you?" she shouted. "You promised to return me to my husband and then you force me back onto this ship? Where are we going?"

Vinchi gestured toward her appointed corner. "Sit and get out of the way. Unless you prefer to go below deck again."

Still steaming, Margreet plunked herself down, preferring fresh air and light.

Vinchi's ship changed course. As it left the sea, the crew lowered the sail and rowed down a river flanked by fields and forests.

Margreet shivered, huddled in the corner on the deck at the back of the ship. The seamen rowed slowly and steadily as the ship headed for a still pocket of the water by the riverbank. This seemed a strange place to dock. Here, trees lined the river, but rolling fields lay beyond the shoreline, lined with furrows of harvested crops. In the distance, low mountains lined the horizon. She suspected they still might be in Daneland, but she wasn't sure. She knew very little about this part of the world.

Margreet hated Vinchi and the boy for breaking their promise to reunite her with Gershon. As she'd pointed out to Vinchi during the past few days, she hadn't asked for help and certainly didn't need any. What happened between Margreet and Gershon should remain their business, and no one had the right to interfere.

She touched the simple silver ring on her finger that Gershon had given to her on their wedding day. It marked her as his property. It meant she belonged to Gershon and no one else. Why didn't these fools understand?

Perhaps they see you belong to no one but yourself, a small voice whispered inside her head.

Margreet froze, startled by the voice because it hadn't spoken to her for years. Why had it suddenly started talking during the past day or so? Her mother had taught her to listen to that voice and follow it without question. Her mother said it was a light within that would guide Margreet like a beacon.

But like everyone else, her mother had listened to the voice inside herself, and it had led her to death.

No. Margreet would not follow that path. The only way to survive was to ignore the voice.

The ship jerked to a halt and gently rocked while a few crew members jumped onto the nearby riverbank, tethered the ship to a tree, and put the wooden board in place, making a walkway to shore.

Margreet jumped to her feet and stayed on Vinchi's heels. "If you don't take me back to Gershon this instant, I will make sure he kills you!"

A pained expression crossed Vinchi's face fleetingly, surprising Margreet. This marked the first time she'd said anything so harsh to Vinchi, but he should have expected it. She couldn't imagine what pained him.

"He'll kill me whether you tell him to or not," Vinchi said, supervising the landing.

The boy interrupted, asking Vinchi a question in the Northlander language. In response, Vinchi rolled his eyes and shook his head. The boy cast a disappointed look at Margreet.

"Tell me what you are talking about," she demanded of Vinchi.

He ignored her, gesturing for the boy to leave the ship. Turning to Margreet, he said, "You're next."

She folded her arms and stood her ground. "I'm waiting right here until Gershon comes and finds me."

"Then you will stay in the company of the crew, and I will not be there to keep them in line," Vinchi said quietly. He turned his back to her and followed the boy off the ship, leaving Margreet alone on the deck.

She took his point. Margreet had been safe among men who were used to bedding any woman they chose, regardless of the woman's wishes. She'd been safe because Vinchi had told his crew the moment they'd set sail that he'd personally throw any man overboard who dared to touch her.

She hurried to catch up with him, following him along the wooden board until her feet landed on dry ground. "You've always been pleasant to me in the past. Why are you so cruel to me?"

Vinchi turned sharply to face her, and Margreet didn't have time to slow her pace. She bumped into him, then took an embarrassed step back. "Perhaps," Vinchi said coolly, "it has something to do with your plan to order your husband to kill me."

Oh. The man had a point.

"I apologize," Margreet said, meaning it. "I promise I will not tell Gershon to kill you. But I am not responsible for the decisions he makes on his own."

The harsh expression in Vinchi's eyes softened and he smiled sadly. "That," he said, "I already know."

The boy called out to them, gesturing for them to follow.

"Let's go," Vinchi said as he walked toward the boy.

Glancing back at the ship, Margreet saw the crew watching her. One of the men gestured for her to join them on deck, and the other men smiled.

Suppressing a sudden shiver, Margreet ran to catch up with Vinchi. "And what of the boy?"

"What do you mean?"

"Will he keep his hands off me?"

Vinchi laughed until tears streamed from the corners of his eyes.

Margreet frowned, peering with even greater suspicion at the boy waiting patiently for them in the harvested field. She couldn't imagine what Vinchi found so amusing.

"Trust me," Vinchi gasped as he tried to catch his breath from laughing so hard. "The boy poses no threat to you."

⁓⁓

They traveled for days. Fields that had radiated vibrant greens and crimsons and ambers weeks ago now lay wasted, their hacked stalks and vines now dry and brittle after savage frosts. The ground they walked upon, once soft and forgiving, felt hard and unyielding through the thin soles of their shoes. Instead of a bright and pleasant dome, the sky looked weary from bearing the weight of thick, gloomy clouds.

Astrid jumped in surprise at the strike of an ice pellet against her face. A farmer's family had given them a warm place to sleep last night, in addition to enough food to get them through the next day or two. The icy wind blasted across her face and through her clothing. Astrid wished she'd accepted the farmer's offer to stay and blacksmith for him, mending his damaged plow, making nails, and repairing other tools that had gone too long without attention.

But what about Margreet, trudging by Astrid's side? They'd stolen the woman away with just the clothes on her back, and she'd been shivering since they'd left the ship. Vinchi had quickly given his cloak to Margreet. It measured far too long and dragged around her feet, threatening to trip her. And now Vinchi had started shivering, even though they walked at a steady pace that would have caused anyone to break out in a sweat only a week or so ago. Now armed with Falling Star only, Astrid traded her ax and other daggers to the farmer for food and a good cloak for Margreet, who now held it wrapped tightly against her body. An ice pellet bounced off the top of Margreet's exposed head, and she flipped up the hood to cover her hair.

Vinchi squinted up at the sky and then pointed across the field at a line of trees. "There's the entrance. Going through the forest is the fastest way."

Concern creased Margreet's forehead as she asked Vinchi a pointed question.

At first Vinchi shrugged, taking a quick glance at their surroundings. He answered, but Astrid understood just one word: "Aguille."

Margreet shrieked and backed away.

Vinchi spoke to Margreet calmly, gesturing to the hail that now came down in sheets, white icy pellets the size of pebbles bouncing off the hard ground.

Margreet shook her head in vehement disagreement, holding out an open palm toward him as a warning to keep his distance from her.

"What's wrong?" Astrid asked.

"Margreet doesn't want to enter the forest."

"Why?"

"It's a place that upsets her."

Margreet kept up a rapid stream of babbling, but once more Astrid understood one word.

"Limru!" Astrid said. She raised a questioning eyebrow at Vinchi.

"Limru is deep inside the Forest of Aguille," he said. "She doesn't want to go anywhere near Limru, but it's our most direct and safest route."

"There is a well in Limru—"

"The Dragon's Well," Vinchi said.

"You know it?"

"I know of it." Vinchi paused, glancing at the forest.

Good, Astrid thought. *The water from the well can help us. It can heal us. Make us stronger. We'll need all the help we can get if Gershon catches up with us.*

Margreet spoke more firmly, pointing at the forest.

Astrid followed her gesture, squinting. There seemed to be something odd about the entrance to the forest, but it was difficult to see from this distance, especially through the hailstorm. "What is it?"

"I don't know," Vinchi said. "She said something blocks the way into the forest, but I can't tell from here. We'll have to get closer."

Vinchi spoke quietly to Margreet, pointing to the stormy sky. Her face drawn with fear, she nodded.

Astrid winced with every step as they crossed the hail-covered field, wishing her shoes had thicker soles to protect against the sharpness of each ice pellet. They walked with their heads down, pulling hoods close to their faces to protect from what seemed like a never-ending onslaught.

Approaching the edge of the Forest of Aguille, Astrid looked up briefly. A towering wall of brambles formed a natural wall around the forest, leaving only a narrow gap that formed an entrance. What she saw next made her cry out, causing them all to come to a sudden stop.

Dozens of men and women stood in front of the entrance to the forest. They were solid, but they had no color at all. They were completely transparent.

Frozen in place, they looked like people who had been turned into ice by some type of horrific magic.

Chapter Thirty-Six

Astrid stared in wonder at the dozens of ice people blocking the entrance to the forest. Frozen in place, each one held up their hands and arms, seeming to warn the living to stay away from the forest. Many of them showed open mouths, shouting silent caution to those with warm flesh. The ice people stood shoulder to shoulder, forming a startling barricade. Hail pellets still rained down, adhering to the ice people, making them more solid and real.

"What is this monstrosity?" Vinchi said.

Margreet shrieked at the sight of the ice people, flinging her hands across her face in horror.

Fascinated, Astrid took a step forward. It looked as if a master carver had created statues from ice instead of stone, an impossible task. Although the weather had been growing increasingly cold, the temperature hadn't been cold enough to freeze blocks of ice the size of people, and there certainly hadn't been enough time to carve dozens of lifelike statues.

Margreet cried out, pointing at the ice people. She spoke rapidly to Vinchi, who translated for Astrid. "Margreet says she saw them move."

"That's impossible." Astrid approached the ice people slowly, watching them closely with every cautious step.

But then she saw it, too.

One iceman appeared to lead them. He stood in front of the group with a sword held high above his head, looking ready to cleave in two anyone who dared come close. Astrid didn't see his frozen body move. Instead, she witnessed the hail striking the iceman's skin and running down before freezing into place.

But she also saw movement within the iceman like fog rising on a warm spring morning after the rain. Like a mist drifting behind his transparent skin.

Understanding hit Astrid like a punch in the gut. Turning to Vinchi, she said, "Step closer and look at his face."

"I'll stay where I am." Vinchi wrapped an arm around Margreet's shoulders. "Are you mad? Don't you recognize danger when you see it? This is the work of a powerful sorcerer."

"No," Astrid said. "It's not. It's the work of someone who knows we're being followed. Someone who knows how to scare the living away from the forest we need to enter."

Vinchi shook his head, rejecting her opinion. "We have to go back."

"Look at him," Astrid said softly. "The man in front. The one with the sword raised over his head."

Vinchi squinted. "I am already looking at him."

"Look closer." Astrid reached her hand back toward Vinchi, hoping he would take it. "They aren't made of solid ice. They've been coated with a layer of ice. The same would have happened to us if we hadn't been shaking it off."

Vinchi's arm drifted down from Margreet's shoulder and he took a step away from her. His face strained in disbelief. "That's impossible."

Astrid walked up to the first iceman, smiling and taking in every detail of his long and lean face. The curly hair cropped close to his head. His lanky limbs. And the icy replica of the sword hanging by Vinchi's side that had once belonged to the dragonslayer. "Hello, DiStephan," she whispered.

CHAPTER THIRTY-SEVEN

"How is this possible?" Vinchi said as he stepped next to Astrid, staring in amazement at the perfect icy image of DiStephan.

"They're ghosts," Astrid said. "DiStephan must have asked for their help. He must have seen we were coming this way and assumed we'd need to make our way through the woods. They must have all stood in front of the road going into the woods and let the hail freeze solid on them."

"How can hail freeze on a ghost? Wouldn't it pass right through them?"

Astrid shrugged. "I took Night's Bane so I could spend time with DiStephan once I knew he had died. He said he had limited strength. When he travels with me, he can make small things move, like throwing a handful of dirt into a lizard's face. Maybe they have enough strength to stand up against hail." She gazed up at the ghost of Starlight that DiStephan held above his head. "Or to remember the weapons they once held in their hands."

Margreet called out behind them. Vinchi motioned for her to join them, pointing at DiStephan's icy figure and calling out with confidence.

Turning back to Astrid, Vinchi said, "But why would he do this?"

Astrid smiled and gazed into DiStephan's icy eyes. "It's what he does. I've had no training as a dragonslayer, so I learn from experience. DiStephan travels with me and ahead of me. It's how he watches over me. It's his way of helping me stay alive while I learn my new trade."

As Margreet reluctantly joined them, Vinchi pointed again at the ice people, apparently relaying the guess about who they were and what they were doing.

Margreet's face paled as she listened to Vinchi, and she quickly scanned the faces of the ice people as if looking for someone familiar. Her gaze locked on the figure of a woman back near the tree line.

"Margreet?" Astrid said, following the woman's gaze.

Margreet's attention snapped to Astrid, who gestured to walk forward. Margreet nodded.

Astrid noticed that tears welled in Margreet's eyes but assumed the cold air caused them. She waited while Vinchi and Margreet stepped slowly and carefully, winding their way between the ice people while Astrid paused and laid a gentle hand on DiStephan's ice-cold face for just a moment, careful not to linger for fear of melting away his menacing expression.

CHAPTER THIRTY-EIGHT

The hail pounded against the overhead canopy provided by the trees like raindrops on a wooden rooftop. Beneath the canopy, the air felt cold and dry. Margreet pulled the cloak tight against her chest, and she hurried to keep up with Vinchi and the boy as they wound their way through the wicked forest. Brown, brittle fallen leaves and pine needles littered this narrow dirt path, unlike most roads that ran through the woods. Margreet's shoe snagged on a gnarled root hidden beneath the leaves, and she caught herself from falling. She swore under her breath, watching the man and boy navigate effortlessly ahead.

Ridiculous path. Why couldn't it be a normal road wide enough for a cart and horses instead of barely allowing enough width for one person to pass?

Footsteps shuffled behind her. Catching her breath in fear, Margreet looked back but no one walked behind her. She paused just long enough to see a small brown bird with a tufted head hopping among the leaves, peering beneath them for insects. It wasn't a brigand or a dragon, after all. Through Vinchi, the boy had explained to Margreet that the smallest birds or animals sometimes made enough noise to sound like a herd of cattle crashing through the forest. Margreet hadn't believed it at first, but now she gave credit to the boy. He seemed to understand the forest far better than Margreet or even Vinchi.

Taking one last glance to make sure nothing but the bird made the threatening noise behind her, Margreet took several hurried steps to catch up to Vinchi, who walked directly in front of her. Squirrels chattered and complained high up in the trees near the path and deep in the woods. The birds that had either decided to stay for the winter or were passing through on their way to warmer climates sang brightly, claiming their territory. And every so often something deeper and heavier seemed to trudge among the trees far to either side of the path.

Vinchi's presence calmed her nerves. Even though he didn't have the size or power of her husband Gershon, Vinchi knew how to use the weapons he sold and would be useful if they were attacked.

A stray piece of hail filtered through the overhead canopy and plopped on the end of Margreet's nose. She quickly brushed it off. Normally, the drumming high above their heads would have soothed her, but she was preoccupied with missing her husband. Shuddering, she remembered the gazes of desire and entitlement cast toward her by Vinchi's men during the time they were at sea. True, she'd heard Vinchi tell them more than once to keep their hands to themselves, and, thankfully, they'd obeyed. But while in Gershon's presence, no man dared to do so much as look at her. As long as she counted herself as Gershon's wife, she could count on his protection from other men, and she took comfort in that knowledge. It hadn't been long since she'd learned how cruel and cold the world could be toward an unclaimed woman.

She hadn't thought about it in a long time—not since she'd married Gershon.

But now that they traveled in these woods—a place Margreet recognized—those unwelcome memories were drifting back into her head.

The boy cried out, but she couldn't tell if he'd made the sound in fear or surprise. The boy darted down the path and disappeared around a bend, and Vinchi raced to follow. Fearful of being left behind, Margreet ran to catch up.

She found them standing at the edge of a clearing within the heart of the forest. The size of a small village, a circle of grass lay before them like a patch of harvested land surrounded by towering stalks of grain. In the center of the circle, a cluster of ancient trees with immensely thick trunks towered above the forest, spreading hundreds of branches like a spoked wheel to protect the clearing from the elements. The high branches of the ancient trees overlapped the top of the forest surrounding the clearing.

Tears welled in Margreet's eyes. She remembered how gold and silver chains had once hung from those mighty branches, gifts from those who had come to pay respect to the gods. She remembered the days when no thief would dream of stealing any of the treasures left by worshippers because even thieves asked the gods for help and protection.

It was unthinkable to steal from a god.

Now, bones littered the ground beneath the ancient trees. Thousands of bones. Hundreds of victims had been hung by their hair, and now only the hair remained on the limbs, replacing the gold and silver that had once adorned them.

This clearing of majestic trees had once been the Temple of Limru.

Now it looked like a nightmare.

Margreet sobbed, sinking to her knees. She hadn't wanted to see this place ever again, and now she could no longer block the memory of her own mother screaming as the horrible men had tied her by the hair to a tree limb, kicking and screaming before her own weight caused her to crash to her death on the ground below.

All the while, Margreet had hidden, clutching her hands over her mouth and willing herself to be silent so the horrible men wouldn't find her and string her up by her hair, too. Torn between the urge to dash into the fray to fight the men with her young hands and the desire to live, Margreet had chosen to follow her mother's orders and save herself. But for days after, she'd been unable to utter a sound, still terrified that someone might hear her and kill her.

Now, alone in the forlorn temple with a weapons trader and a boy, Margreet cried the tears she'd spent a lifetime feeling too terrified to set free.

CHAPTER THIRTY-NINE

Astrid stared at the enormous trees towering above them and the clearing surrounding them. Fighting back a lump in her throat, she finally recognized bones piled up under the trees and long locks of hair tied to their branches. She felt an urge to whisper. Clearly, something terrible had happened here, and she wanted to be respectful of the dead. "What is this place?"

"The Temple of Limru," Vinchi said softly, his face drawn and pale. He stared at the trees.

Limru. Of course. Her brother Drageen had told her how a king claiming a new god marched his armies through the Southlands, slaughtering everything in their path—including Limru.

"Are we in the Southlands now?" Astrid said, feeling a sudden urge to look back and make sure no one stood behind them.

Vinchi nodded. "Just barely. Limru borders the Midlands."

Astrid cleared her throat, gathering her thoughts as she remembered what Drageen had told her. "I heard the tribes that worship tree spirits roam the Southlands." While Astrid never paid much attention to such things, she understood some people believed tree spirits were messengers to the gods of the land and sea and air and fire.

Vinchi automatically looked at Margreet, who knelt weeping by his side. "They once did," he whispered. He knelt next to Margreet and spoke quietly to her.

Astrid's eyes widened as she watched them. Since the day she'd met Margreet, she'd seen the woman scream and yell and cower in fear. For the first time, Margreet exhibited genuine pain, crying as if she'd received word that her only friend had died.

The Southland tribes, Astrid thought. Could Margreet have belonged to them? Did she once worship the spirits of trees?

Standing, Vinchi said, "This place upsets her. We should keep moving."

The more Astrid watched Margreet cry, the more she saw herself in the woman. Not even a year had passed since the burning of Guell and the murder of most people who lived there. Astrid easily remembered how she'd felt in the days that she'd been captured by Drageen's men and taken from her home only to escape and return to find her friends and neighbors dead.

"What happened to her?" Astrid said, sinking next to Margreet, who now hugged her knees while weeping.

"She won't tell me. She only says she wants to go home to Gershon."

"I don't know what they did to you or who they are," Astrid said to Margreet.

"But I appreciate what you feel."

Startled, Margreet lifted her head, catching her breath in surprise to find Astrid next to her.

Before Vinchi could translate Astrid's words, she placed a gentle hand on Margreet's knee.

Margreet jerked back as if Astrid had touched her with a red-hot piece of iron, her eyes wide with terror as she barked an order to Vinchi.

Vinchi sighed. "She wants me to remind you that she's married and her husband will slice your head off with his sword if you touch her again."

Astrid realized she'd let everyone believe she was a boy in order to protect herself. Vinchi had seen through her ruse, but Astrid had become so relaxed when the three of them began to travel together that she'd forgotten Margreet didn't know the truth. "Tell her who I am."

Vinchi sank down to sit next to them. "How much should I tell?"

"Everything."

Vinchi considered her words before launching into his explanation to Margreet, who looked at him in disbelief.

Astrid recognized her own name when Vinchi spoke it, as well as DiStephan's. She recognized the name of Guell. But it wasn't until she heard Vinchi mention her last name—Scalding—that Margreet gasped and took a closer look at Astrid.

No longer crying, Margreet pointed at Astrid's face and chanted a familiar rhyme.

Astrid didn't understand the words Margreet said, but she knew the cadence. In Astrid's language, the words were:

Mind yourself
Mind your thoughts
Or Scaldings
Tie you into knots
They take you
Into their tower
Walk inside
Where dragons glower
Rip your head
Leave you for dead
Making sure
The dragons get fed

Astrid first left Tower Island as a child, and she'd encountered children in her own land who knew this rhyme. She'd never dreamed people in other countries knew it, too.

Margreet kept chattering, now touching her own face with her hands and pointing at Astrid again, saying, "Scalding! Astrid Scalding!"

"She says she should have realized it was you because of your scars," Vinchi said. "She says she thought you died when you were a child."

Astrid steadied herself, remembering how she'd learned the truth about herself just months ago. Drageen knew her body could produce the bloodstones that would make him invincible, whether against dragons or the king's armies sweeping through

the Southlands. Drageen had probably made sure Astrid didn't die in childhood because he knew he'd need her years later to produce his bloodstones. "Tell her I know
what it feels like to lose everything you hold dear," Astrid said. "And tell her I think
we should honor the dead at Limru in whatever way is most respectful to them."

Margreet listened closely as Vinchi translated. Her eyes welled with tears, but
she seemed to will herself not to cry again. Gazing at Astrid, Margreet nodded and
told Vinchi what the dead would want.

CHAPTER FORTY

While Astrid and Vinchi scaled the sacred trees to cut down the hair of victims tied to their limbs, Margreet chose a place in the clearing, halfway between the edge of the forest surrounding it and the Temple of Limru. She squinted as she looked upward. The limbs of the sacred trees spread high above, spreading across the clearing to rest on top of the shorter forest trees. Most of the forest trees were evergreens, but the sacred trees had shed their leaves, shaped like the hands of giants and still tinged with orange, many weeks ago. The clouds peeking through the limbs hung so low that they drifted through them.

Judging by the brightness of the sky, Margreet guessed sundown would come in a few hours.

Quickly, Margreet chose the best stones she could find in the forest and laid them on the brown grass to form a circle large enough to hold Vinchi's ship. Again, moving quickly, she pulled the dried grass growing a forearm's length behind each stone and threw it into the circle.

"North from which the water flows," Margreet chanted softly to herself as she worked. "South from which the earthen rows. East from which the daylight grows. West from which red sunsets glow." Suddenly realizing she chanted from old habit, Margreet jerked to a stop, looking around anxiously to make sure no one could hear her.

Vinchi and Astrid were still far away in the midst of the temple of sacred trees, lost in their own work. They were too busy to notice Margreet at all.

"Watch your mouth," Margreet admonished herself. "Do you want to end up hung by your hair like your mother?" Heart racing in fear at the very thought of it, Margreet took out her anger on the brown grass by ripping it out by the handful. "I hate you!" she told the grass, keeping her voice low so that only the ground could hear her. "You evil, horrible blades of wickedness!"

It felt good to run her fingers through the dried grass as if it were a head of hair. It felt good to take a strong hold on a handful of blades. It felt even better to grunt while she braced her feet against the ground and jerked the dead vegetation out by the roots. She exhaled in relief, tossing each handful into the center of the stone circle.

Margreet would never allow herself to end up like her mother, who had refused to betray her gods in the face of the soldiers of the Krystr after they'd murdered Margreet's father and every other man in their village. The Krystr soldiers had recognized the village and its people as the Keepers of Limru, those dedicated to the temple and those making a pilgrimage to worship there. The villagers should have run away at the first word of soldiers marching in the Southlands, but they were convinced they could protect the temple.

Instead, half of the villagers had been slaughtered in battle and the others had been sacrificed in the temple as a warning to anyone who would not discard their beliefs in order to join forces with the soldiers of the Krystr.

Margreet couldn't understand it. Until the soldiers of Krystr invaded their homeland, she'd never heard of anyone failing to respect the gods of another. The very thought of it baffled her. She understood war. She understood that men always wanted more land, more water, more food, more animals, more gold, more silver, more everything.

But what could be gained by forcing others to believe exactly the same thing?

On the day she watched her mother die, she'd taken her dying words to heart: save yourself. Any woman who failed to marry was asking for trouble. Marriage meant safety. Choosing a good husband ensured a woman's security for life—or for as long as her husband lived, whichever came first.

And Margreet had chosen very wisely indeed. The day Gershon met Margreet, he had been shy and tongue-tied, even though he had no problems speaking to anyone else. He'd showered her with compliments. On the day he'd asked for her hand in marriage, he had stuttered and stumbled over his words. Margreet agreed to be his wife, and he had cried with joy. He'd looked as vulnerable as a newborn calf trying to stand for the first time on its wobbly legs, melting Margreet's heart.

She'd never imagined that any man could ever want her so desperately and with so much hope. For the first time since her mother had been murdered, Margreet believed she had true value in the world. If Gershon thought so highly of her, that meant something, didn't it? Like most traders, Gershon wore his wealth in the form of silver bracelets and rings. On their day of marriage, he had removed a silver ring from his littlest finger and placed it on one of hers as a symbol showing the world that she now belonged to him.

Now, kneeling and creating an outer circle of dirt by yanking dry grass up by the handfuls, Margreet realized it had been a full day since she'd felt the pangs of missing her husband.

Wiping the dirty palms of her hands against her cloak, she looked at the silver ring she'd worn since her marriage day. Once upon a time, she'd been happy as Gershon's wife. She wept whenever he went trapping and rejoiced every time he came back home, not even caring whether he'd met with success or failure. Margreet knew all too well from her own experience that life presented constant challenges. Some months were bountiful, making life easy, and other months were fruitless, making life difficult. But Margreet believed that as long as one had a will to survive, one could always find a way to do so. And as long as she had love in her life, she needn't worry about anything else.

But that was once upon a time.

Soon after they were married, Gershon's manner toward her changed. Where he'd once been kind and loving, he now became demanding—treating Margreet like his servant, not his loving wife! He presumed she owed him a great deal, and he seemed determined to make sure he got his due.

She sometimes wondered if an evil spirit had possessed him, controlling his thoughts and actions. How could a man who had been so loving and kind toward her suddenly treat her so miserably? It made no sense.

Margreet had heard stories of wicked people and sorcerers. She wondered if someone had cast a spell on Gershon. The more she wondered, the more she began to believe it. Nothing else made sense.

Margreet sat back on her heels, studying her work. She'd created a circle of stones, keeping them close together. She crouched halfway around the outside of the stone circle, having already cleared the grass behind half of it with the other half to go. Her arms ached, but she didn't mind. Whenever she paused to think about what they were doing, tears of relief ran softly down her face. Margreet still was surprised that Astrid Scalding had suggested they take care of the dead in a respectful way. In a way that honored their own beliefs, not those of the Scalding woman or even Vinchi.

At the same time, Margreet pondered something Vinchi had whispered to her quickly: that Astrid Scalding had suffered her own hardships, which were similar to Margreet's.

Bones had littered the temple ground for too many years, and the hundreds of scalps of hair tied to the limbs of the sacred trees made Margreet ill. But the act of creating the stone circle and clearing the grass behind it calmed her, as did the actions of Vinchi and Astrid Scalding.

She hadn't felt this calm since she'd lived in her own village with her own family.

No matter how she tried, Margreet couldn't imagine Gershon making the same decision that Vinchi and Astrid Scalding had made. In fact, Gershon probably tracked them at this very moment, and Vinchi and Astrid Scalding could be risking their own lives for the sake of honoring the dead and restoring the temple.

No. Gershon would never do anything to honor Margreet's people. Not even before he'd been possessed by an evil spirit.

The tears stopped running down Margreet's face, and she wiped them away. For the past several months she'd struggled to be kind to Gershon in hopes that he'd regain his senses and they could return to the happiness they'd known after they were first married. But maybe Gershon had never been possessed. Maybe his true nature had finally surfaced.

Margreet reeled at the thought, placing her hands on the ground to steady herself. In her own village, she'd seen several strained marriages. She'd known husbands and wives who argued so much that they went at each other's throats like rabid dogs. She'd known some men who treated their wives like slaves. Margreet had always wondered how anyone could be so stupid to choose such a mismatch of a mate. For the first time, she began to understand how that kind of mistake could happen.

It happened because a man presented himself in one light only to prove that he lived in a very different kind of darkness.

Margreet twirled the silver ring around her finger, wondering what her life might be like without Gershon in it. How could she possibly survive without him? The thought struck terror in her heart. But now the thought of returning to him scared her even more. She fiddled with the ring.

One moment she wanted to cling to it for life. The next moment she wanted to take it off and fling it into the woods and be rid of it forever.

But that wouldn't do. If Gershon trailed them, she didn't want to leave anything so obvious for him to find.

Margreet fingered the silver ring she'd worn every day since their marriage day. She'd treasured it as if it had been made of gold, but now she realized it was just payment someone had once given Gershon in exchange for a bit of fur.

She'd loved Gershon. But that was once upon a time.

She returned to work, her energy renewed and focused as she ran her fingers through blades of dried grass and mercilessly yanked them out of the ground by their roots.

CHAPTER FORTY-ONE

Vinchi watched Margreet as she completed the stone circle, laid an ankle-deep layer of fallen leaves from the sacred trees inside it, and started a fire in a tiny pit she dug outside the circle. With Astrid's help, he had moved all the bones and scalps within it.

His concentration broke the moment Astrid asked if there was anything else Margreet wanted them to do on behalf of the dead.

Vinchi paused, and he noticed Margreet look up at the mention of her name, raising a questioning eyebrow and waiting for his translation. He didn't realize he'd been staring at her.

"She is being respectful," Vinchi told Margreet. On one hand, he was glad Astrid had decided to reveal her identity and even happier the women seemed to be getting along. On the other hand, he wished that one or both of them were willing to learn each other's language instead of relying on him as a go-between. "Is there any ceremony or ritual we should perform to help the dead find their way to the spirit realm?"

Margreet stiffened as shame shadowed her face. "I no longer follow those barbarian beliefs. Everyone claims the Krystr belief now."

"No one here will judge you," Vinchi said softly. He pointed at Astrid. "She's a Northlander who believes in shapeshifting. I'm a Southlander who believes in nothing."

Margreet's gaze snapped back to him, and her eyes narrowed in suspicion. "Nothing?"

"I believe we're born, we live, we die. That's all."

"But what about the place of beauty that the Krystr followers claim as their own? Or the spirit realm that barbarians believe exists?"

"They're no more real than tales of fairies and such," Vinchi said. "I believe in what I can see and lay my hands upon." He gazed at her, wishing her could touch her. Wishing more than ever that he'd met her long before she'd known Gershon existed.

The expression in Margreet's eyes softened. For a moment, she seemed to know his thoughts.

Vinchi winced when Astrid jabbed his arm with a sharp finger. "Well? What does she say?"

Before Vinchi could answer, Margreet said, "The man—that's you—should stand to the North, and she should stand to the South. I will give you fire and tell you when to use it."

Margreet gathered small, fallen branches, and Vinchi passed along her instructions to Astrid, who took her place between the outside of the stone circle and the sun skimming the horizon. Vinchi walked outside the stone circle and stopped directly across from her.

Behind Astrid and outside the stone circle, Margreet lit the ends of two branches. Margreet murmured something, but Vinchi couldn't make out the words. Holding a burning branch in each hand, Margreet looked up toward the sky and she raised the fire above her head.

Vinchi caught his breath as shadows and firelight played across Margreet's face. Surrounded by darkening woods, she looked magical and ethereal. A breeze lifted her hair away from her face. Her skin glowed and her voice grew strong while she chanted.

"South from which the earthen rows."

Lowering one arm, Margreet pointed one lit branch toward Astrid while keeping the other aimed at the sky. Margreet kept chanting until Astrid accepted the makeshift torch from her.

Now Margreet walked counterclockwise, lowering the remaining branch and pointing it toward the contents of the circle. Halfway between Astrid and Vinchi, Margreet chanted, "East from which the daylight grows."

Vinchi shivered with anticipation as Margreet swung the last flaming branch toward him. She approached, chanting, "North from which the water flows." She stood so close to him that the heat from the fire raised beads of sweat on Vinchi's forehead. Margreet flipped her wrist, pointing the flame toward the sky again. She handed over the branch and walked past Vinchi to complete her journey outside the circle.

She had never looked more beautiful. Vinchi marveled at Margreet's ease and confidence. A softness about her co-existed with her strength.

He wished Gershon would never find them. Since they'd left the Northlands, Vinchi sensed he was sharpening the metal of his own spirit in the same way he sharpened the weapons he sold. He wouldn't mind at all if Gershon died while trying to find them, leaving Margreet free to live the way she wished.

Even if it meant living without Vinchi.

Margreet stood in a space halfway between Vinchi and Astrid, the final quadrant of the stone circle. She nodded to the others and said, "West from which red sunsets glow."

Vinchi and Astrid lowered the torches Margreet had given to them, lighting the dry leaves inside the circle.

The fire caught quickly, racing from the Northern and Southern sides to meet in the middle where the flames roared and towered high in the air, casting a golden glow on the sacred trees behind the stone circle.

Vinchi caught his breath as the heat threatened to singe his hair, and he stumbled away from the stones and into the dirt ring outside the circle that Margreet had cleared. Even several steps away, the heat felt intense. His heart raced. He was a product of the Southlands, where the gods were ancient but very straightforward. He'd grown up learning to honor and pay homage to the gods by taking tokens of food and drink inside stone temples and hoping his prayers would be answered, which seldom happened. These days, he kept up his worship whenever he returned home but only to please his parents and keep peace among those who had high expectations of him.

Margreet conducted her old practices, and he watched in awe, wondering if maybe he'd been worshipping the wrong gods.

The fire roared and the leaves burned. The thousands of bones resting on top of those leaves shifted, scraping against each other, groaning like an old man trying to get comfortable in bed. At the same time, Vinchi's nose twitched at the pungent smell of burning hair. Looking into the stone circle, he saw ribbons of hair glowing orange as the strands curled and dissolved in the flames.

Smoke twisted and rose from the stone circle fire, taking its time to collect and gather into the shapes of people.

Vinchi's jaw slackened, and he watched in wonder. Made entirely of smoke, hundreds of people took shape inside the circle, some rubbing their eyes as if waking up after a long night's sleep: women, men, and children.

A thought occurred to Vinchi, and he swallowed hard, troubled by it.

What if these were the spirits of the people from Margreet's home village? What if they were the people who had been murdered here? The Keepers of the Temple of Limru?

A woman made of strands of white and gray smoke turned to look at Vinchi. Her eyes were empty and hollow sockets.

Vinchi froze in terror. But then he realized that the woman made of smoke resembled Margreet, and his fear eased into compassion. Could this be Margreet's mother?

The woman of smoke nodded and smiled at him, seeming to read his mind. Then she turned back to the other smoke people and reached out to them.

For the first time, Vinchi realized how firmly his thoughts were grounded in the physical world. He'd never given much thought to the spirit realm before, but now his eyes were open and he stared at what appeared to be a glimpse into that world inside the stone circle Margreet had created.

The smoke woman who resembled Margreet rose slightly in the air. The flames near her climbed. She scanned the edge of the circle.

I'm part of this, Vinchi realized. *I gathered their bones. I climbed the trees and cut down their hair. I placed them inside the circle. I helped bring them here.*

The smoke woman hesitated for a moment and then darted to the West, where Margreet stood.

Vinchi strained to see across the fire and the hundreds of smoke people who were now moving within the circle, seemingly recognizing each other and rejoicing. He thought he saw the smoke woman raise her hands to the edge of the stones and Margreet reach up to touch them.

In a sudden whoosh, the fire skyrocketed as high as the treetops. When the flames dropped as quickly as they had risen, the smoke people remained in the air, now rising up through the canopy of branches made by the sacred trees and toward the night sky. Soon, they'd be gone.

Vinchi looked across the stone circle again, where the burned leaves had begun to smolder.

Now on her knees, Margreet held her hands to her heart, gazing upward.

Vinchi strained to see the expression on Margreet's face, even though the dying fire still cast a golden glow upon it. She seemed to look hopeful.

And for that, he was grateful.

CHAPTER FORTY-TWO

"It moved!" one of the men Gershon had paid to join him shouted.

"That's impossible," Gershon said. He still worried about the time lost because he'd been unconscious for days. He had pushed the men he'd hired to travel each day, making them keep their eyes open and resist the temptation of sleep.

But now that they'd reached the edge of the Forest of Aguille, the men held back, afraid to move forward.

Dozens of men and women made of ice stood at the entrance to the forest.

"It's magic," one of Gershon's men said, "of the worst kind."

"There!" another man shouted, pointing at the ice people. "Another one moved!"

Gershon's handful of men backed away, leaving Gershon standing several paces away from the frozen ones. But Gershon took comfort because the divine creature Norah, who had saved his life, and her manservant Wendill had crept toward the ice people to inspect them.

"Mistress?" Gershon inquired meekly. He'd learned she had little use for people, so he tried to bother her only at important times. "Do you believe the Scalding came this way?"

Norah ignored him, as usual. She ran a fingertip along one of the figure's icy forearms and up to his shoulder while she peered into his transparent eyes.

Wendill answered. "Is this a likely place for the man to come?"

The man. Wendill referred to Vinchi. Gershon's blood still boiled whenever he thought of the last sight he'd seen before fainting from the evil, tiny dragon's bite: Vinchi reaching for Margreet's hand. One thing Gershon wanted even more than reclaiming Margreet—his property—was teaching Vinchi what a mistake he'd made in stealing another man's wife.

Gershon considered Wendill's question: could Vinchi have led Margreet here? "He sailed South. That much we've been told by those who witnessed it," Gershon said, thinking out loud. Gershon had insisted they stop at the most likely Midlands port that Vinchi would have chosen. Sure enough, someone at that port saw him sail this way. He squinted at the ice people. "But what are these abominations?"

"Ghosts," Wendill said brightly. "This is what happens when ghosts stand still and allow themselves to be coated with hail."

Gershon backpedaled, stepping back until he bumped into his fellow men. Anyone in their right mind knew ghosts were extremely dangerous and to be avoided at all costs.

Wendill smiled before turning his back on Gershon, whispering to Norah.

"There's another way through the forest," Gershon stammered. "If we head West for two days..."

"You do that," Wendill said, casting a quick glance over his shoulder before he returned his attention to Norah.

Gershon recoiled as if Wendill had punched him in the gut. The divine creature Norah had saved his life. Didn't that make him special to Norah and therefore her manservant? Gershon clearly remembered Norah's touch and the sensation of rising out of a deep, deep sleep that had lasted for days. Most people never woke up from such a sleep.

Afterwards, everyone had looked at Gershon in awe, as if he were as divine as Norah. As if he'd accomplished something wonderful and inspiring simply by waking up at her touch. Typically, folks showed respect to Gershon because they feared him. But the type of respect they paid him now appeared more clean. More pure. He preferred that their eyes held hope instead of terror.

"Should I go with you?" Gershon called out, even though the men standing behind him shuffled their feet anxiously, clearly ready to leave.

He watched in horror as Norah delicately tapped at the transparent eyeball of one of the frozen ghosts until it broke. A steady stream of white fog poured out of the broken eyeball.

"She's setting free the ghosts!" one of the men shouted.

Shrieking, the men that had accompanied Gershon, Wendill, and Norah here to the Midlands turned and ran back in the direction from whence they'd come.

Too afraid to move, Gershon watched numbly. The stream of white fog swirled around the icy figure before disappearing into the forest.

"Go with your people," Wendill said absentmindedly.

Gershon reminded himself that he tracked, trapped, and skinned dangerous animals for their fur. He'd had many frights in his day, but he always found his courage even at times that it seemed to have vanished forever.

She saved me once, Gershon thought, staring at Norah, who now approached another figure made of ice. *If I travel with them, she'll protect me. She'll keep me safe from ghosts.* "Mistress," Gershon called out weakly. "I'd be honored to stay by your side."

Norah spun to face him, her face flushed with anger. "Go!" she hissed.

Astonished, Gershon stood his ground, not knowing what else to do. She was his savior. How could she speak to him like that?

Norah bared her teeth, hissing again before turning her back on Gershon.

He stood for several more seconds before he realized that if he didn't wipe the tears welling in his eyes, they might turn to ice before he could rejoin the men walking away from this ghastly place.

Chapter Forty-Three

At the same time Astrid, Vinchi, and Margreet made their preparations to heal Limru, Wendill gazed with a twinge of regret at Gershon, whose shoulders slumped in defeat and anguish. He walked away from the edge of the forest with the few men he'd brought with him. Oddly, Gershon had been good for Norah. Since the day Wendill had met her, Norah had lived inside herself, withdrawn and sullen. But when she'd touched her tongue to Gershon's face and unintentionally brought him out of a deep sleep from which no one expected him to awake, Wendill had quietly watched her change.

Although Gershon had been mistaken in believing her to be an agent of the new god Krystr—a god unknown to Wendill, which baffled him—Gershon had been quite accurate in his inclination to worship Norah.

Gradually, she had accepted Gershon's fawning. Norah had been timid at first, but having a strong man like Gershon make himself meek in her presence had worked wonders. She'd become more comfortable among strangers.

Although Wendill had become strangely fond of the man and would miss his presence, he couldn't help but smile every time he imagined what Gershon's face would look like if he learned Norah's true identity.

At the sound of cracking ice, Wendill turned back to Norah, who tapped the nail of her forefinger against the eyeball of the iceman who seemed to lead the other frozen figures guarding the entrance to the forest. She punctured the icy shell, and Norah covered her mouth with both hands in delight, mesmerized by a white wisp of fog streaming through the tiny portal she'd created. The ribbon of fog twisted and turned, and Norah said, "Pretty!"

But the fog shifted into the shape of a man, making Norah recoil. Edging her way to stand behind Wendill, she hissed, "Dragonslayer!"

"No need to worry," Wendill said in the most soothing voice he could muster.

Wendill didn't recognize the face formed by the fog, but he believed Norah. Wendill always recognized a dragonslayer even though he could never describe how. He often sensed something in the dragonslayer's expression that gave him away. How wonderful that Norah had already developed this skill. It would serve her well.

"You're safe. Dragonslayers are friends. They're our allies."

Wendill sensed her step away at his words. Turning slowly to face her, she stared wide-eyed at the spirit of the dragonslayer that still floated above the icy shell he'd allowed the hail to form around him, willing to be entrapped inside the ice until it melted—or in this case, until Norah unintentionally released him.

The dragonslayer's spirit smiled briefly at them before whisking into the forest. Perhaps he had important tasks to attend.

Norah sank to her knees, reaching for the ground to steady herself.

Wendill knelt beside her. "The dragonslayer girl—the one we follow—you are bound to her just as I was bound to the dragonslayer father of her father."

"No," Norah whispered. Tears spilled down her cheeks.

Wendill hesitated. Perhaps he had said too much too soon. These things had to be handled delicately. He noticed a small stone on the ground near Norah. He picked it up and handed it to her. Nodding toward the ice people, he said, "They're trapped, too, like the dragonslayer before you set him free. They're trapped like I was inside Dragon's Head. Like you were on Tower Island."

He watched Norah study the stone after letting him place it in the palm of her hand. She shivered hard and wiped the tears from her face. Still studying the stone, she rose to her feet.

Suddenly, she threw it, smashing open the ice figure next to the one that had held the dragonslayer.

A wisp of fog emerged from the broken ice figure, but it took no form. Instead, it merely drifted into the forest.

Methodically, Norah picked up stone after stone, hurling each one harder than the last, until all the ice figures lay in shards at the edge of the Forest of Aguille.

CHAPTER FORTY-FOUR

Gershon walked in stunned silence, following his men without paying attention to where they led. First, his wife—his greatest possession—had been stolen from him by a fellow merchant whom he'd trusted for years. After being poisoned by a dragon conjured out of nowhere by the boy, Gershon had fallen into a deep sleep only to be awakened by Norah, a glorious agent of Krystr.

And now even she had betrayed him.

Had the entire world turned against him?

"We're here," one of his men said.

Gershon snapped out of his misery long enough to notice they'd arrived at a small village of a few dozen wattle-and-daub houses surrounded by harvested farmland on one side and cattle on the other, grazing on the last pale blades of grass before they dried up for winter. He followed his men down the village's dirt road and into the largest house. Gershon paused at the threshold, his vision fading as he stepped out of the light of day into the dimness of the house. He reached out for the doorjamb and held onto it to steady himself. His men greeted the homeowner and spoke quietly.

"And who do we have here?" a friendly voice bellowed.

"Gershon. Who are you?"

The friendly voice laughed in response. Gershon's eyes adjusted to see a short man with bushy brown hair standing before him. "Clerk Thomas. Welcome to my home." The man's blue eyes seemed to twinkle. Gershon took in his odd dress of a white smock covered by a belted brown robe.

That's right. The man claimed to be a clerk, a man who spread the word of the new god.

Gershon's men made themselves at home around the hearth in the center of Clerk Thomas's home. Two young women wearing simple blue smocks and white cloth bound around their heads to hide their hair tended the fire and steaming broth and potatoes cooking in iron pots. When one of Gershon's men slapped the bottom on one of the women, she cried out.

Glancing over his shoulder, Clerk Thomas said, "No need for that, Cyntha. These men are my friends, and I expect you to make them at home while I walk with my new friend." He turned back and smiled at Gershon. "My new friend Gershon."

Gershon watched his men squeeze Cyntha's bottom hard enough to make the girl wince. Gershon had gone for days without having his wife at hand for his convenience. Without the release she provided, he felt taut and brittle. Damn the woman!

For the first time, Gershon wondered why she hadn't fought back against Vinchi and the boy at the time they stole her. Margreet was a spry little thing. Many times she'd wriggled out of Gershon's grasp, which had excited him and made her ultimate surrender even that much sweeter.

Gershon stood twice the size of Vinchi, so Margreet should have been able to free herself from that wretched merchant with little effort!

But you've seen the way he looks at her, a tiny voice in the back of Gershon's mind said. *What if she finally looked back?*

"Follow me," Clerk Thomas said, breezing past Gershon and out into the sunlit village.

Gershon staggered to keep up, the world now going white as a result of stepping from the dim house into the light.

"I understand you believe you encountered an agent of Krystr."

Gershon nodded. "She saved my life."

"I would beg to differ."

Gershon stumbled and bumped into Clerk Thomas, who seized Gershon's arm and kept him from falling flat on his face. The clerk seemed surprisingly strong for a man of small stature.

Regaining his balance, Gershon stood up straight and tall. "I knocked on the very door of Death itself. I was attacked by a monster, a dragon, and slept for days. No one expected me to live, and yet she sucked the poison out of my skin and gave me new life. How could she not be an agent of Krystr?"

Clerk Thomas knelt by a patch of dried plants outside his home. "In the spring, the most beautiful flowers grow here. Lovely things. Lovely colors of purple and pink and red. They grow bountifully, and when they're ripe for the taking, I pluck them." He rose and motioned for Gershon to keep following him as he strolled through the village. "Has it never occurred to you that the one you claim as your savior is a woman?"

The clerk's question stunned Gershon into silence. In truth, Gershon had failed to consider this fact.

"Women are here to serve men," Clerk Thomas said. "And the world was a perfect place when only men lived here. The Krystr tells us that when men grew arrogant and needed to be reminded of their own weakness, a woman was sent to show that weakness to them. If we had been able to curb our arrogance and simply rejoice in the world, no woman would ever have been sent to ruin it."

Gershon frowned. He'd heard part of this story told in various ways before, but some of the details were new to him. "The world was once perfect?"

Clerk Thomas nodded. "We would be living in the most wonderful world imaginable had not a vixen succeeded in tempting men and causing us to fall in disgrace for our weakness in succumbing to something beneath us."

"A woman," Gershon said.

Clerk Thomas nodded. "A woman." He glanced up at the sky as if speaking in front of a divine audience. "So how could an evil creature be an agent of Krystr?"

Gershon's heart sank. How could he have been duped so easily? How could he have let himself be humiliated by a woman? "It's impossible," he said, his voice cracking with shame. "Krystr's agents are good, not evil."

"And all women are evil."

"Yes," Gershon whispered. "I know."

"It has come to my attention that some of the best clerks are men who have experienced the torment of women. They speak courageously from personal experience. There is no one better to warn others of the importance of minding their women with even more care than they mind their cattle or pigs or sheep."

Gershon shook his head. "I trap animals—I don't keep them. I have no interest in giving up my trade." Even now, possibly the lowest moment of his existence, Gershon knew the one thing he could trust was his work. It felt good to trap animals and kill them and skin them. No woman could take that away from him.

"There is no need to give up anything." Clerk Thomas smiled. "I'm a farmer and yet I'm also a clerk. And as I reap the benefits of my farmland, I also reap the benefits of my workers and followers."

"Benefits?"

"Here, for example." Clerk Thomas stopped in front of a modest wattle-and-daub house. "One of my farmhands and his new bride." Without another word, Thomas entered the small house.

Not knowing what else to do, Gershon followed.

This time, his eyes adjusted more quickly to the dim light inside. A pretty girl in a green smock sat by the hearth and cut vegetables. A man, presumably her husband, sat in a corner fiddling with an ax.

"Is she serviceable?" Thomas called out.

The man rose to his feet quickly, followed by his wife who bowed meekly. "The blade needs sharpening," the man said. "But the handle is loose. It could use replacing."

"And it's a fine day to look for good wood to replace that handle." Clerk Thomas said cheerfully.

Worry creased the husband's brow, and he stepped closer to his wife, whose face looked flushed from sitting so close to the fire. "I had planned to spend the day with my bride. I was too tired to see much of her during harvest."

"You've the entire winter approaching. You'll have so much time to spend with her that you'll be sick of her company by spring."

The man reached for his wife's hand, and she clung to it gratefully. "With all respect, clerk-"

Thomas maintained his cheerfulness. "Respect comes from actions, not words. I suggest you spend the next hour finding the best piece of wood possible to replace your handle."

Still, neither the man nor his wife moved.

"My dear," Clerk Thomas said to the girl. "Tell your husband to go on his way."

"It's fine," she said with too much brightness in her voice as she kept clinging to her husband's hand. "Everything will be fine."

Gershon fidgeted when the husband stared at him.

Clerk Thomas laid a strong hand on the man's shoulder, pushing him out the door. "We need to ask your wife her opinion of clerks." After the husband stumbled onto the road, slouched in defeat, Clerk Thomas slammed the door shut. Facing the girl, he said, "Tell my friend Gershon what women think of clerks."

Her eyes glazed and she stared into empty space. Gershon recognized the expression. He'd seen it on Margreet's face whenever he struggled with her to convince her of the time for his release.

"Clerks are the most trustworthy men," she said. "They are the best men. The most handsome."

Clerk Thomas spoke softly. "My friend Gershon may decide to study with me. Can you show him what a clerk can expect from his patrons?"

She moved stiffly, as if not thinking, and raised her smock up to her waist, revealing her nakedness underneath.

Gershon watched in stunned silence. Each man owned his wife as personal property. No woman ever showed her body to anyone other than her husband or, if unmarried, her lover.

Clerk Thomas had already unbelted his robe and shrugged out of it. Startled, he stared at Gershon. "How could I forget my manners?" Thomas said. With a fresh smile, he gestured toward the girl and asked Gershon, "Would you care to go first?"

CHAPTER FORTY-FIVE

The night they set the spirits at Limru free, Astrid, Vinchi, and Margreet camped on the outskirts of the temple. The next morning, Astrid stood outside the stone circle, now filled with ashes. It didn't make sense. Bones shouldn't reduce that quickly to cinders. And the dried leaves fueling the fire had burned far longer and hotter than any leaves she'd ever known.

She hadn't needed to ask the others if they saw the smoke spirits rise from the fire. Astrid recognized this truth from the shock and awe on Vinchi and Margreet's faces last night in the glow of the firelight. For a moment, Vinchi looked like he tried to speak with one of the spirits until it darted toward Margreet. Then Astrid had seen the spirit's face and noticed the resemblance between that spirit and Margreet. The spirits left soon after they took form, rising up through the enormous limbs of the sacred trees of Limru and into the darkening sky.

But the fire had burned inexplicably for hours, and the embers glowed through the night, casting an eerie white glow on the stones forming the circle. Astrid had come awake in the early morning hours and knelt outside the stone circle to watch the last embers' light wink out of existence. Only then did the eerie glow fade from the stones.

Later, Vinchi awoke and started a breakfast fire. Margreet and Astrid sat on the logs next to him. He reached into the pouch hanging from his belt, handed something to Margreet, and spoke in her language.

Margreet sat quietly for several minutes, staring at the object in her hand.

Straining to see what it was, Astrid asked, "What did you give her?"

"I found it when we gathered the bones," Vinchi said, staring at Margreet. "It is the sign of the Keepers of Limru. An iron pin in the shape of a tree."

Astrid glanced at the pin on Vinchi's hat that identified him as a member of the weapons guild. "Did the Keepers wear them the way you wear yours?"

Vinchi's voice softened. "In the old days, yes."

Margreet closed her fingers around the tree-shaped pin, walked toward Astrid, and sat next to her. Margreet placed the pin in Astrid's hand and spoke foreign words.

"She wants you to have it," Vinchi said.

"Didn't this belong to her people? Shouldn't she keep it for herself?"

Speaking quickly, sensing Astrid's hesitation to accept the gift, Margreet closed Astrid's fingers around the pin.

Vinchi rubbed his eyes. "She says it belongs to you now."

Seeing the determined set of Margreet's mouth, Astrid nodded her thanks and began to attach the pin to her shirt.

Margreet and Vinchi protested in unison. As Margreet pointed to the pouch on Astrid's belt, Vinchi said, "Never wear it outside of the Northlands. It could attract the attention of the people who killed the Keepers."

Nodding, Astrid tucked the pin inside her pouch. She then said, "Can you take me to the Dragon's Well?"

She couldn't tell Vinchi or anyone else about Taddeo. What could she say? That the animals that Vinchi and everyone else believed were dragons were actually lizards that were overgrown as a result of being overly impressed with themselves? That true dragons were shapeshifters that often took the shape of men and women whenever they ventured outside of their caves? That Taddeo had told her she needed to drink from the Dragon's Well in order to become whole again?

Vinchi questioned Margreet, and she answered him.

"She knows where it is. The well is inside the temple. Among the trees."

"Will she show us?"

Again, Vinchi posed the question.

Margreet wrapped her arms around her bent legs, tucked to her chest. She considered them both carefully for a few moments, but mostly she considered Astrid. Margreet spoke, and her voice softened.

"Margreet wants to eat first. Then, she says, she'll show us where the Dragon's Well is located." Vinchi fed a series of small sticks into the new fire. "I've heard stories that her mother was one of the Keepers of Limru. I think I saw her ghost last night and that Margreet saw her, too."

Margreet looked up at the mention of her name, and she studied them closely.

"Yes," Astrid said. "I noticed."

Vinchi nodded. "I suspect she's willing to show the well to you because you set her mother and the others free."

"We all did. The three of us."

"But it was your idea," Vinchi said. "Had it not been for you, we would have left Limru the same way we found it."

⁂

Later that morning, Astrid followed Margreet into the temple of Limru. Vinchi had claimed he wanted to bury the fire they'd used properly with dirt, but Astrid suspected he feared going in the temple. He'd looked terrified at the sight of the ghosts taking form last night. If any lingered in the forest, they would probably scare the life out of him by sheer accident.

Astrid agreed he should douse the fire instead.

Stepping mindfully over gnarled roots, Astrid reconsidered her goal. Initially, she'd rejected Taddeo's suggestion that she drink from the well to renew her lost arm and solidify the scars that sometimes wandered out of place on her skin. But now that she'd seen Limru, Astrid knew she'd be foolish to waste this opportunity. It seemed that only Northlanders drank dragon's blood, which meant they were the only ones who could see her phantom arm. It made no sense to risk strangers witnessing her using her phantom arm and assuming she used some kind of sorcery.

And the more she thought about it, the more she wondered if she should offer water from the Dragon's Well to Margreet. Even though Margreet had all her body parts intact, she seemed to have a weakness in her own spirit. It was as if she didn't know what kind of place she could have in the world outside of being Gershon's wife.

Even though Astrid had never married, she understood what it felt like to not know one's place in the world. If not for DiStephan and Lenore and Randim and Donel—and even Taddeo and Norah—Astrid might just as easily be in a place like Margreet's.

Like the stones Margreet had laid out last night, the sacred trees grew in a circle. Their trunks were thick with rough bark, and a few of their limbs grew down until they touched the ground before rising skyward, seeming to reach with the intent of scooping the women up into the air. Despite the chilliness of approaching winter, grass grew thick and green in the center surrounded by trees.

Margreet spoke, pointing toward a few wooden planks near the base of a tree.

Astrid helped her lift the first plank covering the well. Its rim rose slightly above the ground, and its stone walls sank deep into the earth. Unlike the circle Margreet created outside the temple by gathering rocks, these stones had been carved to fit together and form a smooth and polished surface from the lip of the well at ground level to its depths below. The women lifted all the planks, revealing a bucket hanging from a rope looped around a hook inside the lip of the well.

I'll take the first drink, Astrid thought, *then I'll offer it to Margreet.*

But when Astrid unlooped the rope from its hook, Margreet protested, her face creased with worry.

"It's fine," Astrid said, knowing Margreet understood nothing she said but hoping she'd hear Astrid's intent. "I have permission to drink." Before Margreet could protest again, Astrid dropped the bucket into the darkness of the well until it thudded to a stop.

Astrid frowned and Margreet kept protesting her concern. Testing the rope, Astrid noted its slackness. The problem wasn't that the bucket had reached the end of its rope. Instead, the bucket seemed to have reached the bottom of the well, even though there had been no splash.

Quickly, Astrid pulled the bucket back up, horrified to discover no water inside the bucket. Not even the outside showed any signs of being wet.

The Dragon's Well that Taddeo had said would heal her had gone dry.

CHAPTER FORTY-SIX

Vinchi paced by the remains of their breakfast fire, now dead and gone. He'd stirred the embers to make sure none of them were still alive. The ground had gone hard enough from the cold that it made no sense to try to dig it to cover the embers, so he'd gathered a few dozen small stones to pile on top of the fire's remains, just to be safe.

Despite the cold, his armpits were damp with sweat from taking care of the fire. His heart raced with anxiety. With every day that passed, he worried about dying at Gershon's hands.

What was I thinking? Vinchi wondered. He gazed up at the morning sky, worried that the wispy white clouds were a false promise of hope. What if the harmless wisps gave way to dark, heavy thunderheads? What if the winds grew strong enough to pick Margreet up and take her skyward? What if the ground shook apart and devoured her? What if the oceans rose and a rogue wave dragged her out to sea? What if—

"Stop it," Vinchi whispered to himself. Nothing like that would happen. Even if Gershon came searching, how likely was it that he could actually find them? Vinchi could take Margreet to the deep Southlands where he still had family, and he could marry her and protect her and cherish her—

"The well is dry," Margreet said.

Vinchi looked up sharply, feeling guilty and not understanding why. "Dry?"

Margreet let the skirt of her dress skim the ground, not bothering to pick it up. Though belted, the skirt still hung a shade too long. Dirt stains that had never washed out darkened the hem. Morning dew on the dried grass made the hem wet, as well.

Astrid trailed Margreet, her gaze downcast and distant. Astrid looked as if her thoughts were oceans away.

Vinchi repeated his comment, this time in the language Astrid understood. "Dry?"

The muscles in her jaw flexed as she swallowed. "We should go to Guell," Astrid said. "All of us. We'll be safe there."

Vinchi's immediate thought was to run and hide. To cower in a place where no one would ever find him. "Guell?"

"Guell?" Margreet said.

"Astrid's home," Vinchi said. Switching back to the Northlander's language, he said, "That's impossible. And what good would it do us?"

"Most people are afraid to go to Guell because of Dragon's Head and the dragons it attracts. Everyone in Guell will stand by us. Margreet will be safe there—we all will."

Vinchi shook his head as he suppressed a shudder. "But Gershon has no qualms. He'll travel anywhere."

"He won't suspect we're there. He won't think to look for us in Guell. And if he does, he'll have to face an entire village."

No, no, no, Vinchi thought. *I need Margreet in the Southlands. Once she's there—once she has a chance to get to know me and my family and friends. And Gershon has never been in the deep Southlands. He won't know where to find us.*

He looked up at the sky again, bright and pale blue, still dotted with wispy cloudlets. In a few weeks, crossing the sea back toward the Northlands would be too risky. The colder the air grew, the higher and more violently the waves churned. Few ships attempting to cross the winter sea survived. Not to mention the fact that the mountain passes leading to Guell would probably be blocked by several feet of snow. If they left now, this moment, the odds of crossing the sea and the mountain passes were still good, but so were the chances of running into Gershon or people who could report to him.

No. Better to follow Vinchi's way.

"Why is she talking about Guell?" Margreet said, folding her arms across her chest as she pursed her lips in discontent. Margreet had never been one to show patience at being left out of a conversation.

But she would have to wait a bit longer.

"I told you," Vinchi said to Astrid. "It's impossible. At this time of year, the sea's too rough to cross. We'd perish."

"But—"

"And even if we survived the crossing, the mountain passes would be filled with snow. We can't get to Guell until it all melts, and that's usually sometime in spring. We'd be stuck at the town where we took Margreet, and folks aren't likely to be welcoming of us."

"What are you saying about me?" Margreet said.

Vinchi turned to face Margreet. "We're talking about a way to keep you safe."

Both women stared at him.

"That's not my language," Margreet said coolly. "You're still speaking the tongue of the Northlanders."

Vinchi swallowed hard, hesitating before he looked at Astrid's face, her jaw clenched in anger. He winced, realizing he'd forgotten which language he spoke.

"We were talking about going back to Guell. Why didn't you tell her that?"

"No need to get her hopes up," Vinchi said smoothly, scrambling to figure out a way to placate both women. He couldn't suggest heading for his own home immediately. It would look too suspicious. He had to find a way to make it seem like the most logical and safe solution for all of them. It was best to stick to the destination he'd recommended several days ago.

Astrid took a few steps forward, suspicion lacing the look in her eyes.

Margreet stared intently at her. Maddeningly, even though the women didn't speak the same language, there were times that they seemed to understand each other quite well. Margreet turned to face Vinchi with the same suspicion in her own eyes.

"Then what," Astrid said in a tone as chilly as the wintry air, "do you suggest we do?"

"Keep our original plan," Vinchi said with complete honesty. "Gershon will never find us there."

"Tell me what you're thinking!" Margreet demanded of Vinchi.

Concentrating this time, Vinchi switched to Margreet's language. "Astrid and I will take you to a safe place where Gershon is unlikely to find us but where we'll have shelter from the weather and plenty to eat and drink."

"Is it far?"

Vinchi smiled. "No. We're nearly there."

CHAPTER FORTY-SEVEN

Wendill and Norah walked for several days through the Forest of Aguille. Sometimes the trees were bare bones of trunks and limbs, making it easy to see far into the deadened forest as they marched ankle-deep through brittle, crunching leaves. Other times, pines grew thick among the leafless trees, making it impossible to see more than a few feet in any direction. The air took on the fresh crisp odor that promised oncoming snow, even though the little bit of sky that showed above looked pale and cloudless.

Wendill mulled over how to prepare Norah for what she would soon witness. He hadn't seen the Temple of Limru in many decades. He'd been trapped inside the Dragon's Head outcrop near Guell for many decades, but Taddeo and other dragons had told Wendill about everything that had happened at Limru.

A sharp crack caught Wendill's attention. He slowed his pace, looking to his left. The groan of wood and a dull thud gave him reason to breathe easy. No one followed them in the forest. Most likely, a rotting branch had broken free and fallen.

He turned when Norah tugged on his shirtsleeve. Wendill had encouraged her to walk by his side, but she refused. He didn't know if she felt safer walking behind him or if she copied him to understand how a dragon moves through the world or if she had some reason of her own that he didn't understand.

"Bad man?" Although Norah appeared calm, something about the way she looked at Wendill made her seem concerned.

Wendill reached to place a comforting hand on her shoulder, but she backed away. He silently admonished himself for forgetting her aversion to being touched. He'd never felt that way himself, but he'd been born and raised in the wild, as it should be—not inside a Scalding's cage like Norah. He sometimes wondered if he'd made a mistake allowing himself to be trapped inside Dragon's Head. If he stayed in the world instead of becoming part of it, maybe he could have prevented the capture and murder of so many of his kind by the Scaldings. Maybe he could have saved Norah from her imprisonment. Maybe she would have grown up surrounded by the love and care she deserved and she'd be happy now instead of...

Then again, Wendill reminded himself, *if I hadn't agreed to the entrapment on Dragon's Head, none of us might have survived.*

He smiled at Norah. Better to have her here in her current state than not at all. "Do you smell the bad man?"

She paused, flaring her nostrils and taking a deep breath. She shook her head—

she had caught no scent of Gershon.

"You can trust yourself and what you sense. If you don't smell him, then he is nowhere near us." Wendill paused. "But there is something you should know about where we're going."

Norah watched him steadily, bracing herself for the worst.

"We are going to a place where people used to worship and pay respect to the spirits of the world."

"Spirits?"

Wendill caught his breath, sad to see the confused expression on Norah's face. He never dreamed he'd meet a dragon—even a young one—that knew so little about the world in which it lived.

"Taddeo asked you to guide me to Limru, and you have succeeded."

"Here?"

"Not here. But close enough that I recognize where we are."

Norah's face relaxed as she smiled. For the first time, she looked happy.

"But there is something I must tell you about Limru before we arrive. It is an old place that was once very beautiful."

The smile faded from Norah's face. "Once?"

Wendill hesitated, unsure of what to say next or how to explain what he needed her to know. "There are many kinds of people. One kind understands the world and its spirits. Another kind does not. This other kind hurt Limru."

"Hurt," Norah whispered, seeming to take the word personally.

"But those people are not at Limru anymore. They achieved what they wanted—to hurt Limru and the people who took care of it—and they have gone to other places. They cannot hurt you or me."

"Scaldings!" Norah hissed.

"No, not the Scaldings. I understand how much the Scaldings hurt you, Norah, but know this: the Scaldings are people who can understand us. They can learn how. These other people, the ones who hurt Limru—it will be very difficult to help them understand. It might be impossible."

Norah nodded as if accepting the inevitable, her eyes glazed with puzzlement. But she gestured for Wendill to lead on.

As they pressed forward, Wendill realized for the first time that in addition to preparing Norah for the destruction they were about to see at Limru, he would have to prepare himself as well.

Chapter Forty-Eight

A few days later, Wendill stood among the sacred trees of the Temple of Limru while Norah studied them, keeping close by his side.

Wendill had last visited the temple many decades ago, long before he'd been imprisoned at Dragon's Head. Never before had he seen Limru after autumn had left its tree limbs bare. Even though their leaves were brown and thin as an old man's skin, the trees standing without them somehow appeared more powerful and strong as their thick branches wove high above the tree line of the surrounding forest.

But even more shocking, the sight Wendill beheld looked nothing like what Taddeo or any of the other dragons had described. They'd warned of carnage and destruction, and he saw nothing like that here. True, the gold and silver chains that had once hung on every limb of every tree and glittered among the leaves had vanished. Otherwise, the sacred trees of the temple were just the way Wendill remembered them. "Hello, my friends," he murmured.

"Look!"

At the sound of Norah's voice, Wendill turned and followed the direction in which she pointed. His heart plummeted like a seabird diving into the ocean.

With Norah trailing close behind, Wendill approached the stone circle in the clearing outside the temple. He recognized the work of the Keepers of Limru: a circle, as large as a ship, aligned with the directions and blessed with fire. But as he peered at the contents inside the circle, he felt more confused.

Charred bone fragments rested in a thick bed of soft ashes. As a matter of respect for the Keepers of Limru, Wendill stayed outside the stone circle and simply peered at its contents instead of reaching inside. "Do you see those marks on the bones?" he said to Norah, who now stood so close by his side that she almost touched him. "That is the mark left behind when the spirit has been set free from the bones." Wendill swallowed hard. He hadn't considered that the spirits of the people who died here would have been trapped, but considering the violence and the suddenness of the attack, that probably would have been enough to keep them imprisoned inside the little that remained of their bodies.

Norah crept to the edge of the stone circle and walked slowly. Coming to a stop, she pointed at one of the stones. "Scalding."

Wendill turned to face her. "You sense the Scalding was here?"

Norah nodded, jabbing her forefinger at the same stone. "Scalding!"

Wendill frowned. "The Scalding is a Scalding. Not a Keeper of Limru. How could she know how to do this?"

"Others."

"Others were here? With the Scalding?"

Norah took a deep breath and considered it for a few moments. Then she nodded again.

"But the Scalding didn't stop them." Wendill looked back at the Temple of Limru behind them, its sacred trees standing tall and proud. "She allowed the others to heal the Temple."

Norah stared at the bones and ashes, seeming to contemplate them. Softly, she said, "Well?"

Her question jolted Wendill back into the reality of why they'd come here: the Dragon's Well of Limru. How fitting that Taddeo had suggested the guise of Wendill needing to be healed for the sake of convincing Norah to travel to the one place that had the power to heal her and set her right in the world—and that they'd discovered the place itself had been healed.

"Of course," Wendill said. "Follow me."

Instead of following quietly behind Wendill, Norah practically skipped next to his side, watching his every step as if to make sure she didn't take a wrong step.

Wendill understood. He and Taddeo had been able to lure her into the outside world by promising she could do something that mattered and that would make a difference to all dragons. Although Wendill would benefit from drinking from the well, it wasn't essential to his survival. But Norah's survival depended on it. Norah stood on the precipice of the most important thing she had ever done.

Wendill removed the wooden cover from the well and pulled up the dry bucket from its depths. Picking up a pebble from the forest floor, he tossed it into the well, listening intently until he heard it bounce on the bottom. "The well is dry," he whispered.

"No!" Norah dropped to her hands and knees at the lip of the well, peering down into it. "No!" She ran her hands along the polished stone rim and as far as she could reach down its sides.

Wendill watched in awe. She knew. Somehow, the young dragon knew what was needed, even if she didn't understand it herself.

Rubbing the dry, polished stones, Norah wept. Where her tears landed on the stone surface, its color faded to pale gray, mottling the surface.

Wendill approached her slowly, not wanting to startle her. Kneeling by her side, he cupped his hand at the line of her jaw and caught the tears that fell.

Too upset to jerk away from his touch, Norah cried harder.

Lifting his cupped hand to his face, Wendill drank her tears, which tasted like spring water.

Startled, Norah watched in silence, still weeping. Her tears kept falling on the stone surface of the well, changing more and more of its color to pale gray. Although the well had gone dry, her tears had the power to fill it again.

She pointed at Wendill. "Better."

He examined his hands. His skin looked smoother and the color much improved, more vital. He expected his overall appearance made him look stronger and younger.

"Yes," he said. "Because of you."

Norah cried out in surprise at the touch of a wet flake of snow landing on her nose. She shivered violently.

Wendill stared up at the sky, darkening with imposing, foggy clouds. Soon, the snowflakes would be thick and furious. If Norah had been able to drink from the well, it might have been possible to carry on. But Wendill now realized they'd pushed their luck. Norah seemed too weak to withstand the oncoming storm and the coldness of winter that bore down upon them. Plus, although Norah had the power to replenish the well, it would take months to do so.

"Here," Wendill said, pushing Norah into the well. "You'll be safe here."

Norah cried out as she fell into the depth of the empty well. A soft thud told Wendill that she had landed safely at the bottom.

As a sudden onslaught of snowflakes blinded him with white, Wendill removed his clothes, folded them, and slipped them inside a hollow in a nearby tree trunk. He stretched and breathed deeply while taking one last look at the sky above.

Wendill grew and curled his body around the edge of the Dragon's Well. Transforming into his dragon shape, his body expanded until it covered the mouth of the well completely. Then, amidst the furry of the snowstorm, Wendill changed his dragon body into stone, sealing the well and protecting it from the cold.

CHAPTER FORTY-NINE

Weeks later, Astrid and Margreet sat next to each other on a wooden bench, watching Vinchi teach a handful of teenage boys how to fight with weapons.

They'd traveled for many days, first through the forest and then through a stretch of low-lying hills. Every morning, the increasingly cold air had made Astrid's skin feel so brittle and stiff that it might break. Every harsh breath numbed the inside of her nose and mouth. But every day they walked South, the sky appeared a bit clearer and the climate warmed slightly. Finally, they came upon a fine stone mansion surrounded by a village twice the size of Guell encircled by a trench barricade filled with brambles.

Vinchi had led them to the barricade's gate, where he spoke with the guards and gained entrance for the three of them. Astrid had gazed in wonder at the enormous stone mansion, towering as tall as the treetops of the Forest of Aguille, standing squarely atop the highest hill in the region. Unlike the natural formation of the tower on Tower Island, which had been fashioned by dragons, the stone mansion had the smooth polished lines so commonly made by men. The stones were dark, mottled gray, and they had been fit together like puzzle pieces to form each wall. The simple but enormous structure included a walkway along the perimeter of its pitched roof, constantly patrolled by guards.

Astrid, Vinchi, and Margreet had been escorted from the barricade gate through the village and toward the stone mansion. Astrid stared at the activity surrounding them. Cows and goats grazed on a lawn beside the mansion, while villagers busied themselves around their wattle-and-daub huts, streams of smoke rising from the hole in the center of each thatched roof. The air thickened with the scent of meat being smoked.

Once at the door of the mansion, they'd waited outside for so long that Astrid wondered if they'd been forgotten. Finally, a servant girl had led them inside. The sudden cool, dank atmosphere inside the mansion startled Astrid. She noticed its walls were covered in gigantic, musty tapestries and there seemed to be at least one fireplace in every room. Astrid imagined that's how they kept the place as warm as they could once the weather turned. The muffled hush of the bottoms of their soft leather shoes against the cold stone floor echoed all around them like scampering mice. The air smelled stale, and Astrid suspected it had been hanging in the same room for decades.

The servant girl had led them to a chamber full of carved wooden chairs, more tapestries, and the musky dark furs of bears spread on the floor. A middle-aged man sat alone in the room, leaning back in his chair with his eyes closed. Under normal circumstances, Astrid would have taken him for a farmer from the look of his plain, weathered face. But as they approached, she noticed a faint scar running diagonally across his forehead. It was a clean, straight line—the type a sword would likely leave in its wake.

"Master?" the servant girl said, her brow creased with worry at the peril of waking him.

The man covered his face with both hands, waking up from a deep sleep and shielding the light from his eyes. "Leave me be!" he complained.

The servant girl scampered from the chamber room, not one who needed to be told once, much less twice.

Letting his hands fall from his face and opening his eyes, the master smiled. "Vinchi."

Astrid quickly learned that the man owned not only the mansion and the village but all the surrounding land. Worried about invasion, he'd told Vinchi to come teach his sons how to fight once trading season had ended. That's what Vinchi had done every day since they'd arrived, but Astrid and Margreet had been subjected to the gentler activities of proper women, which apparently boiled down to wasted time doing nothing of importance. Astrid's protests and rejection of such gentler activities had been ignored. No matter what she said or did, Astrid was supervised very closely every day.

It relieved Astrid to see Margreet grow bored so quickly, too. She'd wondered if Margreet would enjoy the opportunity to huddle out of sight with other women and was glad to see Margreet had no more stomach for that kind of thing than Astrid. Although no one would tell Astrid the details, apparently Margreet had said something offensive enough to banish her to the hall where the boys learned weapons skills. Insisting that she needed to stick by Margreet's side, Astrid beamed at the thought of getting her hands on a sword again, even if it wasn't Starlight. She missed the heft of a sword's grip in her hands as much as she missed the heat and smoke of her smithery back in Guell.

Striding along the wall to stay out of range of the boys' sword blows as Vinchi trained them, Astrid knelt by Vinchi's bag of weapons. Sorting through them, she withdrew a metal practice weapon. Somewhat shorter than a dragonslayer's sword, it sported a two-handed grip, dull edges, and a dull point. However, the blade itself was thicker and the weight felt solid in her hands.

"Put that back!" Vinchi shouted from across the hall.

Pretending she hadn't heard, Astrid took a few practice swings.

Vinchi dashed toward her, grabbing the blade in his gloved hands and yanking it away. "I'm earning our keep by teaching the boys, not you." He put the practice sword back in his bag of weapons like a father putting a sleeping infant in its bed. "And you and your errant friend are here for punishment, not study. So sit down and behave yourselves!"

Astrid crossed her arms. "And if I refuse?"

"I'll have you sent back to the Northlands."

"But the mountains won't be passable for months. How would I get back to Guell?"

"That is not my problem." Vinchi smiled sweetly. "It is yours."

Astrid recognized his tone of voice. Vinchi meant every word he uttered. What good would it do for Astrid to return to the Northlands now?

Arms crossed, she paced back to join Margreet. They sat on the wooden bench in the practice hall, and Astrid spoke her mind. "I think you're glad we took you from your husband. I think maybe you took being his wife to heart so much that you forgot who you are, and now you're beginning to remember."

Of course, Margreet still spoke none of Astrid's language and therefore had no idea what she'd said. "You remind me of my friend Lenore," Astrid continued. "She once had a wealthy husband who truly loved her, but the only way she believed she could succeed as his wife was to become like him. And then the only way she could become herself again was to cut off her feet." Astrid made a chopping motion at her own feet, and Margreet's eyes widened in horror. "But she's fine now," Astrid said. "Another man loves her just the way she is. And she walks on spirit feet that come from her belief in them." Astrid paused. "If you believe you can be happy without your husband, then you can fashion a new life out of that belief. Just like Lenore."

Margreet pointed at the boys, scowling and unleashing a tirade of gibberish. Astrid now recognized a few words of Margreet's language: "sword," "dragon," and "incompetent," which seemed to be Margreet's favorite word.

The master of the mansion had twelve children, ten of whom were boys, ranging from a toddler to the eldest who sported a light beard that did little more than hug the edge of his jaw. Vinchi trained eight of those boys, giving most of his attention to the four oldest. Mostly, he kept an eye on the younger ones to make sure they didn't hurt themselves or each other, even though all the boys trained with wasters, wooden versions of swords that bore the same shape and weight.

Suddenly, Margreet jabbed her elbow into Astrid's side, pointing with fury and passion at the oldest boy, who had just fallen to the ground after aiming a missed blow at his brother and being carried to the floor by its momentum. Speaking rapidly, Margreet pantomimed the worst-case scenario: Margreet gestured a stabbing motion at the boy on the ground, grabbed her own neck with both hands, and let her tongue hang out the side of her mouth as she mimicked a slow and painful death. Carrying out the death scene to its conclusion, she made loud choking noises as she deliberately fell off the bench, rolled on the floor a few times, and finally came to a tragic halt, her eyes staring vacantly at the high ceiling.

Vinchi's youngest student, who looked to be about eight years old, giggled wildly. He dashed toward Margreet and stabbed her lightly with the waster.

With the scream of a vengeful ghost, Margreet sat up wild-eyed and reached with tickling fingertips toward the boy's' belly.

Shrieking with glee, he raced to hide behind Vinchi.

The weapons practice came to a silent halt, and everyone stared at Margreet.

The oldest boy turned to Vinchi, complaint in his voice as he pointed first at Margreet and then at the door.

"No!" Astrid shouted, jumping to her feet. Even though she knew only Vinchi could understand her, Astrid shouted, "We're not leaving. Watching you is all we have to do!"

Margreet rose slowly, again talking so rapidly that Astrid suspected she couldn't have understood the woman even if they spoke the same language. Venting frustration, Margreet continued for a few minutes without pausing to breathe.

The four oldest boys surrounded Vinchi, all of them speaking at once.

Vinchi closed his eyes, his face sagging with the despair of wishing to be someplace else.

Finally, the youngest approached Margreet, his eyes large and round with sorrow. He dragged the wooden sword, its point clacking against the floor.

Margreet grew silent as the youngest boy drew near. Without a word, he handed his own sword to her.

Margreet smiled, and Astrid felt entranced, realizing Margreet looked happy for the first time.

The youngest boy spoke solemnly to Margreet. He stared longingly at the door leading to a bright sunny day outside the practice hall.

Equally solemn, Margreet accepted the waster from him. He squealed for joy and raced out the door. Moments later, his young brothers dropped their own wasters and followed suit.

Wooden sword in hand, Margreet mimicked everything she'd watched the boys learn for the past few weeks.

Of course! Just because Vinchi refuses to teach us, Astrid thought, *doesn't mean we can't learn.*

Astrid often peppered Vinchi with questions at the end of each day out of curiosity. The techniques Vinchi taught were nothing like her dragonslaying skills, which were specific in their own right.

From what Vinchi had told her, Astrid recognized Margreet's actions. First, Margreet adopted every guard, a starting position for a fight, which was often a position one took at the end of a given blow. Margreet called out the name of each guard as she took it. Then Margreet delivered a precise version of every blow Vinchi had taught, again calling out the name of each blow as she made it.

Actually, Astrid realized, *she's quite good.*

Clearly, Margreet had been doing far more than just complaining about the boys' mediocre skills and calling them incompetent. She'd been paying close attention to everything Vinchi had said.

Just like Astrid.

Astrid noticed Vinchi's gaze settle on Margreet. She practiced each guard and blow until the remaining brothers clamored for his attention. Only then did he turn his back on Margreet, who methodically went through her paces at the opposite end of the practice hall.

Once the boys were fully engrossed again in their own drills with each other, Astrid walked to the corner where the younger boys had dropped their wasters. She picked one up. Like Margreet, she mimicked everything she'd learned by watching the boys.

Margreet approached, pointing her own waster at Astrid. The dragonslayer smiled, surprised not only by the smirk on Margreet's face but the wicked expression in her eyes.

CHAPTER FIFTY

"No, that's not right at all," Margreet said. She gestured for Astrid to freeze in place, while Margreet put her own waster on the floor of the practice hall. Knowing that Astrid Scalding understood nothing she said, Margreet was convinced she could still convey her meaning. She took a few steps back, studying Astrid's position: wide stance, one leg forward, arms extended as she delivered a blow meant to cleave an opponent's head in half.

Astrid wobbled for a moment, and suddenly everything became clear to Margreet. "Of course," Margreet said. "Your balance is bad because your feet need to be wider apart." Kneeling by Astrid's front foot, Margreet pushed against the inside of the woman's foot. "Move this foot."

But the Scalding woman didn't budge. Instead, her face reflected confusion.

Honestly, Margreet thought. *This is a woman who kills dragons?*

Finally, the Scalding woman asked a question, but Margreet had no idea what she said. Standing, Margreet decided the best way to communicate. Margreet would act like a mirror image and demonstrate correct form.

Now standing directly in front of Astrid, Margreet placed her feet exactly like hers. Pointing at her own feet, Margreet said, "You stand with one foot far ahead of the other but look like you're walking on top of a fallen log. That is why you have poor balance." For emphasis, Margreet leaned slightly to one side, having to wave her arms wildly to keep from falling down.

Astrid frowned. Clearly, she understood none of Margreet's meaning.

But Margreet wouldn't allow herself to feel discouraged. "Now," Margreet said, "imagine that instead of trying to keep your balance on top of a fallen log, you now straddle it with your feet on solid ground. That means one foot is still stepping far ahead of the other, but your feet are now wider apart."

Margreet demonstrated by widening her feet a bit. "And now, think about taking an even wider stance." Margreet widened her feet a little bit more. "Now, look how steady I am. I can lean this way and that way, and I'm in no danger of falling over." The width of her stance resulted in Margreet's knees bending deeply and leaning with no danger of wobbling.

Frowning and looking unsure, Astrid struggled to widen her own feet, keeping her knees bent.

"Now, raise your sword and bring it down again." Empty-handed, Margreet raised an imaginary weapon above her head and brought it straight down, taking a forward but wide step as she delivered the blow. When her front foot landed, she pointed at it, saying, "See where my foot is." Standing straight up as she brought her feet together, Margreet took a step back and gestured toward Astrid. "Now you try."

Slowly, Astrid raised the point of the waster above her head and then took a step forward and to the side as she slowly brought the sword back down, landing with her knees bent and with every sign that she stood her ground, stable and solid.

"Good!" Margreet said. "And again." She gestured for Astrid to deliver the same blow while taking another step forward.

This time, the Scalding woman took less time and showed more confidence as she maintained her wide stance while delivering the next blow at the air in front of her.

Margreet smiled. She found this far more enjoyable than sitting on a hard wooden bench watching the boys or—far worse—sitting in some dreadful, musty room listening to excruciatingly boring privileged women complain about their riches. "Now," Margreet said, "we will train in the same way as the boys. Let's begin side by side. We will deliver the same blow from above the head across our end of the practice hall."

Picking up her waster, Margreet delivered a couple of blows as she stepped forward with each one and stopped to point across the floor, showing the path they would take. Astrid still looked confused, so Margreet physically placed her in the starting position, pushing the waster Astrid still had in hand above her head. "Now, stay there," Margreet said. She took the exact same position at Astrid's side. "Ready...strike!"

As Margreet stepped forward and delivered the blow, Astrid remained frozen in place.

Margreet walked toward Astrid and grabbed onto the wooden blade near the crossguard, which was all she could reach with Astrid holding the training weapon above her head. "Ready," Margreet said slowly and clearly, looking into Astrid's eyes. Margreet said, "Strike," and she forcibly brought the blade down, pulling Astrid to make her step forward. "Ready," Margreet said, raising the blade high again. On "strike," she forced the blade down and pulled Astrid forward once more. When Margreet said, "Ready" and raised the blade again, Astrid brightened, babbling incoherently but excitedly.

Margreet smiled, motioning for Astrid to join her side at their original starting position. "Ready...strike!"

This time, Astrid brought her blade down and stepped forward in unison with Margreet.

Overjoyed, Margreet turned her head to look at Astrid, who smiled back at her. Nodding her approval, Margreet looked forward, focusing on an imaginary opponent whose skull she intended to open. "Ready...strike!" Again, the women delivered the same blow and footwork, side by side.

Throughout the day, Margreet and Astrid drilled together. It wasn't until their work ended and they joined the master and his family for dinner that Margreet thought about Gershon for the first time that day. She experienced just a momentary thought, a brief remembrance of herself as a married woman despite the fact that she was beginning to feel like a maiden again.

Margreet smiled with surprise at how much that feeling delighted her.

This is right, the small voice inside her said. *This is good.*

Margreet kept smiling. For the first time since she'd escaped the attack at Limru, she listened closely to that voice instead of brushing it away.

CHAPTER FIFTY-ONE

That night, Astrid kept to her new routine. After the sun had set and all lingering light had vanished from the sky, she joined Vinchi and Margreet in the great hall at a table near that of the master and his family for light supper. After washing their hands in bowls of water brought in by servants, Astrid and her companions sat together at a table covered with a plain linen cloth, wiping their hands dry on the end that hung near their laps.

Astrid still had to remind herself to wait patiently for one of the master's sons to speak before the servants delivered food to the tables. The boys took turns, and tonight the youngster who had handed his wooden sword to Margreet during practice stood and spoke quickly. He acted hungry and anxious, just like Astrid. At dinner, the boys spoke the Northlander language to stay in good practice. "Thank you Krystr for giving life to man and food is life. We beg forgiveness for sharing this food with the lower kind, but we know the females cannot help what they are. We forgive your mistake in making them, we men."

No matter how many times she witnessed it, Astrid couldn't help but press her lips together in frustration as she watched the males at the master's table say in response, "We men," while the women and girls looked down in shame. Margreet always did the same, and no matter how many times Astrid spoke with Vinchi about it, he wouldn't encourage Margreet to do otherwise, claiming Margreet showed wisdom in fitting in and that Astrid endangered herself by holding her head up.

Hogwash, Astrid thought.

When she glanced around her own table, Astrid paused and smiled.

For once, instead of bowing her head in shame like the other women, Margreet sat with her arms folded, her face drawn in the most serious expression Astrid had ever seen her muster. Margreet stared into empty space.

Astrid cleared her throat until Margreet cast a glance at her. Looking directly into her eyes, Astrid smiled.

One corner of Margreet's mouth turned up slightly, enough to make Astrid break out into a grin.

She started at the moment Vinchi, sitting next to her, smacked his knee directly into hers, making it smart. Wincing, Astrid turned to complain only to be silenced by the frightened look in his eyes.

He'd warned her many times during the past weeks to remember that they were no longer in the Northlands or even the Midlands. Here, in the Southlands, they had entered territories already conquered by the armies of Krystr and monitored by his servants, the roving clerks. The master of this mansion had succeeded in preventing any clerks from making themselves at home here, but bands of them wandered the countryside and were likely to arrive for a visit—possibly even a long visit—at any time.

It was, therefore, in Astrid's best interest to act with caution except when alone with Vinchi and Margreet. In fact, he'd advised her to follow Margreet's lead in humbling herself whether in the company of men or women or children.

Astrid imagined his horror now that Margreet followed Astrid's lead instead.

Even more reason to convince Margreet to begin a new life in Guell once the winter snows had melted in the Northlands, making it possible to travel through the mountain passes again.

While the master and his family ate a meal of white bread, venison stew, and pastries, Vinchi, Margreet, and Astrid received small loaves of bread with the insides hollowed out and a large wooden bowl of the stew to pour into the hollow of the bread. Pepper spiced the stew, laced with cloves and heavy with garlic. At the end of the meal, Astrid palmed a small wedge of cheese. She slipped away from the table at the same time the master's wife prepared to sing the evening's entertainment. Even though Astrid believed it a poor excuse, she'd asked Vinchi to explain to their hosts that because she was a Northlander, Astrid normally slept longer hours in the winter and shorter hours in the summer due to her body being attuned to sunlight. Margreet glared in envy as Astrid left, but this time Astrid paid her no mind.

At night, the rooms and hallways of the stone mansion glowed from the flames in the fireplace and the flickering light of torches sconced on the walls. Outside of the Great Hall, warmed mostly by the bodies of all the people inside it, stark and chilled air drifted through the building. Walking through an empty chamber, Astrid borrowed a bearskin cloak draped across the back of a chair before she went out into the frigid night.

She strolled around one side of the manor, and the frozen brown grass broke under every step. Cattle lowed nearby. The light from the sparse quarter moon caught the light parts of their black-and-white patterned skin, making the grazing animals look like misshapen ghosts floating above the ground. Her eyes adjusted to the point where she could see the shape of each animal's body.

Astrid smiled as an owl screamed like a woman being murdered in the distance. Long ago, she'd learned to recognize the difference between an owl's screech and a woman's voice, even though both sounds made the hair on the back of her neck stand up.

She ran a hand around her neck, rubbing the skin to warm up. A few months had passed since Trep had used his dagger to cut her hair off close to the scalp at Astrid's request. Her hair had grown about a thumb's length since then, hugging her head in straight but shaggy locks. She smiled as she ran her fingers through her own hair, suddenly missing Trep and the way he called her "Girly." She laughed, remembering the time she thought he looked glad to see her despite his true joy in winning a bet based on the day the blacksmiths would see her again.

This had become her favorite time of day. Astrid strolled to the back of the mansion and sat on a large rock by the tiny pond the servants had created for the children. This was when she remembered Guell and everyone she'd left behind. She thought of Donel and all the times he'd shown up at her doorstep, begging her to take him on as an apprentice. She thought about Randim and the other blacksmiths, wishing she could be with them in the heat of the smithery. She missed the smoke and the solid feel of striking iron on an anvil. She even missed clearing the slag, the metallic flakes that seemed to emerge magically from the iron after striking it. But she also missed the company of men who understood her in ways that no one else could because they were blacksmiths, like her.

Astrid kept thinking about Lenore, who once had married a wealthy man and lived in a manor like this one. Now Astrid clearly understood why Lenore could never be happy in such a place. After spending time with the master of this mansion and his family and observing the way they lived, she felt a deeper appreciation for everything Lenore had told her. Despite the mansion's beauty, it looked too big and too formal. At first, Astrid had been impressed with the sheer size of the building and felt enchanted walking from room to room. But it didn't take long before she began to see the place as impractical, drafty, and cold. She missed the cozy warmth of her small home back in Guell almost as much as she missed the warmth and companionship of her friends.

She shivered, feeling the cold from the hard stone seep through her clothes. Glancing up, she smiled at the sparse clouds in the night sky and the brightness of the moon and the stars. It wouldn't be too much longer.

Almost on cue, mist began to rise from the pond in wispy, pale sheets.

Astrid drew her knees to her chest, hugging them close for warmth but also because she knew that if she tried to touch him, she'd feel nothing but the cold mist.

A familiar shape pressed itself into the mist and took form as it drifted toward her. Astrid smiled and said, "Hello, DiStephan."

CHAPTER FIFTY-TWO

"Every time I ask Vinchi about all of us going back to Guell, he makes up an excuse," Astrid said to the misty shape of DiStephan sitting next to her. "He's afraid we'll run into Gershon, but I think it's worth the risk."

Astrid imagined it took all of DiStephan's strength to keep the mist in the shape he'd had when alive. Mist rolled across what seemed to be invisible skin and the shape of the clothes he'd worn as a dragonslayer. It clung to his face, allowing Astrid to read his expressions. Under the moon and the stars, his ghostly body glowed eerily, although not quite as frightening as the reflection on the spotted cows that made them look like spirits hovering off the ground. That had been a disturbing sight the first time Astrid had seen them.

DiStephan's misty face hadn't changed. He seemed to simply be listening, as he often did on these frigid nights.

"I want Margreet to come to Guell. She doesn't seem to miss Gershon—not any more. And she's not prissy like some of the people here. I think she'd have no problem rolling up her sleeves and working in the fields."

The spirit extended his arms, holding his hands together in a grip, and the mist spilled down and took the shape of a sword.

"Yes!" Astrid beamed. "Isn't it exciting? It was wonderful training with Margreet today. Did you see us?"

DiStephan's ghost didn't need to nod his head. His face, now beaming like Astrid's, was all she needed to see.

"They have a blacksmith, and he hates me. Said he wants nothing to do with a woman 'pretending' to be a blacksmith. Can you imagine?"

DiStephan's ghost shook its head, his happy expression fading.

"It's all right," Astrid said quickly. "I don't mind. I know my anvil waits for me at home. I don't have time for blacksmithing now anyway. I'll be too busy learning about swords with Margreet. Then once spring comes, I'll take Margreet back to Guell. I've decided Vinchi can come, too, if he wishes."

She paused. "You know he won't give Starlight back to me because he says you've been friends since you were boys. Is that true?"

The ghost nodded.

Astrid sighed. "All right then. He may want to avoid Gershon, and there's no safer place to hide than Guell. I've seen the skins Gershon sells. He may be skilled at killing bears and wolves, but he didn't have a single lizard skin. I'll wager he's terrified of them, and that's probably why Guell isn't on his trade route and probably never will be." A new thought silenced Astrid for a moment, then she said, "If you and Vinchi were friends, does that mean you were also friendly with Gershon?"

DiStephan's ghost shook his head.

"But you knew him."

This time, the ghost nodded.

"And Margreet? Did you know her?"

The ghost nodded again.

A flush of happiness hit Astrid like the sudden whoosh of a fire. Learning she met the same people that DiStephan had known during his life made her feel closer to him. She could pretend he was still alive.

By asking a series of simple questions, she learned that DiStephan had recognized the problems Gershon and Margreet shared and seemed troubled, even though he'd never seen Gershon strike his wife. DiStephan had seen only signs of the aftermath and hadn't known what he could do to help the woman, especially because she didn't seem to want any.

She knew how seriously DiStephan took his responsibilities as dragonslayer. It must have pained him to see a woman in need of help, all the while not being able to find a way to give her what she needed.

"You helped us," Astrid said quietly, just now understanding the degree of truth. "I recognized you at the entrance to the forest. You stood and let the hail coat your spirit body to form a shell. And the others—were they spirits you met in the forest?"

The ghost nodded.

"Were they spirits of the Keepers of Limru? The ones murdered by the followers of Krystr?"

The ghost nodded again.

Astrid remembered the way Margreet had chanted at the Temple of Limru on the day they'd created a funeral pyre for the people killed there.

Overwhelmed, Astrid's eyes filled with tears.

She started at a cool, damp touch on her cheek. DiStephan's ghostly hand lingered, ready to wipe away her tears. Astrid took a deep breath to collect herself. "It's all right. I was just thinking about Margreet. They were her people. Did you know?"

Again, the ghost nodded.

"They helped you. By helping you, they helped us. And then we set them free."

The ghostly fingertips trailed down Astrid's cheek, making her shiver.

"Margreet knew, didn't she? When we first saw you and the other spirits cased in ice, she must have recognized them. That's why she helped us set them free."

The ghostly fingertips faded, leaving only half of DiStephan's hand intact.

Astrid glanced at the tiny pond. A slight layer of mist drifted through the tips of the dead grass blades. DiStephan had probably exhausted himself from holding a recognizable form together for so long. "I should go back inside."

But she sat, as always, until DiStephan's ghost had dissipated completely, leaving no hint that he had ever sat by her side on that or any other night.

Sighing, Astrid rose, stretching her arms wide and yawning at the night sky.

Turning to leave, she froze.

There, in the moonlight, were tracks she had seen only once before. Tracks she'd discovered by Sigurthor's dead body in the mountains of the Northlands.

Wide eyed, she stared in disbelief at the tracks the size of a man's foot with the claws of a lizard.

They were the tracks of a monster.

CHAPTER FIFTY-THREE

Early the next morning, Astrid cornered Vinchi in the practice hall before the boys arrived for their daily work with weapons. Although the winters were mild like autumn here in the Southlands, Astrid's breath hung lightly in the chilly air. No one bothered to use the fireplaces in this room. Once the boys arrived and began their work, the room naturally warmed up to a comfortable temperature. But right now, whenever Astrid inhaled, the air left a chalky taste on the back of her tongue.

"A monster has followed us here!" she whispered to Vinchi.

"What?" Every morning Vinchi sat on a bench and rubbed linseed oil into each waster to prevent it from cracking or breaking during practice. Winter's dry air affected the wooden weapons.

"A monster. I saw it in the mountains. In the Northlands. I don't know how it followed us, but it has. Everyone is in danger!"

Vinchi poured oil the color of liquid amber on a rag and rubbed the blade of the waster in hand slowly, letting the wood drink in the liquid. "What kind of monster are we talking about?"

"I don't know."

"What does it look like?"

Astrid shrugged. She sat down on the bench next to him and pointed at the fuller carved down the length of the blade. "You missed a spot."

Wrenching his mouth in a peeved expression, Vinchi handed the waster and rag to her. "Then fix it." He picked up a dry waster, poured a dollop of oil in the center of another rag, and went to work. "Did you actually see this monster?"

Happy to have something to do, Astrid rubbed the oil hard into the waster's fuller, what some people mistakenly called the "blood channel," thinking it a place for blood to run down a sword during battle although in reality the fuller made the sword lighter. Or, in this case, made the waster lighter. Answering Vinchi's question, she said, "Not exactly. Not the monster itself. But its footprint is behind the mansion, and I saw the exact same footprint in the Northland mountains by the dead body of a merchant."

Vinchi paled as he looked up from the waster. "A merchant?"

"Sigurthor. He's a Northlander. He always brought sweet onions to Guell." She hesitated. "DiStephan loved those onions. He said they reminded him of home—where he and his father came from."

Vinchi appeared understandably shaken. No merchant wanted to hear about someone like himself being murdered on the road. Vinchi's hands trembled as he ran the oiled rag over his waster. "Why do you think those footprints belong to a monster? Couldn't they have been Sigurthor's footprints? Couldn't he have simply died a natural death? It happens to merchants all the time while they're traveling."

Poor Vinchi, Astrid thought, torn between feeling sympathy and embarrassment for a man so clearly afraid to die. "No," she said softly. "The footprints I saw in the mountains were unlike anything I've seen before, like half-man and half-lizard. The foot of a man with the claws of a lizard. And I saw the precise same footprint behind the mansion last night!"

Vinchi focused his attention on the waster, now rubbing oil into the trickier parts—the crossguard, grip, pommel, and all the nooks and crannies between. "You saw it at night? How sure can you be of what you saw?"

"Quite sure. There was plenty of light from the moon and stars."

"And did anyone else see this 'monstrous' footprint?"

Astrid hesitated, not wanting to let Vinchi or anyone else know that she'd found a way to spend time with DiStephan's ghost. The ghost seemed like all she had left of him, and she didn't want to share it with anyone, certainly not with curiosity seekers who had only heard of ghosts but never seen one. "Yes. I was alone."

Vinchi breathed a heavy sigh and then smiled. "Well, there you go. It was night. You were alone in the dark. Of course one's mind will play tricks—"

"No!" Holding onto her waster's grip through the rag, Astrid pounded its point against the floor, and the clattering sound echoed through the empty practice hall as Margreet entered, yawning and stretching. Raising her voice, Astrid said, "I will not have you make me out to be imagining things. I know what I saw!"

"Of course you do." Vinchi's voice dripped with insincerity.

Margreet marched toward them, calling out. She pointed at Vinchi.

Switching to Margreet's language, Vinchi's tone became quiet and apologetic. He seemed to be offering a reasonable explanation.

Interrupting him, Margreet's footsteps echoed loudly across the stone floor until she halted at Astrid's side. Margreet clamped a solid hand on Astrid's shoulder, this time jabbing the forefinger of her free hand from Vinchi to Astrid.

Hanging his head, Vinchi stared at his feet and answered Margreet.

"What is she talking about?"

"Nothing," Vinchi said quietly.

Margreet slammed an open palm down on the empty space on the bench between Vinchi and Astrid. She then said something softly to Vinchi.

Astrid strained to hear, even though she knew Margreet's words were none she could understand.

"She thinks we're arguing about whether I will train just the boys or you and Margreet. She says she's decided you're her friend now, and that I must train you both with equal care."

Beaming, Astrid looked up at Margreet, still standing by her side.

Margreet nodded and patted Astrid's shoulder, still glaring at Vinchi.

"And have you answered Margreet?"

"I told her the boys must come first. That is why I'm here and why all of us have a bed to sleep in and food to eat. But whenever I can leave the boys to practice on their own, I will work with you."

"And the monster?"

Vinchi looked up quickly.

"I can probably draw what I saw for Margreet, and we can show the master, and—"

"I'll take care of it," Vinchi said quietly. "I'll talk to the master directly and tell him what you saw. He can have his staff look into it. There's no need to frighten anyone unnecessarily."

Vinchi looked up at Margreet. Astrid noticed for the first time that his concern for her seemed to run much deeper than she'd ever suspected.

Chapter Fifty-Four

In a remote corner of the Southlands, Gershon fought boredom at the daily service held after sunset and before supper. Now dressed like Thomas in a white smock and brown robe, Gershon sat on a bench in the front row of a simple meeting house in the center of the village. Thomas stood in front and droned on about the teachings of the Krystr. Gershon shivered, drawing the robe tight around him, tortured by the scent of smoke and the promise of blazing heat from hearth fires in surrounding houses. Thomas claimed their belief should provide all the fire they needed to stay warm, but the village men huddled close together on the benches behind Gershon.

"...And when the Creation God invited the Mighty Krystr to come out of the sea, the Krystr was like all other Men of the Sea. He was all man except for his fish tail, but then the Creation God cleaved that tail in two, and they grew into legs."

The first time Gershon had heard this story, it took all his willpower to keep his eyes from rolling toward the sky. Who ever heard of men coming out of the sea? He'd heard his share of sailors' stories about creatures swimming in the waves that were half fish and half man. Gershon had been tempted to believe them at first. After all, the ocean seemed a vast and mighty place. How could one tell what kind of world lay in its murky depths?

The first time Gershon crossed the sea from the Northlands to the Midlands, he sailed on a ship with a crew that swore they saw such creatures on every voyage. Sure enough, they'd skimmed alongside a rocky shore far from any village, and the crew had excitedly pointed toward a narrow island of stones that paralleled the shore. As the crew trembled and stared, Gershon had squinted and made out a colony of seals. Later, he'd discovered no one else on board had the good vision to see well at a distance.

"The Krystr stood and walked until his feet and legs became strong and sure. He then called to his brothers who still swam in the sea and convinced them to breach themselves on the shore, promising to show them a mighty new way to be in the world."

At first, Gershon had enjoyed these stories. Of course, they were outlandish, but he'd heard equally bizarre tales of gods and goddesses from the High Northlands to the deepest regions in the Southlands. Every country or region or empire had such stories. He'd heard of gods taking the guise of all manner of animal and bird, including many strange combinations of various animals that clearly had never existed. Gershon took Thomas's stories about the Krystr to be nothing more than stories, just like all the others he'd heard in his travels.

"Krystr followed the example of the Creation God and cleaved all the tails of his fellow men into legs. He then taught every new man how to walk upright and hunt and gather food, because food on land isn't plentiful like it is in the sea."

It had been a long winter. Here, hills rolled gently and the days were pleasant even though the temperature dropped sharply at sunset. At first, Gershon had been happy to have a place where he felt he belonged. After that thief Vinchi had stolen Margreet, Gershon had been lost and confused. Despite their habit of argument, Gershon could always count on his wife for a unique opinion. He often disagreed with her, but she always gave him something to think about, and that often helped him in business arrangements. Although he'd briefly considered returning to his habit of trapping, he found it easier to follow Thomas than strike out on his own without Margreet.

"And life was good. Men left the sea and made a new home on land. Man became the king of all animals, thereby proving Man's superiority to all living creatures. On land, men found their own perfect world of fields and valleys, streams and mountains, hearth and home. But that perfect world was destroyed when females decided to breach themselves, all because they wanted to follow men out of the sea."

Margreet had always traveled with him, whether he hunted in the Northlands during summer or the Midlands during winter. He missed how good it felt to have her make his meals and mend his clothes. But he'd also grown used to her company and it seemed strange to have not seen her at all during the past few months. In some ways, Gershon didn't feel like himself and wondered if he might be turning into someone different.

"Men found a Sanctuary of their very own on land. A place where they could find peace and happiness. A place where they could dominate the world, which is right and true. A place where each man could fight and claim his own territory for himself. Where he could even dominate other men, if he so wished, for he had the freedom to do so. But when females breached themselves in an effort to follow, men took pity upon them and clove their tails into legs. Women destroyed the Sanctuary of Man by calling female gods into creation. If women had accepted their fate as creatures of the ocean—if they had accepted the attention of men who returned to the sea when they wished to spawn with them—we would still live in a perfect Sanctuary today. Instead, women have ruined the world of men. It is our duty to make sure they don't destroy the little we have left."

Gershon shifted on the hard bench, searching for a way to find comfort. In a way, Thomas's words made sense. If Margreet would only mind him, they'd have no arguments. If they had no arguments, he would have no need to strike her in order to remind her that the role of the man in their marriage belonged to him. And if he had no need to strike her, Vinchi never would have stolen her away.

Gershon reconsidered his anger toward Vinchi. Perhaps Vinchi couldn't help having a soft heart. Maybe a woman had hurt Vinchi and worn him down, leaving nothing but a shell of who Vinchi used to be. Gershon remembered times when Margreet had worn him down to a point where he considered giving in just to make her stop talking. But Gershon had a deep well of fortitude, and he'd always managed to pull himself back up even though he'd been beaten down by the woman who'd accepted the duty of making his life easier, not more difficult.

Maybe Gershon didn't believe in men who came out of the sea with fish tails and a god that had turned their tails into legs, but he began to see a hidden meaning in Thomas's words. The world could be a sanctuary for men if only women didn't struggle so hard to ruin it for them.

Gershon turned a renewed attention to Thomas, this time listening for the deeper meaning in his words instead of taking them at face value. Surely, Thomas would say something that would help Gershon understand the best way to punish Margreet as soon as their paths crossed again.

CHAPTER FIFTY-FIVE

For the seventeenth time that morning, Astrid fell to the hard floor of the practice room after being thrown off balance by Margreet. Astrid winced as she landed on her side, certain bruises already covered her body from the morning's work, even though they'd only been practicing for an hour or so. She grinned at the sound of Margreet tapping the point of her waster against the stone floor as she called out to Astrid, most likely spurring her to hurry back up on her feet to face off against Margreet again.

What they learned from Vinchi failed to compare to the skills for slaying lizards. Astrid's slaying skills were about staying alert and avoiding the animal while trying to get close enough to climb on its back and then get a clear shot of stabbing the back of its neck. She knew about avoidance and waiting for the perfect opportunity and taking advantage of the opportunity once it presented itself.

As much as Astrid enjoyed using a waster, she yearned to touch a real sword, especially one forged by her own hand. She missed the comfort of the leather grip and the clean, sharp feel of the way the blade cut through the air while swinging it at a lizard to keep it from charging.

The techniques Vinchi taught were for a sword shorter than a dragonslayer's sword, something meant to kill a man instead of a lizard. Even though the waster was the same size and shape of a small sword, it felt ungainly in Astrid's hands. Because the sword Starlight had become so much a part of her, she struggled trying to learn how to use a sword that seemed so vastly different.

Standing behind Astrid's crumpled form, Margreet tapped the point of her waster against the floor, faster and louder.

Astrid remembered the patience with which DiStephan's ghost had taught her how to use Starlight, the sword she'd originally forged for him, and how quickly she'd taken to it.

Speaking rapidly in an irritated tone, Margreet marched to face Astrid but stopped in mid-sentence.

Vinchi called out from across the room where he worked with the boys, but Margreet waved him off. Taking a tentative step forward, she sank to her knees.

For the first time, Astrid saw the expression in Margreet's eyes soften. Margreet spoke, and her voice grew soft and concerned, still speaking rapidly.

Astrid understood nothing Margreet said. Even so, as usual, Astrid imagined Margreet's meaning and answered, knowing Margreet would understand nothing she said. "I'm used to being good at what I do, and this is going terribly. We've been training for how many weeks now?" Astrid paused and counted on her fingers. One, two, three, four, five, six, seven, eight. She held up eight fingers.

Margreet's eyes glazed over for a few moments while she stared at Astrid's fingers, but then they lit with recognition. She shook her head and showed Astrid nine fingers.

"Nine weeks!" Astrid corrected herself and held up nine fingers to match what Margreet showed her. They both let their hands drift to their sides. "I'm terrible at reading what you're about to do with your sword, which means I'm far too slow in making a decision about how to respond." She waved a hand toward the boys grunting and groaning and shouting while they trained with Vinchi at the opposite side of the practice hall. "We work twice as hard as those boys and spend far more time at it than they do. And you're marvelous. You're so quick and decisive and strong." Astrid paused. "And I'm not. I used to be quick and decisive and strong, and maybe I still am when it comes to lizards. But not when it comes to fighting men. I don't want to fight men."

"You're a dragonslayer," Vinchi said, walking toward them. "Sometimes you have to fight men."

"I've fought men," Astrid said, looking up at him. "I'm saying I don't like it."

"But you like killing dragons?"

Vinchi's question gave Astrid pause. "Only when I'm defending my people or myself. I take no pleasure in killing for the sake of killing."

"And what if men attack?" Vinchi said. "Are you going to simply stand by or kill the same way you'd kill a dragon?"

Astrid knew she shouldn't be shocked by his question, but she felt like she'd stepped onto an ice-covered lake only to hear the ice crack open beneath her feet. On one hand, she wanted to always be ready to fight whether the foe was man or beast. At the same time, she couldn't shake the memory of being tortured by her own family on Tower Island.

She didn't want to be like them. She didn't want to live up to the name of Scalding.

Margreet looked steadily into Astrid's eyes and spoke softly. Her tone remained calm but earnest. Astrid decided that whatever Margreet said, it sounded logical. Maybe her words simply encouraged Astrid not to give up.

Finally, Margreet rose slowly to her feet, quiet now as she extended an open hand to Astrid, who accepted it and let Margreet help her stand. She kept talking softly for a few more minutes, placing a gentle hand on Astrid's arm.

Astrid breathed deeply, letting herself feel calm while realizing that every day Margreet reminded her very much of her friend Lenore back home in Guell.

CHAPTER FIFTY-SIX

Daylight dimmed, and Vinchi made his usual rounds of circling the practice room to light the candles set in iron sconces shaped like ram horns on the walls. Throughout the winter, he'd had to set about this task by mid-day because the sun set so early. But now the sun rose higher in the sky and sank more to the West than the South.

As Vinchi drew closer to the women, Margreet signaled her intent to take a break and sat down on the bench where she and Astrid had once done nothing but watch. She dipped a wooden cup into a large bowl of water next to the bench and drank.

Astrid watched the boys run out of the room, which they normally did at the end of each day. Once Vinchi stepped close enough to hear, she said, "You're taking your time. Have you forgotten there's a gathering to attend?"

Vinchi had wrapped a wick around the point of a metal practice weapon, lit it, and took delight in extending the practice sword up to light the sconces high above his head. "The boys simply left to make themselves useful. The clerks departed this morning, so there will be no more gatherings until they return next year."

Turning toward Vinchi, Astrid said, "Have you spoken to the master about the tracks I saw outside? About the monster?"

"Yes." Vinchi paused underneath a sconce he'd just lit, holding his flame-tipped sword to one side while watching to make sure the fire had taken. The light flickered and a steady ribbon of black smoke streamed from the scone. He raised the sword again, repositioning himself to get a better angle for lighting the candle within. "He sent the servants out to investigate, and they say it's a wolf print. Sometimes they circle the mansion at night during the winter. You shouldn't be going out there. It's too dangerous."

"That was no wolf print," Astrid said. "I've seen plenty of wolf tracks, and I know what they look like."

A strong flame flickered above, and Vinchi hurried to the next sconce. "There's a different type of wolf here in the Southlands. It's bigger and stronger. Its paws are shaped differently."

"Then what was such a beast doing in the Northlands?"

Vinchi lit the last sconce successfully and gazed around the room to admire his own handiwork of lighting the place before extinguishing the wick on his sword point and removing it. Gripping the blunt-edged blade with his leather-gloved hand, Vinchi walked toward Margreet and extended the grip to her.

In wide-eyed surprise, Margreet took a last gulp of water and grinned. She wrapped her hand around the grip of the iron weapon.

"What are you doing?" Astrid said, suspicious of his answers and even more suspicious that he seemed to be changing the subject.

Margreet stepped out onto the practice floor. She lunged, thrusting the blade forward and followed up by slashing the air in front of her with diagonal cuts. Her face glowed in the soft candlelight. Like always, she'd tucked part of the hem of her skirt into her belt, revealing glimpses of her calves and clearing the way for her footwork.

"What are you doing?" Astrid crossed her arms, still gripping her waster in one hand, its blade crossing her body like a shield. "You told us everyone has to train with wasters for at least a year or two before they're ready to use metal. Why did you give that to her?"

Vinchi withdrew a second iron practice weapon from his belt and handed it to Astrid.

Despite her suspicions, she took it, grateful for the elegant feel of its grip and appreciating the fine balance of the weapon.

"We can't stay here forever. If the clerks are moving on, then more people will be on the roads, which is what we should be doing. The two of you aren't ready to progress to iron, but I fear it's more important for us to do whatever is necessary to prepare for the journey ahead." Vinchi cleared his throat. "I'm taking you to my family home in the Far Southlands. My relatives can protect you—"

"Margreet, you mean." Astrid put the waster to one side and gripped the iron weapon. A dragonslayer's sword provided a long grip for both hands, but this shorter sword forced the hands to jam close together, which she found odd and disconcerting. "How do you think your family will react when you show up with another man's wife?"

Vinchi flushed and he stuttered. "I will explain the danger she faces from her husband. They will understand."

Astrid studied him closely but he avoided her steady gaze. "I think they'll understand far more than you wish."

Vinchi faced Astrid. He positioned himself with his back to Margreet as if he couldn't bear to look at her. "What else can I do? Desert her and you both?"

Astrid held the iron practice sword out to one side and leaned slightly on it. "Did you know that in the Northlands, the law allows a woman to break ties with her husband if she feels mistreated by him?"

Vinchi shrugged, his face slack with misery. "But Margreet is no Northlander."

"Did you know that any woman who chooses to live in the Northlands is bound by its laws? And that if a woman moves to the Northlands, she can draw upon any law that suits her. Immediately."

Vinchi shook his head, unconvinced. "But what about Gershon? He would follow us and—"

"And in a town like Guell, everyone would stand by her side. Just like everyone would stand by your side if you were her husband."

Vinchi's jaw slackened in surprise, and he had the look of a deer finding itself caught in the sight of an archer.

"She could break her marriage simply by gathering witnesses at the foot of her marriage bed—any bed will do, in this case, I think—and announce her break with Gershon. She could marry you whenever she wants. Even on the same day." Astrid paused. "From what DiStephan told me of your homeland, I believe you have no such laws. I believe that once a woman marries, she must stay with her husband for life and cannot marry again, even if her husband dies."

Vinchi looked away quickly, as if Astrid had secretly discovered he'd been thinking about all these things.

"But that is not a problem if we all go to Guell," Astrid said quietly.

They stood in the flickering candlelight of the practice room, watching Margreet while she joyfully swung a weapon of iron against an imaginary foe.

Chapter Fifty-Seven

"Awaken."

The familiar voice sounded distant. Wendill shifted in his sleep. Every joint and muscle ached. He'd been sleeping in the same position too long.

Gradually, Wendill began to notice the sounds of bare branches groaning as they rubbed against each other and chirping birds claiming their territory. The smell of damp earth surrounded him, and his mouth tasted of chalk and dust. He shivered at the chill that permeated his body.

Wendill remembered. When Norah had fallen into the Dragon's Well at Limru, he had curled himself around the mouth of the well, transforming himself into a rock dragon of his own making to seal and protect the well throughout winter. Now came the time to wake up and transform his stone body back into flesh and muscle and blood.

His wakefulness increased, and Wendill poured his thought into his body, willing the transition. On Dragon's Head, he'd been trapped until the sacrifice of the Scalding had broken the barrier embedded in the stone surrounding him, but here Wendill's transformation could come easily.

He reached far underground with his awareness, searching until he sensed thin ribbons of water. He called to them through the earth and drew them into his body. Slowly, his stone-being softened and transformed. He uncurled his body from the mouth of the Dragon's Well, mindful of the aches and pains resulting from a long period of immobility. Once straightened, he rose slowly from his hands and knees to face the one who had called him to awaken. "Taddeo."

His fellow dragon now gazed beyond the Dragon's Well at the Temple of Limru, whose branches were just beginning to sprout yellow-green leaf buds, giving the temple a warm glow. "The last time I was here," Taddeo said softly, "this place had been desecrated in blood. I did not expect you and Norah to restore it."

"We did nothing. This is how we found it when we arrived."

Taddeo's jaw slackened in astonishment. Wendill smiled. Few had the ability to surprise Taddeo, and Wendill relished this moment, already thinking how he'd remember it fondly for many years to come. After all, Taddeo had always been the one who seemed to know everything, and very little escaped his notice.

"But there was an agreement," Taddeo sputtered, now distressed. "No dragon would ever clean up the blood spilled by man in a sacred place."

Wendill's smile widened. "No dragon did."

Taddeo paused, squinting while trying to make sense of it.

Even though Wendill enjoyed toying with Taddeo, experience had proven that such enjoyment tasted sweetest when short lived. "Norah detected evidence of the Scalding. We believe she restored the temple."

"Astrid?"

"Norah found her scent everywhere. In the trees, on the grounds, around the fire pit where bodies were burned. It must have been the Scalding."

Wendill loved the Temple of Limru at this time of year. Although the tall tree-top branches still formed a canopy covering the temple, sunlight streamed through, coaxing new blades of grass to shoot through the temple floor, along with early purple and white flowers of spring. In just another week or so the branches would leaf out and shade the temple throughout the day. This time—this day—felt like transformation at its best.

"Where is Norah?"

Wendill stepped toward the polished stone edge of the mouth he'd protected throughout the winter and looked down into the well. He'd pushed Norah into the empty well to keep her protected, and now her body floated vertically in clear water.

Startled by the sight, Wendill dove toward the well's edge, skidding across the ground on his stomach. He plunged one arm into the icy water. His skin numbed quickly, but his hand sank into Norah's soft, floating hair, and he grabbed a fistful, hoisting her to the surface. Now reaching with both hands under her armpits, Wendill hauled her out of the water. "Norah!"

Taddeo knelt, placing his hand on her face. "She is alive. Bring her to the pit, and I will build a fire."

Wendill scooped Norah's drenched, unconscious body into his arms and followed Taddeo through the temple to the fire pit filled with the scorched bones of the Keepers of Limru. "I regret having failed you," he said to Taddeo. "I did not imagine her tears would fill the well so quickly."

Taddeo laughed. "Norah is fine. What else makes you think you have failed?"

Wendill hesitated, recalling everything Taddeo had asked of him to make sure he hadn't forgotten any part of it. "I haven't accomplished what you wanted."

After gathering broken pieces of fallen limbs and moss dried from winter, Taddeo arranged the kindling inside the pit. "What has happened is far better than what I had hoped." Taddeo paused, rearranging a few pieces of wood. "And we are on the verge of something that will make our goals far easier to achieve."

"Going home? Is it time?"

Taddeo nodded. "There is much to be done before we can find our way and it may take a great deal of time, but we will soon begin that journey."

CHAPTER FIFTY-EIGHT

Just like every morning since they'd begun traveling to Guell, Margreet woke at the earliest hint of light before dawn. She felt somehow connected to the sun. Or maybe she woke early because she wanted to get an early start on each day and make the most of it. Whatever the reason, her favorite time of day happened now, with the whole world quiet and still, and she could take all the time she wished to simply watch the colors of the sky change from indigo to pale blue. A few wispy clouds ribboned this morning's sky, and she smiled with the anticipation of watching them turn pink and orange.

Weeks ago, Vinchi had traded one of his best weapons with the master of the mansion for horses, bedrolls, and food. Happy with the attention Vinchi had given his sons over the course of the winter and early spring, the master had been generous, providing them with good-natured horses and a wealth of provisions. They'd traveled up through the Southlands and into the Midlands. Last night they'd made camp by the flatlands, good farming land that stretched far to the horizon.

Margreet breathed in the chilly morning air, hugging her bedding tight around her body while she sat up, watching the sky. Only months ago, she had dutifully followed her husband from country to country, territory to territory, keeping camp every time he hunted and tending to his needs after he sold those goods at market. It had been a simple existence and one to which she gave little thought. Under his wing, she'd been protected from the worst cruelties of the world.

On the other side of the fire pit they'd created the night before, Vinchi rolled over in his sleep and a twig cracked beneath him. Margreet watched him until he snored, indicating plenty of time before the others would wake up.

The last several months had been odd. At first, she'd been mortified by being spirited away by Vinchi and Astrid, missing Gershon every minute of every day. Without him, Margreet had felt exposed in the world and trembled at the thought of the danger that most likely lurked around every corner, certain she'd be facing death without Gershon to protect her and keep her safe.

But no danger had emerged.

Instead, Margreet watched her bruises heal and remembered what it was like to have none. For weeks, she'd flinched every time a man had raised his hand for any reason, even if just stretching. Margreet believed she'd become adept at keeping her flinching hidden. Or maybe the others were being kind by pretending not to notice. Either way, she thought of Gershon less and herself more. One week she'd forget her husband existed. The next few weeks, she noticed a deep, dark rage toward him seething in her gut.

And then there was Limru. They'd encountered the frozen icy ghosts by the Forest of Aguille, and Margreet's worst fear had come true. Except for the man up front—the ice ghost she'd seen Astrid embrace—Margreet recognized every face. They'd been her neighbors and friends. They were the Keepers of Limru, and the army of Krystr followers had murdered every one of them.

Margreet had experienced shame walking past the ice ghosts. Why should she have survived when they hadn't? Even though she'd followed her mother's wishes and escaped the slaughter, she wondered if it would have been better to disobey and die by the sides of those who loved and knew her.

The first thin slip of yellow emerged above the horizon, and the sky brightened, pushing the indigo aside.

Margreet had looked for her mother among the ice ghosts, but she wasn't there. But later, after Margreet had called upon everything she'd learned from the Keepers of Limru to honor the dead and renew the temple, she'd seen her mother's spirit rise in the smoke from the fire. Her mother's smile assured Margreet that she'd done the right thing, after all. If she hadn't escaped, no one would be left to do this work, and the spirits of the Keepers of Limru could have been trapped forever. Margreet had set them free, and she realized that she had become a Keeper. The last Keeper of Limru.

Margreet hugged her knees to her chest, watching the wispy clouds drift above the flatlands and change from black to dark red to orange. She knew Astrid worked as a blacksmith and a dragonslayer—Margreet had been fascinated whenever the blacksmith of Limru had let her watch him work. The way the clouds changed made her think of the way that iron changed when plunged into the heart of a fire.

Maybe that's what's happened to me, Margreet thought, staring at the clouds. *Maybe I've been plunged into the heart of a fire and my colors are changing.*

Margreet stood and took a few steps toward the naked fields before her. She twisted the silver ring on her finger for the first time since Limru. She remembered the day Gershon had taken it from his own littlest finger and placed it on hers. Their marriage day. She took the ring off and held it in the palm of her hand.

With all her might, Margreet threw the silver ring high into the air and far away. For a moment, the ring caught the sunlight and sparkled and it spun at lightning speed, end over end, sailing through the air. Somewhere, far out into the field, it landed, kicking up a small cloud of dust.

Margreet's heart raced. For the first time since the slaughter she'd witnessed at Limru, she felt free.

She smiled at the sound of Astrid's whisper in the Northlander language. Margreet turned to see Astrid sit up, while Vinchi still snored nearby. Astrid rubbed her eyes, took a moment to smile at the sunrise, and then gestured as if she wielded a sword.

Margreet whispered back, "Good morning," in her own language. Although the women had learned a few words of each other's language, once they'd begun training together, they'd found they could understand each other quite well without language, something that baffled and seemed to annoy Vinchi.

Several minutes later, the women walked out onto the nearby flatlands with metal practice weapons in hand and began their daily ritual of weapons work in the light of the rising sun, their shadows stretched long and lean across the land.

Beware, the small voice whispered inside Margreet's head. *Be alert!*

Margreet stepped back and held up a warning hand to Astrid, who dropped her weapon to her side. Slowly, Margreet gazed around them, looking for signs of danger. But they were alone. No one could hide on these flatlands, and there was no one else in sight but Vinchi. Margreet shrugged and beckoned to Astrid to resume their practice.

A few minutes later, Margreet's foot caught in a rut left in the field from the fall harvest. She cried out as she crumpled to the ground, letting her weapon fall to one side.

Startled, Astrid babbled with worry, her face drawn and pale. Gently, her hands cradled Margreet's ankle.

"I'm fine," Margreet said, poking and prodding her own ankle to make sure, even though she'd felt nothing pull or pop. The rut had simply tripped her.

That was why the voice had warned her. It knew she would soon be at risk. Margreet had taken precaution. She simply hadn't known what kind of precaution to take.

Astrid spoke again, looking into Margreet's eyes.

"Truly, I'm fine." Margreet let Astrid help her back up on her feet.

Astrid pointed toward the camp where Vinchi still slept, speaking with worry.

Margreet tested her ankle. Dull pain throbbed deep inside. Maybe she'd twisted it, after all. She walked around in a circle. She clenched her jaw as if that could make her feel better. It was good enough to use, and Margreet cared about nothing else.

Finding a better patch of land, Margreet waved Astrid over. "Let's practice here. There aren't any ruts."

They continued practicing, but after they were done and Margreet glanced skyward, she noticed all the wispy clouds had disappeared and darker ones loomed on the horizon.

CHAPTER FIFTY-NINE

Trudging across open fields on a muddy road rutted by the recent passage of carts driven by merchants who should have known better and ridden horses instead, Gershon decided to make his move today.

Thomas walked several paces ahead, heeled by a well trained clerk. Thomas spoke loudly and enthusiastically, while the clerk nodded. They acted oblivious to everything that struck Gershon as obvious: the beauty of the day. The sky shone clear and vivid blue. The sun's warmth raised a few beads of sweat on Gershon's forehead. They'd spent the past few weeks walking through hills and valleys and past farmland breaking free of winter's cold embrace. Now, the distinct tang of salt water hanging in the air replaced the fresh, clean scent of pine. The horizon looked hilly with no body of water in sight, but Gershon convinced himself the next town might likely be a seaport.

Gershon tired of conversations consisting of nothing more than Thomas lecturing excitedly about the Krystr—or Thomas talking about himself. It hadn't been long before Gershon learned that, no matter what Thomas claimed, the man constantly needed all eyes on him and all ears trained on every word he said. At first, Gershon experienced a sense of relief because it meant no one questioned him or asked why he wanted to become a clerk. But now he missed his old life, even without Margreet. He missed the lovely solitude of hunting in the woods, discovering fresh tracks, and making a new kill. He missed preparing the fur of the animals, not to mention the looks of delight from people that saw his work in the marketplace.

Gershon didn't need fancy words or ideas or beliefs. These past few months had taught him that he needed nothing more than his work, and the rest of the world be damned. Until, of course, he was ready to take his furs to market.

"Thomas," he said abruptly, startling himself because he hadn't planned to say anything until they reached the seaport.

The clerk shot an angry look over his shoulder, but Thomas paused and took a step to one side, waiting for Gershon to catch up. "Brother Gershon?"

He cleared his throat to stretch time so he could decide the best thing to say. He stepped between Thomas and the clerk, and the three of them walked forward in step with each other. "I believe the time has come for me to return to my worldly work."

Thomas laughed. "But you are doing that work already right here with me. There is no need to worry!"

"I have no worries," Gershon said, "except that I should be working on my own in my trade as a trapper."

"Liar!" the clerk spouted. "You joined Brother Thomas in good faith, and he will not permit..."

"I can speak for myself," Thomas said cheerfully. Nodding toward the clerk, he added, "Although I do appreciate your concern for my well being."

Placated, the clerk nodded his head abruptly before looking daggers at Gershon.

Turning his attention toward Gershon, Thomas said, "Pray tell...from where does this sudden wanderlust come?"

The clerk shook his head in disgust and softly muttered, "Lust!"

Gershon cleared his throat again, silently reminding himself that Thomas had proven himself to be far more crafty than he'd originally seemed. In town after town, Gershon had witnessed Thomas use smooth words to convince villagers to give them food and shelter. Although Thomas didn't have the clout to help himself to women in the same way he did with the villager's wives in the town where he made his home, Gershon had noticed more than one wife glance at Thomas with either glee or disgust after her husband had been kept busy elsewhere, often with the clerk or Gershon.

It didn't sit right with Gershon. Helping yourself to another man's property boiled down to theft, pure and simple, whether that property be a drinking cup, a goat, or a wife. Once, when he'd broached the subject with Thomas, it resulted in a stream of excuses and nonsensical explanations that ended with Thomas speaking about himself—as usual.

This time Thomas cleared his throat, raised his eyebrows questioningly, and waited for Gershon to answer.

"There is some truth to wanderlust being part of my nature," Gershon said, choosing his words carefully.

The clerk grunted and looked like he'd just smelled something putrid.

"It's a nature not uncommon in my family. My father was a fur trader like me, and his father before him." Gershon shot a pointed look at the clerk, who ignored him. "It's an honest trade."

"Of course," Thomas said, his voice as soft and gentle as spring rain. "How can anyone criticize a trait required in a honorable profession? But you are a soldier of the Krystr now. You have new responsibilities. New priorities. The world is a place full of barbarians, and your newfound calling is to help them." Thomas paused for effect. "That was the agreement you made in exchange for the food and shelter I provided over the course of the winter. Not to mention the training in the ways of the Krystr."

"And the training is far more valuable than food or sleep!" the clerk added.

Thomas waved a shushing hand at the clerk, keeping his gaze on Gershon. "Are you shirking your training?"

The man is a weasel, Gershon thought. *An exceptionally smart one.* "Of course not." Gershon now realized that to break free of this weasel and be rid of him for good, he should lie. "When I go back to my worldly trade, I will travel far and wide into territories where no one has heard of the Krystr. What better way for me to spread the teachings of him than to go directly to the barbarians themselves?"

Thomas's eyes brightened with greed. "And you would convince them that they must share their wealth with the agents of Krystr?"

"Without hesitation," Gershon said, his voice now as smooth as Thomas's had been moments ago. He knew what Thomas meant—Gershon would collect valuable goods and give them to Thomas. "They know me. They trust me. More important, many of them fear me." Gershon paused to gaze at the fields surrounding them and pointed to a distant farm where a man drove an ox and plow. "Think of me as the plow that will prepare the land for your seed. I will do the hard work, and you will reap the benefits."

The clerk pursed his lips, ready to question Gershon's words. Before the clerk could open his mouth, Thomas spoke excitedly. "Yes. I see the possibilities." He took a deep breath, and his voice became more calm and even. "Forgive me for doubting you, Brother Gershon. We have suffered pretenders in the past who drank of our good will and banqueted on our kindness, only to disappear when we needed them most. You do understand."

"Yes," Gershon said, mustering all his will to keep from smiling, "I understand quite well."

For the rest of the morning, Thomas returned to dominating the conversation about his favorite topics, and Gershon let his mind wander. The scent of salt in the air grew stronger and more intoxicating. Before the day's end, he could be on board a ship sailing toward the Northlands or the other side of the Midlands. In either case, he'd likely arrive at a good time to hunt. He'd be glad to be rid of these ridiculous men forever and start his life anew.

⁂

By noon, they reached the outskirts of a seaport. A stray cat sat on the edge of the wooden boardwalk serving as the town's main avenue. Its fur was orange and thick, and the cat busily licked its paws and ran them across the top of its head. An open and empty clamshell lay at the animal's feet.

The simple wooden houses lining the boardwalk were gray and weathered from the sea air. The air weighed thick with the briny and tart smells of fish and clams and shrimp. Although the sun's rays were still warm, a sharp breeze whistling down the boardwalk made Gershon shiver. As they walked into the heart of the seaport, dozens of people crowded the boardwalk: seamen hauling coils of rope or cargo, merchants bargaining for better rates of transport and passage, and townspeople bartering for food and wares.

Gershon's heart lightened at the joy of being in the thick of normal, reasonable people again. Until now, he'd never realized how much he loved his work and his life, and he readied himself to begin with renewed appreciation.

But he stopped short at the sound of a familiar voice.

Gershon scanned the crowd until he saw her, the light in his heart going out like a candle's flame extinguished by the wind, not believing at first what he saw.

In the middle of the boardwalk, Margreet walked toward him, flanked by Vinchi and the boy who had kidnapped her.

Chapter Sixty

Margreet caught sight of her husband. Her eyes widened and her heart seemed to stop beating for a moment. In that moment, she realized that for the past several days she'd forgotten he existed, caught up instead in the excitement of starting a new life in Guell.

Without thinking, she choked on empty air. She jerked to a halt and clutched Vinchi's arm out of the habit of reaching for the nearest man to protect her.

Deep in conversation with Astrid, Vinchi stopped at Margreet's touch, his smile transforming into an alert expression of concern as Margreet curled her fingertips tighter into his forearm. "What is it?"

Margreet imagined herself frozen like the ice ghosts that had guarded the entrance to the Forest of Aguille. She couldn't will herself to speak or move. Instead, she kept seeing what her life had been like during the past few years. She remembered the terror she'd experienced after witnessing the Krystr army's attack on the Temple of Limru and its Keepers. Guilt washed over her again for being the only survivor of that attack. She remembered the first day she'd met Gershon. His gentleness and kind voice. And later his promise to protect her from anyone who might do her harm. The way she'd come alive again the first time they'd made love. The adventure of travel that gave her the opportunity to journey by his side.

For a moment, she wanted to race across the boardwalk and through the crowd so she could jump into his arms and remember how safe she'd once felt there.

"Margreet," Vinchi whispered urgently. He and Astrid reached for the daggers tucked under their belts. "What troubles you?"

She realized they didn't notice him in the crowd, and only then did she realize he dressed in a simple robe belted at the waist like the much shorter men flanking him. "Gershon," she whispered.

At the mention of his name, she saw her husband's gaze drop to her hand on Vinchi's arm. Even from this distance, she recognized the darkening of her husband's face. Quickly, she let go of Vinchi's arm and let her hand drift back to her side where it belonged.

Astrid whispered, "Gershon," noticing him at last.

Vinchi spoke rapidly to Astrid in the Northlander's language and then took a deep breath. To Margreet, he said, "We can protect you."

Even though she watched her husband stare at her with growing rage furrowing his brow, Margreet whispered. "I love him."

Vinchi spoke rapidly again to Astrid, who shushed him.

Margreet yelped at the hands grasping her shoulders and turning her. For a moment, Margreet didn't recognize Astrid who held on tightly to her shoulders.

Looking steadily into Margreet's eyes, Astrid spoke the only words she'd ever learned of her language. "Dragon," Astrid said slowly. "Sword."

"You must excuse me," Margreet said out of habit. "My husband is waiting for me."

"Incompetent," Astrid said, holding on tightly to Margreet, refusing to let her go. Astrid looked at Gershon and said it again. "Incompetent."

"No!" Margreet protested, still forgetting Astrid couldn't understand her. "Of course we argue. Every married couple fights. It's to be expected—that's part of what marriage is. Sometimes he gets carried away. It doesn't mean he doesn't love me."

Tears welled in Astrid's eyes and she held on steadily. "Incompetent," she said softly.

"He is not incompetent—he is my husband! I love him." Margreet wriggled but failed to escape Astrid's grip. Frustrated, Margreet cried. "He is my protector!"

Astrid whispered one last time. "Incompetent."

"Margreet!"

She looked up, and the sound of his voice made her feel that she was awakening from a dream.

Gershon walked toward her now, the men still flanking him.

Feeling Astrid's grip fall away, Margreet turned to face him. Now all the other memories came rushing back. The sting of his hand across her face. The soreness of her face after being punched. The feeling of hopelessness that her life would ever improve.

"Our marriage is over," Margreet said fiercely, standing tall. "Be on your way."

For a moment, a flicker of relief seemed to cross Gershon's face.

"How can you let a lowly, evil creature speak to you that way?" one of the robed men said to Gershon.

Gershon looked briefly into her eyes as if searching for approval and then looked away. It was what he did every time he lied. "She is nothing to me. I can serve the Krystr better without being burdened by this woman."

Vinchi and Astrid tried to lead Margreet away, but the robed men blocked them. "This is an atrocity!" one of them said. "The Creator God sees all and knows all. These cannot be followers of the Krystr—otherwise, they would obey their duty and give her to you for your own purposes."

The crowd circled them now, quietly watching.

The older robed man spoke to the crowd directly. "By the law of the Creator God, let our god prove this man to be right and true to his word. Let the Creator God prove this wretched woman to be a liar and a creature of evil!" He paused purposefully and for effect. "I call for a trial by combat."

The crowd broke out into excited conversation, and a few people cheered.

Margreet breathed a sigh of relief as Vinchi and Astrid pressed close, wedging their shoulders against hers. She knew enough about the followers of the Krystr to know what the robed man had just done. Gershon would fight on his own behalf against a man who would fight on Margreet's behalf. The followers believed their god already knew which one of them told the truth: Gershon or Margreet, and surely that god would side with Gershon. If Gershon won the battle, Margreet would suffer the fate of his choosing, which would likely mean imprisonment or death. Margreet's only chance meant finding a man who could defeat Gershon in battle.

Turning to Vinchi, who had paled with fear, she said, "Will you fight for me?"

"I can't."

"But you are an expert swordsman. You teach people how to fight. Who better than you?"

Vinchi took a deep breath, appearing to steady himself. As the crowd around them dispersed in anticipation of the impending trial, he placed a tender hand on Margreet's shoulder. "You forget—we're in Daneland now. Here, the law says you must fight on your own behalf."

Suddenly, Margreet's hands turned numb. "What?"

"You," Vinchi said, "are the only one allowed to fight Gershon."

CHAPTER SIXTY-ONE

An hour later, Margreet held a black woolen sling containing a large rock in her hands. The cloth scratched her hands, and it smelled like a sheep that had been drenched in a summer downpour. She took slow, deep breaths in an effort to control the terror she felt at the thought of facing her husband in their trial by combat. But the sky remained clear and the sun warmed her face. That simple comfort gave her strength.

"The footwork is much the same," Vinchi said as Astrid paced at his side. "And when you use the sling, it's much the same as delivering an overhead blow with the sword. You use the same double-handed grip—just grip the sling, not the sword."

Along with the entire population of the seacoast town, they'd walked a stone's throw from the houses on the outskirts to the beach beyond the harbor's boardwalk. Here, sand mixed with dirt, rocks, and broken shells from where the seabirds had dropped shellfish to break them open. Down the beach, Gershon dug a pit while his robed companions watched, their distant voices offering advice.

Margreet watched her husband dig, overwhelmed with sudden emotion. "Don't let them bury me in that pit." Her voice trembled, and she wiped the tears from her eyes before they could fall. "If he kills me, I want to be with my own people, not here."

Vinchi's soft touch on her shoulder startled Margreet and she turned to look at him.

"No one will be buried in that pit," Vinchi said. "I already told you what that pit is for. Remember?"

Margreet cleared her throat and regained her focus. "It's the pit he'll stand in when he fights me."

"And how deep will it be?" Vinchi said.

Margreet looked at him with a steady gaze. "Deep enough so that my feet will be at the same level as his chest."

Vinchi nodded. "The Danelanders are good people. They believe you must fight your own trial, but they make sure it will be a fair fight. That's why they make him dig the pit himself—to tire his arms. And while he's digging, we have time to practice."

"But he'll have a dagger," Margreet said.

"And he might get a cut or two at your feet. But you have a big rock that you'll be swinging at his head. Remember your footwork, and you should be fine." Vinchi paused. "You are by far the best student I have ever taught, Margreet. If you were anyone else, I'd have concern. I wouldn't let Astrid fight him. She may be a good dragonslayer, but she'll need years of training before she can defeat someone like Gershon."

Astrid looked up at the mention of her name.

Vinchi let his fingers trail as he drew his hand away from Margreet's shoulder. "But you can do this. Remember that."

Taking a deep breath of sea air, Margreet nodded and took a firmer grip on her sling.

෧෪

An hour later, a few hundred villagers circled around the pit, careful to stay a good distance from its edge to give Margreet the freedom to walk around it. Gershon's robed companions took his shovel and melded into the crowd while he sat on the pit's edge and jumped to the bottom. His jaw set in determination, he withdrew a dagger from his belt.

One villager stepped forward to explain the rules. "The man must remain in the pit at all times, but the woman may circle or back away from the pit's edge as she wishes. They will fight only as long as the sun remains above the horizon, preferably until one of them dies. If they both survive until dark, then they will walk their separate ways tomorrow, and no winner will be declared. If one passes out after being struck, the time given to recover will last until the sun's highest point of the day or its lowest, whichever comes first."

As the crowd cheered all around her, Margreet had never felt so alone in her life. She wanted to leave Gershon and start a new life in Guell. She didn't want to kill him. She wished she'd come a day later or earlier to this town, but maybe Gershon still would have been here.

Maybe he would have been in any town where she sought passage to Guell. Maybe she should see him one last time. Maybe it would help her remember who she had been before becoming his wife. Maybe she needed to remember how she'd lost her way so that she would never lose it again.

A town official stepped forward and made a dropping signal with one hand. He shouted to the crowd that cheered in response. He then gestured to Margreet and Gershon before darting back into the crowd.

Vinchi believes in me, Margreet thought. *I can do this.*

Gripping the sling so tightly that her knuckles whitened, Margreet kept her knees and body low as she took big, wide steps toward the pit and took a swing at Gershon's head.

He ducked, and the missed blow threw Margreet so far off balance that she stumbled.

Gershon took a weak stab at her ankles, missing by several inches.

Surprised, Margreet looked down and into his eyes. She tottered away from the pit's edge to regroup.

"Why did you leave me?" Gershon said softly.

"I didn't leave. I was kidnapped."

"But you let him take you. You let him touch you."

Margreet was confused, one moment savoring the freedom she'd discovered without her husband and the next moment remembering that being his wife meant being legally bound to him. "What could I have done? How could I have stopped him?" Margreet walked slowly around the edge of the pit, and a few women shouted encouragement from the crowd.

"You seem to be doing fine right now. Did he teach you how to fight? Did he put his hands on you?" Gershon ground his teeth, and his face darkened. He threw himself against the pit's wall, stabbing as far as he could reach toward Margreet, missing her as she pivoted back on one foot.

"Of course he taught me. He taught me to protect myself from men like you!" Margreet pivoted forward again, swinging with accuracy and grazing the side of Gershon's head.

Before he could react, she stepped away from the pit again.

Gershon clutched the side of his head, gazing at his wife in horror. "You struck me!"

"You challenged me to this fight!" Strangely delighted that she'd struck a partial blow, excitement rushed through Margreet's veins. "You could have walked past me when you saw me. You didn't have to let anyone know I'm your wife. We could have been free of each other so easily."

Furious, Gershon scrambled to climb out of the pit, but the town official ran forward, waving his arms and using his foot to shove Gershon back into the pit. After issuing a warning, the official retreated again.

Margreet circled the pit slowly, watching Gershon turn so that he always faced her. He has the advantage of timing, Vinchi had told her. No matter how fast you try to move around the circle, he can turn faster. But there are other ways to defeat him.

"You have lain with him," Gershon said, his voice low and guttural. "I can smell him on you."

Several paces back from the edge of the pit, Margreet rose from her fighting stance, released one hand from the sling, and placed both hands on her hips as she stood tall. "I have done no such thing! I have been faithful to you since the day you claimed me as your wife!"

"Liar!"

Stepping forward, Margreet gestured wildly with her free hand as she typically did every time they argued. "I am no liar! And what of you, Gershon? Have you remained faithful to me? Or have you been bedding any woman who looks at you twice. Just as you've been doing for the past year."

"How dare you compare yourself to me! I have the right to live as I wish. You have the right to obey me."

Infuriated, Margreet's neck and face burned hot. "How dare you treat me with such disregard! I'm the one who—"

"Margreet—no! Watch your step!"

Margreet halted at the sound of Vinchi's warning voice. Remembering everything he'd taught her during the past months, she quickly checked her position and distance from Gershon and discovered she had stepped nearly close enough for him to stab her.

Regaining her senses, Margreet quickly pivoted a step back, eluding Gershon's stab at her retreating ankle.

"Badly fought," she said softly to Gershon. Regaining her composure, Margreet smiled at his failure.

She knew him well enough to recognize the slight look of hurt in his eyes and for a moment felt sorry for him.

"I never should have taken pity on the likes of you. I should have left you on the streets where you belong." Despite his words, pain stung Gershon's voice. Sniffing, he held up his dagger blade for a moment to wipe it free of dirt.

Margreet responded, just as she had in training to the many cues Vinchi had provided. Taking advantage of Gershon's momentary lapse of attention, she sprang forward and delivered the mightiest swing she could muster to the side of his head.

The rock inside the sling connected with a meaty thud, and Gershon had only time enough to look up at Margreet in wide-eyed surprise before he collapsed on the bottom of the pit in which he stood.

Chapter Sixty-Two

The villager, who had signaled the beginning of the trial by combat, rushed to the edge of the pit and jumped inside, disappearing from view.

Margreet bit the inside of her cheek to keep from crying. How could she have done something so horrible? What if she had taken the man's life? When she'd hidden during the slaughter at Limru and later seen the carnage left behind, she'd promised herself she'd never hurt any living thing, not even the men who destroyed the Temple of Limru and its Keepers.

Not even the man who had murdered her mother.

Margreet believed that if she allowed herself to give in to blood lust that it would overpower her and make her no better than the murderers she despised.

And now she might have killed the man who had taken her in after the slaughter at Limru, given her shelter, and helped her want to keep living. How could she have killed Gershon?

She wished she'd never met Vinchi and Astrid. She wished they'd never stolen her away from Gershon. How were they any better than her husband? Taking her away without asking Margreet if she so desired? If she'd stayed with Gershon, they'd at least both be alive, and Margreet's hands would be clean of his blood.

She stood frozen in time that never seemed to end.

"He lives!" the villager cried from inside the pit. Placing both hands on the edge of Gershon's pit, the villager hoisted himself out of it. He shouted to the crowd, "Gershon sleeps, but he lives."

Margreet's heart lightened, and she silently thanked the gods of Limru for their mercy.

Turning toward Margreet, the villager reminded her of the rules. "By law, his time to recover is the sun's highest point of the day or its lowest, whichever happens first." The villager pointed toward the sky. "Today the sun reaches its highest point when it rises above that tree."

Margreet followed his pointing finger to see a lone tree at the edge of the village, and the sun slightly to its right. It wouldn't take long before the sun hung directly above the tree.

She breathed a sigh of relief. She'd hit Gershon hard, and he might not wake up until tonight or maybe even tomorrow. All her regrets and anger at Vinchi and Astrid melted away as she beamed, facing them.

Vinchi ran forward to join her side. "No, Margreet! Pay attention! However long it takes, you must keep your attention on him and be ready to fight again."

The fear in his eyes startled her, and she nodded.

"Back to the spectators with you!" the villager yelled, pushing Vinchi away from Margreet. "This is her fight—not yours!"

Taking Vinchi's words to heart, Margreet clung to the sling in her hands, ready to bash Gershon's head again, should he rise from the depths of the pit.

❧❧

An hour later, Margreet sat near the edge of the pit, watching the motionless Gershon. Still holding the sling, she'd spent the past several minutes talking quietly to him. Even though he still slept, she needed to say goodbye to him and decided that he would be able to hear her and understand.

"When I lost Limru and my mother, I lost everything," she said softly. "I assumed I'd never love anyone again. And when I first met you, I saw you as my salvation. I knew you'd take care of me, and that was all I wanted." Margreet paused. "I never imagined how much I'd come to love you."

Gershon had collapsed on his side, and Margreet sat so she could watch his face. For a moment, his eyelids fluttered.

Margreet gripped the sling tighter, ready to jump to her feet and fight him again.

But Gershon's face remained without expression, and his eyelids were still again.

Breathing a slow sigh of relief, Margreet continued. "I admired your strength and the way everyone seemed to hold you in high regard. I appreciated the food you brought home and felt gratitude, knowing I'd never go hungry again if I stayed by your side. That made me want to make your life easier and better in any way I could muster."

Margreet's throat tightened and she paused until she could speak again. "When we first married, I knew that luck had finally come my way. I believed you were a great gift brought to me by the gods themselves. My own life became beautiful and rich and perfect. I'd never dreamed I could love a man the way I loved you."

The corner of Gershon's mouth twitched.

Beware! the small voice inside Margreet cried.

Margreet nodded her understanding. She studied his otherwise motionless form, wondering if he had come awake again and only pretended to sleep.

"But then you struck me," she said softly, the painful memory straining her voice. "I thought you'd simply made a terrible mistake. Everyone has faults, and I was willing to overlook one mistake. I remembered our happy times and knew we could be happy again. No matter how many times you struck me, I always thought we could be happy again."

"Stay alert, Margreet!" Vinchi called.

She stared at her husband's face, unable to decide whether she wanted to memorize it or forget it.

"Wake up, Gershon!" one of the robed men called from the crowd, growing restless and vocal. "Do not let her control you! A man decides his own fate!"

As more people cried out, Margreet focused her attention solely on Gershon. "Let me go," she whispered. "Let us both be free again."

"It's almost time!" Vinchi shouted. "It's close to over!"

Stay alert! the voice inside her warned.

Keeping a careful eye on Gershon, Margreet stood slowly, still clutching the sling. Although she still loved the man she had first known him to be, she felt ready to begin a new life in Guell.

"The trial ends now!" the villager declared. "The Creator God has ruled that the winner of this trial is—"

Happily, Margreet gazed up to see the sun positioned directly above the tree.

She gasped as strong fingers dug into her ankles and yanked her feet out from beneath her. Her head hit the ground with a sickening thud when she fell. Disoriented and stunned beyond reason, she thought she heard Astrid scream as Gershon leaned over the edge of his pit and plunged his dagger between his wife's ribs and into her heart.

CHAPTER SIXTY-THREE

Astrid stood in disbelieving silence, staring at Margreet's collapsed figure and the startled villager who had been interrupted while declaring her the just and true winner of her trial by combat with Gershon.

Gershon pulled his dagger free from Margreet's limp body, and the villager cleared his voice to amend his announcement. "The Creator God has ruled that the winner of this trial is Gershon."

The villagers crowded around the pit fell silent. No one seemed to want to move.

"Is this a dream?" Vinchi said softly. He turned to Astrid, tears streaming steadily from the outer corners of his eyes and down the planes of his face. "Am I dreaming?"

Astrid's throat choked so tightly that she couldn't speak. Instead, she shook her head.

Vinchi screamed like an animal being slaughtered, rushing forward to barrel past the villager and drop to Margreet's side. He pressed his hand tightly against her heart, and Astrid watched as blood stained his hand and clothes.

Astrid hadn't let herself cry since the day she'd first been sold to Temple and he'd thrown the blanket she'd used to hide her scarred body into the smithing fire.

Blacksmiths don't cry, Astrid told herself as she walked toward Vinchi. *It creates a danger in the smithery. You can hurt yourself too easily if you cry when you smite iron. You can hurt yourself so much that you will never be the same again.*

Astrid pushed away memories of the first time she'd seen Margreet, fighting with Gershon at the market. She shunned the discord between herself and Margreet, who initially fought with Astrid and Vinchi in the same way she had with her husband. Most of all, Astrid put aside the happiness she'd known since she and Margreet had become training partners, helping each other learn a skill that could save their lives.

Astrid knelt by Vinchi, placed a hand on the grip of the dragonslayer's sword hanging from his belt, and withdrew it. Rising, she faced the pit.

At first, the villager who had announced the verdict pled with Vinchi and failed to notice Astrid. He spoke a Midlander language that Astrid didn't understand, but she didn't care what he told Vinchi.

Astrid cared about one thing only, determined to see it through.

She saw Gershon, leaning against the pit's wall with one hand covering his face. Did he feel regret?

Astrid didn't care. She held Starlight's grip with both hands, aiming the blade at the top of Gershon's ugly head.

The villager finally noticed Astrid's presence, and he jumped to his feet, leaving Vinchi holding Margreet's body in his arms. The villager jumped in front of Astrid, waving his arms, his face paled in terror.

Astrid shoved the villager aside, using a technique she and Margreet had practiced, shifting her bare hands to hold onto the blade, hooking the crossguard behind the man's knees, and yanking to trip him before he knew what had happened.

She didn't feel the pain as each sharp edge of the blade cut her hands. In practice they always wore gloves to protect their skin. Flushed with anger, Astrid felt nothing as she shifted her hands back on the sword's grip.

She swung her blade from above her head, cutting straight down until the sharp iron cleaved into the edge of the pit.

Shaken, Gershon looked up at her from the opposite side of the pit, his eyes brimming with tears. For a moment, the knuckles on his hand still holding the dagger turned white as he gripped it tighter.

Astrid wanted to drive Starlight through him until he begged her to stop. Or she could spear him through the neck like a lizard. The overwhelming desire to chop him into bits rushed like blood to her head, dizzying her for a moment.

Her arms itched violently and she resisted the urge to scratch them. She knew the scars she'd managed to keep locked in place on her skin all winter long were now crawling all over it. She detected a few scars crawl onto the back of her hand but didn't care if anyone could see them.

Gazing squarely into her eyes, Gershon loosened his grip and let the dagger fall to his feet.

Astrid wrenched her sword free from where she had struck it into the edge of the pit. She pointed it at Gershon's face, knowing he wouldn't understand the words she would say but that he might understand the intent.

Astrid's voice shook with rage when she spoke. "Your hold on this woman is over. You took her life, but you cannot touch her spirit."

She is part of me now, Astrid realized. *I will set her spirit free, but she will always be part of me.* She took a deep breath to steady herself, suddenly aware of Vinchi's heaving sobs behind her. Ready to give Starlight back to him, she hoped the sword would bring some comfort.

Chapter Sixty-Four

Gershon boarded the next ship that sailed from the seaport village, accompanied by the robed men.

Taking pity, an elderly woman brought an armful of wool and linen scraps, taking it upon herself to wrap Margreet's body until it looked like a caterpillar encased in a cocoon. Now wearing clean clothes and skin washed free of her blood, Vinchi lifted Margreet's body and draped it across one horse's back.

Astrid paced the boarded walk by the harbor, watching the horizon. Now that Starlight hung at Vinchi's side again, she kept one hand on the grip of Falling Star in case Gershon decided to return. Even though she noticed the shadows growing longer, she still jumped in surprise each time Vinchi touched her shoulder, approaching her from behind. "It's time," he said.

Nodding, Astrid followed him. She saw no need to speak. They both knew what they were doing and where they were going. It took all Astrid's energy just to keep breathing and the thought of trying to talk overwhelmed her.

They rode until dusk and rose with the sun the following day. Between good weather and the luxury of riding horses instead of walking, they traveled the long distance quickly. At the end of each day, Vinchi lifted Margreet's cocooned body from the horse's back and laid it on a small blanket he used to cover the ground. Vinchi would then make their fire for the night, keeping the body close to the flames to keep the animals away from it. Although wrapped in layers of wool and linen, the odor of decay had become their constant companion.

After the first few days, Astrid dared to break the silence between them one evening. "Does it bother you?" Astrid asked as she arranged the kindling she'd gathered from the surrounding woods.

Vinchi started at the sound of her voice, like a man who had grown accustomed to being alone. "What?"

Astrid nodded at Margreet's body. "You keep her under your nose all day. I could smell you a mile away. Does it bother you?"

Kneeling by the body, Vinchi smoothed out the places where the fabric had wrinkled from the day's journey. "It reminds me of what happened. I told her she wouldn't die." He shook his head in disgust.

"It's not your fault. You didn't kill her."

"Of course it's not my fault. It's yours." Vinchi spoke evenly, but rage bubbled under his words. "If we had stayed on the winter route, if we had gone further south, she'd still be alive."

Astrid opened her mouth, ready to argue, but then stopped. Her shoulders slumped in defeat.

The next morning, they arrived at the Temple of Limru. The sun's rays streamed through the canopy of sacred trees rising above the top of the forest, and the yellow-green leaves glowed like fireflies. The crisp, cool air smelled like fresh earth broken by plants rising through its surface.

Astrid breathed in the difference. No longer a site desecrated by a massacre, the temple's sacred trees seemed to welcome them with open arms.

At the edge of the temple itself, Vinchi dismounted, took Margreet's body in his arms, and carried it into the center of the stone circle she'd created months ago.

Astrid tied their horses to a tree at the edge of the woods and watched him.

After placing Margreet's body in the center of the stone circle, Vinchi reached into the cloth bag hanging from his belt. Frowning, he searched without success. Withdrawing his hand, he pointed at the weapons bag he'd unstrapped from his back and placed on the ground by the horses.

Flint. He needed the flint from his bag to start the fire.

Astrid opened the bag, pushing aside the few weapons remaining. But when she reached into the bottom of the bag, she cried out in surprise as something sharp nicked her hand.

It wasn't the kind of sharpness she'd expect from a weapon. This sharpness reminded her of a lizard catching its claws against her skin in a fight.

Looking inside the bag, Astrid froze. Gathering her thoughts and her senses, she withdrew a leather shoe to which the claws of a lizard had been attached.

It was the kind of shoe that would leave the footprint of the monster that had killed Sigurthor in the Northland mountains near Guell and then stolen Starlight away.

CHAPTER SIXTY-FIVE

Even from a short distance, Astrid saw Vinchi's face pale at the sight of the lizard-claw shoe she held up from his weapons bag.

She withdrew Falling Star as she strode forward, holding the lizard-claw shoe in the other hand. "You're the monster that murdered Sigurthor."

"No!" In an act of surrender, Vinchi held his open palms toward her. "He was already dead when I found him. He'd asked me to meet him, he wasn't there, and I went looking for him. I simply picked up the sword and ran his dead body through with it."

Astrid paused at the edge of the stone circle. "Why?"

Vinchi hesitated. "Because he brokered the marriage between Gershon and Margreet. Sigurthor was supposed to find a wife for me. He took Gershon's money after he took mine. He knew of Margreet and he told Gershon where to find her. He told Gershon instead of me. Margreet met and married Gershon because he paid more to Sigurthor than I did. And if she'd married me, she'd still be alive."

"Why didn't you tell me?" Astrid shook the lizard-claw shoe at him. "And what is this?"

"I had them made special. The lizard claws give more grip in the mountains. They're my climbing shoes."

"Why did you lie? When I showed the tracks to you."

"My own shoes needed mending one night, and I wore the only other pair I own—the ones with the lizard claws. You're not the only one who spent time outside alone."

"But why lie?"

Vinchi swallowed hard, still keeping his palms open to Astrid. "I knew who you were the moment I saw you. I knew if you had gone looking for Starlight, you had probably found Sigurthor. And I'll have no one accuse me of a murder I never committed."

His reasoning made sense, but he'd lied to her. That meant he couldn't be trusted, and Astrid still had a long journey ahead. She said, "Get your things, take your horse, and go."

Again, Vinchi drew his breath in sharply as if preparing to argue, but he paused and nodded his consent instead. He unbuckled the sheath from his belt and handed Starlight to her. "You can make better use of this sword than I have."

Surprised, Astrid accepted the sheathed sword. Wrapping her hand around it brought back memories of DiStephan's embrace, and the sunlight seemed to brighten for a moment. But thinking of DiStephan heightened her disappointment in Vinchi. "You have proven yourself to be a man of low character." She handed the lizard shoe back to him. "Go now. Before I'm tempted to use this sword to convince you."

"I want to stay. I need to say goodby to her."

Astrid pulled Starlight from its sheath and pointed it at him. "I'm the one who protects her now."

Vinchi jerked as if she'd slapped him. His sad expression grew deeper. "If you should ever need me," he said, "I'm going back to the Southlands. I'm done with travel and merchanting." Casting a final long look at Margreet's body, Vinchi mounted his horse and disappeared into the forest.

Astrid had kept the flint she'd found in his weapons bag. She arranged kindling all around Margreet's body, lit it on fire, and stepped outside the stone circle.

Astrid walked to the northernmost point. "I don't know the gods you worship. I barely know my own. I don't remember what you said, but I call on them for help."

She continued to the eastern point. "I call out to the Keepers of Limru, those whose spirits we set free. Margreet helped you. Will you help her?"

Astrid kept walking around the outer edge of the stone circle until she paused at the southernmost point. She didn't know what else to say, so she said two of the three words she'd learned of Margreet's language. Holding Starlight high above her head, Astrid said the words for "dragon" and "sword."

Finally, she walked to the western point of the circle and sat, watching Margreet's body catch fire and studying the smoke rising from it. Sometime later, she thought the smoke briefly took the shape of Margreet, but Astrid couldn't tell if she witnessed the woman's spirit or if the smoke had changed because of a shift in the wind. For hours, she thought about Margreet and Lenore and the new burning desire that kindled the fire in Astrid's heart.

A memory stirred in Astrid's soul. She opened the pouch that hung from her belt, removed the gift that Margreet had given to her since they'd first come here, and pinned it to her shirt.

Whether it would lead to danger or not, Astrid wanted everyone to see that she wore the tree-shaped pin in remembrance of the last Keeper of Limru.

Chapter Sixty-Six

The next morning, Astrid wakened slowly to a strange sensation brushing her nose. She opened her eyes to the harsh light of day, which blinded her for several moments. Her vision adjusted, and she found herself staring into familiar eyes.

"Smoke," Astrid said at the young lizard gazing at her.

She found herself sprawled on the ground by the outer edge of the stone circle, where she must have fallen asleep. While Smoke kept a steady watch on her, Fire and Slag chased each other a few feet away.

"I see you still appear to be coming apart at the seams."

Her eyes still adjusting to the light, Astrid sat up and twisted to see Taddeo walking inside the stone circle.

She automatically tugged her sleeves down to cover as much skin as possible, an old habit from childhood when her scars covered her body and she wanted no one to see them. They'd begun moving the day Margreet had died, and now Astrid seemed to have no control of them.

"I understood you would not travel the winter route. I understood you would stay in Guell and return to your anvil."

Astrid jumped in surprise as Smoke vaulted into her lap and began investigating her clothing in case it might hide secret stashes of food. "A merchant stole Starlight, and I had to get it back."

"You can always make another sword."

"Not like that one," Astrid said softly, suddenly happy to see the young lizards again. Happy they'd survived the winter. Happy they were alive. "I made Starlight for DiStephan. It's all I have left of him."

The brittle, burned bone fragments of the Keepers of Limru crunched underneath Taddeo's feet with every careful step he took. "But you said you only protect the people who pay you. You said the foreigners can protect themselves." He knelt and laid a gentle hand on the most recent bones burned inside the stone circle. "You said they were people who would think nothing of invading Guell were it not protected by Dragon's Head and the lizards that come to lay their eggs there. You said they were people who would raid your village and steal your goods."

Awash with sudden anxiety, Astrid lunged. Smoke protested with a clucking sound and tumbled unharmed from her lap. She rushed to the edge of the stone circle but hesitated to enter the sacred space. "Please," she said softly. "Let her be."

Smiling, Taddeo stood. "You did this?" He spread his arms to include the entire stone circle and the Temple beyond it.

"Some of it. I helped." Astrid pointed at the bones by Taddeo's feet. "She built the circle and put the dead at rest."

"How is that possible?"

"She was a Keeper of the Temple."

Taddeo's jaw slackened in genuine surprise. "The Keepers were murdered."

"One survived."

Taddeo nodded, absorbing the information. "A foreigner."

"Yes," Astrid said. "A foreigner."

"But you wanted nothing to do with foreigners."

"I was wrong," Astrid said softly. "I first met her as a foreigner, but she became my friend."

"I see. So you have changed your mind about foreigners. Perhaps not all of them are so bad."

"Yes," Astrid said. "I've changed my mind."

Taddeo sighed heavily, walked across the circle's interior, and stepped across the stones enclosing it to join Astrid's side. "I did not give you much choice when Norah claimed your arm. She was dying, and it was the only way to save her life. I believe the time has come to allow her to return the favor."

"I'm not dying."

Taddeo placed the same gentle hand on Astrid's shoulder as he'd just placed on Margreet's bones. "No. But your pain is palpable."

Astrid felt a sudden lightness of hope. "Can you stop it?"

"No. But you can feel better."

Astrid followed Taddeo into the Temple of Limru. "That's the Dragon's Well," she said, remembering it. But months ago, it had been dry. Now it brimmed with clear water. Astrid pointed at the water. "Where did that come from?"

Instead of answering, Taddeo gave her a slight smile.

"Scalding," Norah said lightly as she rose from the center of the well, her hair and clothes dry as water dripped from her. She smiled and held a hand out to Astrid.

"When you were children," Taddeo said, "she could have devoured you whole. It was your family that placed the two of you inside that cage, and they manipulated you both. They knew a young dragon like Norah would never have the heart to kill you, even if it meant she starved. When she chewed you, it was to drink as little of your blood as she needed to survive. That is why your skin is scarred. Because she chose to let you live while keeping herself alive at the same time."

Norah floated in the air above the well, still holding one hand out to Astrid.

Taddeo's words confirmed something Astrid had always suspected. How else could she have survived being caged with a dragon for so many years?

Then she remembered a dream she'd had many months ago. A dream of Norah allowing Astrid to consume one of her fingers.

Stepping forward, Astrid reached out to Norah, who floated down to her level. Intuitively, Astrid cupped her hands together: the flesh-and-blood hand and the invisible one. Norah's fingers turned to water, falling into Astrid's hands.

Astrid drank, and the water tasted the sweetest she'd ever known. It cooled her mouth and throat as it sank into her body.

"Who do you choose to be now?" Taddeo asked.

"What?" His question startled her. "I know who I am. I made that decision months ago."

Taddeo smiled. "That is not a decision you can make just once and be done with. It is a decision you make with every thought and action from day to day. You are not who you were when you gave your arm to Norah. You are not who you were when you set a dragon free and trapped your brother inside Dragon's Head." Taddeo paused. "You are not who you were even when you found the sword I removed from your home."

Stunned, Astrid said, "You're the one who took Starlight?"

Taddeo simply smiled. "I needed to convince you to travel the winter route. It is part of the dragonslayer's duty."

"But Vinchi found Starlight by Sigurthor—are you the one who killed Sigurthor?"

"No one killed him. Sometimes people simply die."

"But you took Starlight!" Astrid clenched her jaw as her blood raced. "I would be in Guell now if it wasn't for you! And Margreet would be alive!"

Taddeo's eyes blazed. "All of it unnecessary if you'd accepted your duty to travel the winter route like a true dragonslayer." He then pointed at Astrid's phantom arm. "Decide who you are now, before it's too late."

Astrid cried out, feeling as if she'd been set on fire from within. Every muscle throbbed with searing heat. Her blood seemed to boil while coursing through her veins. The moment she breathed, she thought she saw flames erupt from her mouth.

"Decide!" Taddeo cried. "Blacksmith or dragonslayer!"

Astrid silently made her choice: dragonslayer.

As suddenly as the pain had claimed her, it released Astrid. Once again, she sensed the cool sensation of water sliding down her throat and into her belly.

At the same time, she felt whole and solid.

Taddeo latched onto both of her hands and held them up. "What you see before you is what everyone will see from now until you die whether they drink dragon's blood or not, whether they are shapeshifters or not."

Astrid's skin had smoothed, and she sensed the scars locked into the pattern of a dragonslayer's sword down her spine and sternum, where they belonged.

And her arm was whole again, no longer a phantom that only some could see.

"And now," Taddeo said, still smiling, "there is something I would like you to do for me."

CHAPTER SIXTY-SEVEN

Because Astrid still suspected Taddeo of killing Sigurthor, she refused his offer to travel quickly with his aide. Instead, she traveled by horse, and he met up with her every evening until they reached a seaport and boarded a ship together. They left Norah, Wendill, Smoke, Fire, and Slag behind in Limru.

Astrid didn't need to ask why. Norah had found a home at Limru, and at the time Astrid met the dragon Wendill, she sensed he had taken it upon himself to stay within arm's reach of Norah. Astrid still didn't know if Smoke, Fire, and Slag were lizards or young dragons. Perhaps Norah would take care of them.

Or perhaps she'd eat them for supper.

Either way, Astrid had more pressing matters at hand.

After a few days gliding through a calm sea, Astrid and Taddeo approached their destination shortly after sunrise. The tower gleamed golden in the early spring light, its color shimmering across the dark blue sea as if the sun were falling toward them, spreading its brilliant light everywhere.

When they landed at Tower Island, the guardsmen at the gate opened it the moment they recognized Astrid, bowing as she walked past them, Taddeo at her side. They marched into the courtyard, filled with dozens of Scaldings alongside villagers churning butter, mending wheels, and baking bread in outdoor ovens. Astrid called loudly enough so her voice would carry throughout the courtyard. "Who rules Tower Island?"

The chatter of voices reverberating through the courtyard died down slowly, until only the geese and chickens dared to break the silence with their honks and clucks, searching every corner of the courtyard for a misplaced bit of bread. Cows mooed mournfully from the farmland behind the courtyard, as if they somehow realized they were being excluded.

A man who looked like an older version of her brother Drageen stepped forward. Staring at her in disbelief, he whispered, "Astrid." His eyes widened like those an animal realizing it's being hunted. "You've returned."

"Drageen tried to kill me," Astrid announced loudly. "He is now in the rocks of Dragon's Head."

The man who she suspected was her uncle cleared his throat. "Yes. News of his fate carried here." He looked at her blankly.

Astrid found it easy to distinguish the villagers from her relatives. The Scaldings stood tall, thin, and blond, and they'd all adopted Drageen's face, even the women. But each villager had a unique and individual appearance, looking nothing like a Scalding. The villagers watched in idle curiosity, while the Scaldings' faces strained with fear.

"Who rules?" Astrid said again, her voice louder and harsher.

Her uncle cleared his throat again. "We all do. Or no one, actually. No outsiders have bothered us, so there is no need to change what has been in place for so long."

"That changes today," Astrid said.

The Scaldings grew quiet. Then their faces and bodies shifted until they all looked like Astrid.

She shivered, finding the sight chilling.

"Tower Island was built by dragons and it belongs to them—not you," Astrid continued. "They will allow you to work the farmland and keep your homes, but the tower now belongs to them. None of you will ever enter the tower again."

The growing crowd of Scaldings surrounding her began talking all at once, and Astrid raised her voice again. "Silence! There is no room for protest. I defeated Drageen. That means I am the Scalding in charge of Tower Island. I have struck a bargain with the dragons, and you are fortunate to still be breathing because of it!"

Taddeo leaned toward her and spoke softly. "They know not what they do. They are too weak to hold their own shape when faced by someone far stronger. Not one of them knows how to speak the truth. They are like people who are so terrified when faced by a dragon that they turn into deer."

I am Astrid, she told herself. *And they are not.*

She withdrew Starlight and held it high in the air. "If anyone believes I will not hesitate to use this, step forward and let your head be the first to roll."

Trembling, her uncle took a step back. Like the other Scaldings, he still looked like her. "How can you do this to your own kind?"

Astrid lowered Starlight's blade until its point leveled with his face. "We may share the same blood, but you are not my own kind. You are the ones who stood by doing nothing and would have let me die."

Her uncle opened his mouth to protest, and Astrid took a pivoting step forward, just as Vinchi had taught her when she trained with Margreet. "Say one word and it will be your last."

In unison, the dozens of Scaldings grouped in front of her paled, each staying silent.

Keeping her weapon in hand, Astrid turned toward Taddeo. "The tower," she said, "is yours."

Taddeo bowed to her.

"And now," Astrid continued, "there is something I wish to ask of you."

CHAPTER SIXTY-EIGHT

Taddeo stood atop Tower Island, hands cupped around his mouth and calling out across the sea. Astrid stood by his side.

For the next few days, dragons rose up from the depths of the sea, crawling onto the island and into the tower, a catacomb of chambers rising high above the water. Astrid remembered many of them from the time she'd spent in their underground cave. Here, they acted more at ease and lighter in spirit while they each found a home inside the tower.

One morning Taddeo and a few other dragons followed Astrid to the top of the tower where the large cage in which she and Norah had been kept for so many years still stood. Only two vertical bars were misshaped from where Taddeo had pushed them apart on the day he came to set Norah free.

Some dragons grew until they were as tall or taller than the cage and allowed Astrid to climb upon them. Others created fires and kept them burning strong throughout the day. Astrid had found the village blacksmith and borrowed his tools, fumbling at first with a hammer fashioned for much larger hands until she decided to change the shape of her hand to fit the hammer.

Astrid chose to work alone, so it took weeks. Keeping the base of the cage in place, she instructed Taddeo, wearing gloves to protect his hands from the metal, to pry the bars on three sides of the cage loose from the floor and bend them upwards until they flayed out, parallel with the top of the cage. Once the three sides had been freed, Taddeo increased in size until he could easily bend the top of the cage so that it formed a wall of iron bars with the remaining side below, held firmly in place by the floor of the cage.

For the first few days, Astrid's muscles ached from lack of use at the anvil. Out of practice, it took awhile for her to remember her trade, but then she fell into a natural rhythm of forging something new out of the very thing that had led to her disfigurement.

It took shape slowly, and the shape itself looked simplistic, like a figure a child might draw in the sand. Astrid loosened and splayed out a few iron bars from the one side of the cage that stood in its original place, forming a flowing skirt.

She twisted the bars from the former top of the cage to form a torso, but kept the twisting loose despite its similarity to the technique she used to make a dragon-slayer's sword.

She forged some of the bars from the remaining sides of the cage to form the shoulders and arms, rounding a few bars into a face, although it had no features.

She hammered dozens of bars into wavy lengths and welded them around the face. Finally, she signaled the dragon supporting her to lower her back to the ground.

As the dragons shrank in size and surrounded her, Astrid looked directly up at the iron structure she'd forged: the shape of a woman with a sword raised above her head, her hair flying free and wild.

"Here be dragons," Astrid whispered.

CHAPTER SIXTY-NINE

By the time Astrid had finished forging the structure atop the tower, most of the Scaldings had left Tower Island. The villagers who had farmed and cooked and tended to the Scaldings stayed. Taddeo struck an agreement with the villagers: the dragons would keep to themselves inside the tower and the villagers would serve them as they had served the Scaldings. Rewarded with ownership of the land they farmed, they could trade any goods they made with merchants who visited the island.

Before Astrid boarded the next merchant ship set to sail to the Northlands, she stood outside the entrance to the tower to speak with Taddeo one last time. "You maneuvered a way to free Norah from the Scaldings, and now you've maneuvered me into returning Tower Island to you." She couldn't help but feel suspicion. "What else do you want?"

Taddeo smiled, one hand braced against the doorjamb, making it impossible for Astrid to enter the tower. "You still have much to learn as a dragonslayer. I thank you for your work." He looked deeply into her eyes. "Know there is a powerful bond between dragon and slayer. I had that bond with DiStephan when he lived, and that bond still exists with his spirit. You have a similar bond with Norah."

Astrid shuddered. "We don't need it. My family placed us in that cage together. She chewed me up and left me scarred. You freed her. It's over."

A light danced in Taddeo's eyes. "She was starving," he said softly. "She chose not to kill you and make a meal of you for her own comfort. She drank only what little of your blood she needed to stay alive—and she was your age. She chose to let you live because she values all living things."

Astrid's breath caught, remembering the reason why DiStephan had left Guell, only to be killed. She'd seen him kill a hatchling dragon, and his blood lust had disturbed her because of her own compassion for all life.

"Yes," Taddeo said as if reading her thoughts. "You and Norah are alike in many ways." Taking a more serious tone, he said, "If you ever need anything, call upon her or me for help. You have earned the right to do so." He leaned forward for a moment, his nostrils widening as he inhaled Astrid's scent. "You may need us sooner than you expect."

Astrid remembered a thought that had dawned on her within the past few months. She realized she may have assumed too much. "What happened to DiStephan? Why did he die?"

Still smiling, Taddeo closed the door, leaving her alone outside the tower filled with dragons.

⊰❧

Once Astrid had sailed back to the mainland, she traveled through the North-lands on foot, stopping in every village on the winter route to make sure there had been no attacks by lizards, although she did learn of some sightings. But spring had arrived, after all, and the lizards were returning.

Once inside her own territory, Astrid visited every village under her protection, spending more time simply visiting and learning how the villagers had fared during the winter. With each new village, she realized what some villages were wanting, others had in abundance, such as grains or goods. She advised villagers about potential trades they could make without the aid of traveling merchants and suggested the best possible routes and times to avoid lizards, which were predictable creatures. Astrid had already learned that lizards were reptiles of habit, preferring to travel the same paths and rarely wandering far from them. With a gentle nudge here and there from DiStephan's ghost, in the form of a sudden breeze or dewdrops trapped within a large spiderweb that formed the pattern of an arrow pointing the way, she had already learned a great deal about the migration paths of lizards and shared that knowledge with every village that paid for her help.

Finally, Astrid came upon a very familiar trench filled with brittle, brown leaves, its sides bearing old claw marks.

Astrid withdrew Starlight and thrust its point through the leaves, just to be sure no lizard lay in wait underneath them. She spent the next hour walking through the woods, stopping only upon reaching her own dragonslayer's camp.

She touched an open wound in a tree trunk where Starlight's blade had caught when she'd discovered a lizard in her camp last fall. Here, she'd taken a swing and missed. And in the center of camp she'd found the eggs the lizard had been busy eating at the time she'd interrupted its meal, saving three eggs from certain demise. All evidence that they'd once been here had disappeared, but Astrid smiled at the memory of watching Smoke, Fire, and Slag hatch from their shells.

Astrid continued through the woods slowly, also remembering that she'd left Guell without leaving word with anyone. None of them knew Sigurthor had stolen Starlight or that Astrid meant to get the sword back from him and return home that very day. Of course, now she knew Taddeo had stolen Starlight, all part of a ruse to regain control of Tower Island, the dragons' true home.

But she couldn't tell anyone about that. It wasn't anything Taddeo had requested of her. It was something she simply knew. A knowledge that ran through her veins and beat inside her heart. The mere thought of going against this knowledge made her skin crawl. It would be best for everyone—people and dragons alike—for Astrid to keep quiet.

On the outskirts of the village, she saw the blacksmiths out in the fields, plow-ing and getting them ready for planting crops. Hidden by the woods, she paused and watched them until a lump knotted in her throat. She realized how much she'd missed them.

Because the blacksmiths were in the fields, the air in Guell seemed strangely hollow and empty without the loud, solid rings of hammer against iron. The smithery in the center of the village stood silent, even though a faint scent of old smoke hung in the air. Beyond the smithery, a group of the blacksmiths' wives walked toward the sea, baskets tucked under their arms.

Of course. At this time each spring the tide often brought in a wealth of shellfish, depositing them on the edge of Dragon's Teeth Field, where the jagged rocks protruding from the ground forced tide pools that trapped all forms of game from the sea.

The wives walked away, too busy talking and laughing among themselves to notice anything or anyone outside their close-knit group, a gentle humming drifted on a breeze.

Astrid spun, looking for the source.

A young mother chased her young children, who chased a few geese darting between cottages.

Beyond them, a woman doubled over just outside the doorway to her cottage, brushing her long dark hair.

The lump in Astrid's throat became a boulder, and no matter how she tried, she couldn't speak. Instead, she ran through the roads of Guell as fast as she could.

The woman stood, throwing her hair behind her. It took a few moments, but Astrid saw the recognition in her eyes, watching Astrid running toward her.

Lenore's forehead creased in anger, and she clutched the hairbrush as she balled her hands into fists and jammed them against her waist. "How dare you run off..."

Several paces away, Astrid skidded to a stop, never dreaming the profound joy she'd feel at the sight of seeing Lenore alive and well, even if she appeared angry.

But Lenore's anger faded, taking a close look at Astrid. "By the gods," she whispered, unaware of her fists coming undone and the hairbrush falling from her hand. "What happened to you?"

Still unable to speak, Astrid walked forward, reaching for Lenore's hair, now flying all around her in the wind.

Lenore wrapped her arms around Astrid's waist, holding her close.

For the first time, Astrid realized she'd forged the cage atop Tower Island into the image of Lenore. Astrid had forged Lenore's hair to fly forever free on the island now protected by dragons. All the time she had forged, Astrid had believed that if Margreet had stared upon such an image she would have seen her own strength inside it. If Margreet could have understood that she, like Astrid and Lenore, was an Iron Maiden, she would still be alive and arriving in Guell today. If Astrid could have done more to help her, Margreet—Astrid's friend—would be standing by her side right now.

Finally, Astrid sobbed, sinking her hands elbow deep into Lenore's beautiful, beautiful hair.

CHAPTER SEVENTY

One of the blacksmith's wives ran out to the fields, spreading the news of Astrid's return. Soon, the villagers of Guell gathered around her, peppering her with questions about where she'd been and why she had left without explanation.

With Starlight still sheathed at her side, Astrid wrapped her fingers around the hilt out of habit. "When I realized Starlight had vanished, I figured it had to be Sigurthor who took it. I thought I could catch up with him, get my sword back, and be home by nightfall."

Randim stood with crossed arms and a darkened face. "Why would a merchant like Sigurthor steal a sword? We have traded with him for years. He's an honest man."

"Was," Lenore whispered, slipping her hand through his elbow and loosening his tight stance a bit. "Sigurthor was an honest man."

"When you found Sigurthor," Randim continued, "why didn't you come back?"

"Because Starlight was still missing. I found evidence he'd been murdered—there were tracks. Because I had met no one on the road, I figured whoever killed Sigurthor had continued toward the other coast, so I kept on the path." Astrid pressed her lips lightly together, determined not to reveal that Taddeo had taken Starlight, not Sigurthor, because she believed what he said about her bond with the dragons. It was something she couldn't explain. She simply sensed it in her bones. "After I'd met Vinchi, he admitted he was the one who found Sigurthor's body and Starlight. Vinchi took Starlight, not willing to let a good sword go to waste."

Randim's frown deepened. "And left Sigurthor's body to rot?"

Astrid shrugged. "It was his decision, not mine. All I can guess is that with dragons traveling south at that time, staying to bury Sigurthor could have cost Vinchi his life."

Randim snorted, clearly not convinced.

Astrid shifted uncomfortably from one foot to another, anxious to go to her own cottage and rest. She kept scanning the group, mindful that Trep wasn't in their midst.

"Did you miss the blacksmithing?" Donel said, standing so close that he almost stepped on her feet.

"Yes," Astrid said softly. She wasn't ready to tell them anything about Tower Island. Not yet.

At the same time, a wave of sadness crashed over her. She felt the same as the day she'd come awake to discover her blacksmithing arm gone because Norah had devoured it to stay alive. "But I won't be blacksmithing anymore," Astrid said softly.

"I'll be following the winter route at the end of each dragon season instead."

Later that day, Lenore fed her, and the two women sat together quietly while the men headed back to the fields to salvage the remains of the day.

Astrid readied to walk to her own cottage, but she paused. "I didn't see Trep. Is he all right?"

Lenore nodded. "He took your disappearance hard. Give him time. He will come to you when he's able."

Astrid smiled weakly, taking one more look at Lenore's face and hair before walking away.

As she neared her cottage on the edge of Guell, Astrid limped, suddenly noticing pain in the ball of one foot. She shook her foot, assuming a pebble had managed to fall inside her shoe, but the pain persisted.

She froze at the sight of Dragon's Teeth field, just beyond her cottage, and the wooden walkway running alongside it to the sea.

Astrid removed her leather shoes and held onto them as she walked past her cottage and gingerly onto the jagged, rocky surface of Dragon's Teeth field. The edges of the sharp rocks cut into her painful foot. She winced. Close to the wooden walkway, she hobbled over and sat down on it.

Cradling her foot, she studied the cut skin and noticed a stone inside the cut.

Astrid gasped. Last year her brother Drageen had manipulated her for the sake of forcing valuable bloodstones out of her body. She gazed across the sea at the dark outline of Dragon's Head against the setting sun. Its name came from the shape of the dragon that had once been trapped inside. But now the shape had changed, and Astrid saw the outline showing her brother and his alchemist were still safely encased within the stone. This couldn't be his doing. Besides, he was dead. He had to be dead.

But Drageen had identified the catalyst that made the stones emerge as chaos, and there had been plenty of that in Astrid's life during the past months.

Careful not to pain herself any more, Astrid pushed and nudged the ball of her foot until a stone dropped from it into her hand. She spit on it in an effort to clean it. But no matter how hard she rubbed, the stone looked as black as a starless night, not red like the stones that had once poured from her feet and that she'd secretly buried near her cottage.

She held the stone up in the gentle light of dusk, but it only seemed to grow darker the more she looked at it.

For a moment, Astrid had a strange desire to throw it into the sea and be rid of it. Instead, she looked deeper into the depths of the stone.

Something shifted inside her body, but she couldn't put a name to it. Something just felt different.

Remembering the power of the red stones she'd buried, Astrid put her shoe back on and slipped the dark stone inside.

For now, she would tell no one it existed.

"What do you have to say for yourself?"

Astrid looked up, surprised to see Trep's face, dark and serious.

"Starlight was stolen—"

"I know all about that." Trep paused, biting his lip as if willing himself to be civil. "What were you thinking? Didn't you know you'd be causing Lenore a world of grief? And what of the rest of us?"

"I'm sorry." Astrid's voice choked, but she was grateful to see him.

Trep sank next to her, letting his legs drape off the edge of the walkway. "You exasperate me, Woman."

Woman. Trep had always called her Girly.

"I saw a woman murdered by her own husband." Astrid clamped her hand over her mouth, stopping herself from saying more. She hadn't meant to speak of it at all.

Trep's expression softened. "Tell me."

Astrid drew her legs to her chest, hugging them close and letting her forehead rest on her knees. "She was a foreigner, but she wasn't weak. She was strong. We learned how to fight together, and she was a much better swordswoman than me. Her husband called her into trial by combat—"

"You must have been in Daneland."

"Yes, in Daneland. I was sure she would defeat him, but she hesitated. I don't know what she was thinking. I don't know why she let him kill her." Astrid took a deep breath. "And I should have been able to save her. I should have been closer to the fight. I should have had Starlight in my hand and ready to rush in and—"

"That is against the law," Trep said, watching the sun dip below the horizon, the clouds above turning blood red. "You would not have been allowed that close because it was her fight, not yours."

"But I let her down. I could have been a better friend."

After a few long moments, Trep said, "My sister married a Midlander who failed to treat her well."

Astrid sat up sharply, staring at Trep. She'd never heard him speak of having a sister.

"I begged her to end their marriage. It would have been easy enough, but she took being his wife as a serious duty and wouldn't listen to me." Trep kept staring at the horizon.

Unable to bear the suspense, Astrid finally said, "What happened?"

"I learned everyone must make their own decisions. Even if they're bad decisions."

"And your sister?"

Trep smiled. "He beat her so bad she could have died. When she could walk again, she made her way to the Far Northlands, where he'd never dare venture. She works with the boggers and smelters. She's one of the folks that prepares iron for us to smite."

Astrid sighed in relief. "I'm glad to know that." Secretly, Astrid thought, *Trep's sister is an Iron Maiden. Like Lenore. Like me.*

Like Margreet almost was.

A new thought occurred to Astrid. Margreet had become a fierce fighter, despite a few moments of weakness when she saw Gershon again after being separated from him for months. From everything Astrid had witnessed, Margreet had done her best to fight for a new life. She came close to winning her trial by combat, and Astrid would never know what had gone wrong. Only Margreet and perhaps Gershon knew that particular truth.

What if Margreet hadn't let Gershon kill her? Astrid remembered watching the fight and seeing Margreet look away the moment before he'd risen from the pit and attacked her. She'd fought with every fiber of her being. She'd fought with all her heart.

Of course, Astrid thought, *Why didn't I see it before? Margreet was an Iron Maiden like the rest of us.*

Astrid realized she'd witnessed Margreet learn to stand up inside her own skin. She'd discovered her place in the world, even though it had been short-lived.

The Last Keeper of Limru stood up on her feet and decided who she was. She decided to become an Iron Maiden, and she succeeded. Margreet lost the fight, but the prize she won was herself.

The thought brought solace to Astrid, and she chose to embrace it.

Astrid and Trep sat throughout the night, watching the dusk turn to dark and the sky fill with bright shining stars and a full moon that rose above the horizon glowing pale yellow.

As the night progressed, the moon turned a darker yellow, then orange, and finally blood red as it reached its highest point in the sky.

All the while, Astrid found an even deeper solace in knowing that the same moon and stars were shining on Tower Island and the Iron Maiden, the image she'd forged to caution those with ill intent as they entered the Northlands to think otherwise.

About the Author

Resa Nelson has been the TV/movie columnist of Realms of Fantasy magazine since 1999. She is also a regular contributor to SCI FI magazine and has written nonfiction articles for a wide range of publications, including Amazing Stories, Boys' Life, Lupus Now, and Massachusetts Wildlife. She attended the Clarion Science Fiction Writers Workshop in 1985 and is a longtime member of the Science Fiction and Fantasy Writers of America (SFWA). Her short fiction has been published in Science Fiction Age, Fantasy Magazine, Aboriginal SF, Tomorrow SF, Brutarian Quarterly, Paradox, Oceans of the Mind, and several anthologies. The Dragonslayer's Sword is based on two stories originally published in Science Fiction Age: "The Dragonslayer's Sword" and "The Silver Shoes."

While researching The Dragonslayer's Sword, Nelson took a course in blacksmithing, where she learned how to build a fire and forge iron and steel. She also took a course to learn how to use a medieval sword at the Higgins Armory Museum in Worcester, Massachusetts. She soon joined the Higgins Armory Sword Guild and took more courses in German longsword and Italian rapier and dagger. She also studied foil fencing for a year. Nelson participates in the guild's study of fight manuals from the Middle Ages and the Renaissance and participates in demonstrations of historically accurate sword techniques at the Higgins Armory Museum, science fiction and fantasy conventions, and other venues in New England. The swordwork in this novel is based on her study of these techniques.

Nelson has also studied screenplay writing and participated in the making of three short independent films, two of which are based on her short stories. She has been a quarter-finalist in the Nicholl Fellowships in Screenwriting and a semi-finalist in the Chesterfield screenwriting contest. She lives in Massachusetts.

CPSIA information can be obtained at www.ICGtesting.com
Printed in the USA
BVOW070949270112

281518BV00001B/3/P

9 781606 592823